HEAD IN THE CLOUDS MUCH?

Andy Sexton

To everyone I have met over the years who has inspired me, guided me and supported me. This book would not have made it into print without you. Thank you.

1

Saturday weddings are a pain in the arse. Funerals are far more convenient time-wise, as they always involve time off work. If weddings took a leaf out of funerals' book and were held on a workday, I might even enjoy them. I might even throw confetti. A Saturday wedding is ten times worse when you are involved in it, because it takes up the whole day; no decent morning lie-in, and no sneaking off when you have had enough. Annoyingly, there were two weddings coming up, and I was very much involved in both.

The first of the weddings I had to endure was my brother Roy's. I'd learnt to cope with school friends getting married, but I knew life was well and truly leaving me behind when my younger sibling beat me down the aisle. From the moment he left for university, Roy never seemed to be without a girlfriend. His success with women – despite his unsexy moniker – accentuated my lack of success with men. Christina was by far my family's least favourite of Roy's girlfriends, so it came as an unpleasant surprise when they announced their engagement the previous autumn.

From an outsider's viewpoint, some might say Christina was nice to look at – if swollen features are your thing – but her positive traits ended there. Any outer beauty I'd initially seen had been tainted by three years of getting to know her. Another sore point was caused when Christina announced her plans for the wedding. She wanted three bridesmaids, yet Clare – Roy's older sister, my younger sister – wasn't one of them. Clare's and my role was simply to keep the guests happy. As long as we kept them away from the bride, their day would be a pleasant one.

To piss me off further, the weather was fine on the day of Roy and Christina's mid-September wedding. My hatred for weddings can be multiplied by another ten if it turns out to be a sunny day. It's a waste of sun if you are stuck indoors, and it's a waste of a good outfit if you ruin it with sweat stains. Clare and I stood either side of the church's entrance and waited for guests to arrive. Christina and her family weren't remotely religious, but it didn't stop them choosing the venue for the ceremony. They disregarded our local church in Crockham as 'too modern', preferring an 18th-century church on the outskirts of Cardiff instead. The first person to show up at the church that morning was a smartly dressed young man. His face could have been better, but nothing a few drinks couldn't remedy – and I planned on having a few. My outlook for the day swiftly improved; having somebody to impress always perked me up. My target waited for a few moments, before being joined by another not too shabby-looking young man.

'I bet that's his boyfriend,' I said to Clare.

'I bet you it isn't,' she challenged.

'You *hope* it isn't.'

As the dapper young chaps walked up the gravel pathway towards us, Clare and I grinned our biggest grins. She had turned into a rival.

Despite being two and a half years younger than me, Clare's statistics regarding boyfriends put mine to shame. On average, she changed her beau every twelve months – right before her birthday, canny lass. Admittedly, she'd had no luck with any of them, but at least she pulled and got taken out on dates and had a go at relationships. I had trouble committing to a two-part drama serial, let alone a two-week relationship.

'I'll seat them,' I said quietly, maintaining my grin as I

spoke.

'You get the next ones,' Clare replied through clenched teeth. 'I'll deal with these.'

I took a few steps forward and held out an Order of Service.

Come on, I thought. *Wake up. Think of some quirky things to say. Blokes like quirky.*

'Hi,' I said to the first young man, who was the better looking of the two up close. It was his brown eyes that clinched it. 'Nice day for a wedding.'

'Alright?' he replied without meaning it.

The guy ignored my outstretched arm and passed on by. I checked what I was holding. It didn't say *The Big Issue* on it, so why the frosty reaction?

'Ta,' the second young man said, taking the two bits of folded paper.

He wedged my offering into his back pocket. I'd handed out flyers in one of my many previous jobs, but I was far too sensitive for the role. I took it as a personal attack when I saw my hard work scattered on the ground nearby, like pieces of confetti.

'Nice threads,' Clare said to the first young man, who then gave her a kiss on the cheek.

'Not looking so bad yourself,' he replied. 'So, have you got some of these things for us to hand out?'

'There's a box full of them inside,' Clare said. 'I think your sister is expecting quite a few people to turn up.'

'Our Chrissy loves an audience,' young man number two said, leaning in and giving Clare her second kiss on the cheek. There wasn't even the sniff of a handshake for me from either of them.

I watched as the brothers made their way inside. I'd been made to feel like a spectator at my own brother's wedding; I should have been one of the guests, not an usher.

Clare anticipated my question. 'We got in contact a few

weeks ago about the wedding.'

'Why didn't they contact me? I'm the eldest.'

'Roy showed them a photo of us all. They didn't like the look of you.'

'Did they say that?!'

'No, I'm joking!' Clare said. 'I asked Christina for their phone numbers. I thought I'd better make an effort.'

I relaxed my shoulders. 'I didn't even know she had brothers.'

'Sometimes it pays to listen.'

'It's good to know it's not only you and me that have the privilege of welcoming guests. She must hate them just as much as she hates us.'

Christina having brothers did ring a bell. She must have mentioned it during a conversation I'd pretended to be interested in. I should have known the two lads were related to Christina: they were bad-mannered and were exhibiting the familial swollen features. Both men instantly dropped in my estimation.

The brothers came back out with a handful of programmes and chatted to Clare. When had she become my competition? I still saw her as my little sister – the girl who sucked tea from her baby beaker until she was ten. She loved that beaker. But now she was using a similar action to keep boyfriends happy. Gone were the days of innocent bath-sharing. Growing up, Clare and I were often told that we looked alike, and I'd always found that insulting. Yes, we were blue-eyed and fair-haired as children. Yes, we both went through stages of wearing plaits in said hair. And yes, we both had stints as Angel Gabriel in the school nativity because we had been taller than our peers. Nowadays, however, I found it a compliment whenever Clare and I were compared in any way. Yet we were polar opposites when it came to relationships and our taste in men. I would never hear the end of it from elderly relatives if Clare wed before I did. Things were already heading that way, though. Maybe I should have taken tips from her. It looked silly with four of us crowding the entrance, so I went inside, sat down and kicked off my shoes.

*

The good-looking guests were few and far between. The unfortunate-looking ones were aplenty, and they were all sat on the bride's side of the church. Naturally, Christina walked down the aisle to 'The Arrival of the Queen of Sheba', taking glances left and right to make sure everyone was watching the star of the show. I must admit, Christina did look good... for a prison officer. I'm sure I saw Roy mouth 'Wow' when he clapped eyes on her, though the veil was still down at that point. My parents looked so proud during the ceremony. I knew I wouldn't be stirring up such pride within my family anytime soon. Clare and all my cousins would undoubtedly get hitched and have children. At future family gatherings, those pesky children would know me as That Man Who Always Turns Up Alone. At the rate I was going, I'd be the only adult without a plus one; I'd be the odd person seated at the corner of an even-numbered table.

I had managed to fix a smile to my face for the whole service. But by the time the official photos were taken, my cheeks had no strength to support another rictus grin. My face resembled that of an enthusiastic ventriloquist during the bits when the dummy 'talks', and I spoilt all the snaps I was in. Shame. Not that I expected us to be, but Clare and I weren't sat at the top table for the reception, which was held in a nearby country house hotel. Along with Christina's brothers, we were dotted around the minor tables so we could report back to the bride with people's opinions of how the day was going. I hadn't given her my own honest opinion, as I needed my teeth for the upcoming four-course meal.

Being the eldest grandchild, I had the dubious honour of looking after my gran for the afternoon, so she was sitting on my right. One of my cousins and his new girlfriend also joined us, as did one of Christina's brothers – the one who had taken the Order of Service from me at the start of the day. His place name said 'Martin'. I didn't have a clue who the others sat at our round table were, and I'd no intention of making small talk merely to find out their identities. The dining room itself had been decorated with pink and purple hearts to match the roses in the bride's bouquet, and nylon drapes of both colours flowed across the high ceiling.

'When's dinner being served?' my gran asked as the last of the one hundred and fifty guests took their seats.

'I don't know, Gran,' I said over the noise. 'I haven't been told much of what's happening today.'

'I hope it's soon. I'm hungrier than a tramp's dog.'

She was a proper Cockney, my gran. I once overheard my dad telling her to tone down her accent while she was around the grandkids so we wouldn't pick up any bad speaking habits. He repeatedly corrected her when she misused the English language – telling her off for saying 'we was' and 'could of' – but I loved listening to her raspy, common voice when she was in full flow. After eighty-two years residing in and around the East End districts, however, Gran was moved into a nursing home on the outskirts of Crockham, on my dad's orders.

'Pour this into my water glass, Louis, love,' Gran instructed, even though the young lad pouring the free champagne was still at our table. 'I can't use them poncey glasses.'

After I'd transferred her drink, Gran took a swig. It didn't look right, seeing her dressed up and quaffing champagne.

'So, Louis...' Gran started in a tone I recognised all too

well. 'You found yourself a fella yet?'

I looked at my cousin and rolled my eyes.

'No, not yet,' I replied, just as I did every time she asked. 'Are you comfortable, Gran? I can go and find you a cushion, if you want?'

I made to get up, but Gran put a warm hand on my arm.

'Stop changing the subject,' she said. 'When are we going to see someone take you up the aisle?'

Martin, who was sitting opposite me, sniggered.

I liked that Gran felt comfortable enough to talk to me about men, seeing as my dad tried his best not to acknowledge my sexuality, but there's a time and a place.

'Course in my day, we all got married when we was teenagers,' Gran ploughed on. 'How old are you now, Louis? Twenty-three? Twenty-four?'

'I'm twenty-eight, Gran. Twenty-nine next month.'

'Twenty-eight and still living at home. No wonder you're single,' she said, reaching for her champagne.

No wonder Dad put you in a home.

'You're meant to leave some for the toasts,' I advised.

'Louis, love, I ain't drunk alcohol since your dad chucked me in with them coffin dodgers, so I'll drink when I bleedin' well like,' she said, before downing the contents of her glass.

Feeling as if I'd been told off, I turned my back on Gran and started talking to my cousin. The extended family only met up at weddings and funerals, so we always needed a quick recap of what each other had been up to in the meantime. As my cousin had already gathered, I was still single and still living at home. But then came the question I'd feared more than the one enquiring about my relationship status.

'What are you doing for work these days?'

It had to come. It's one of the main three topics people in their twenties get asked about: love life, living arrangements and work. I hadn't felt ashamed about my failure in the first two departments, as Clare was in the same boat as me. I looked over to her table and wondered whether she was being grilled in the same way I was. Clare did, however, have a decent job as a legal secretary – the one thing that was probably saving her from utter humiliation right now.

'Are you still at the bank?' my cousin carried on probing.

'No, I quit that job. It didn't really suit me.'

'Louis don't like working,' Gran said, talking across me. 'He gave up on his A-Levels and ain't ever stuck to a proper job.'

'You're supposed to have a poor memory,' I barbed.

'So your dad says. But I think I'd know if I was going senile.'

Had Clare been at the table, we would have shared a subtle glance.

'Actually, I've got a job interview next week.'

It was a lie, but I had to say something. Besides, Martin was listening in, and I always upped my game whenever a bloke seemed interested. Every time I glanced over at him, he was looking in my direction.

I've so pulled!

'What's it for?' my cousin asked.

'Hmm?'

'The interview you've got?'

'Oh that. Yes, it's for a job... delivering mail.'

I was totally thinking on my feet. I'd read in the local paper that Regal Post were recruiting staff to help out over the busy Christmas period. I'd dismissed the job straight away because of the early starts, as I was a bit of a lazy bastard, you see.

'Your grandad used to be my mailman,' Gran said, her voice softening. 'It's how we met. I used to look out for him every morning so I could give him a wave. He'd be ever so proud of you, bless his soul.'

'My postman is annoyingly chipper,' my cousin said. 'It's probably because he gets to be outside in summer. I guess it beats sweating your arse off in an office.'

'And they do a good pension,' Gran added.

'You can wear those tight postie shorts too,' Martin chipped in, giving me a wink.

Perhaps Saturday weddings weren't so bad after all.

2

It wasn't until the evening knees-up that I managed to palm Gran off on my parents, giving me some breathing space from the barrage of questions I'd faced earlier on. I'd just freed myself from Gran when Christina finally found some time to speak to me. Roy was a quiet fellow, and we didn't speak to each other much, so I simply shook his hand and congratulated him after the reception. Anything more and he would have come out in a cold sweat. Christina, on the other hand, needed a lot more emotion from me to keep her satisfied.

'Hi!' Christina chirped, before advancing her cheek towards me so I'd kiss it, which I did. 'I haven't got long. The first dance is due to take place in a few minutes. Check my teeth.'

Christina bared her teeth as if she were a dog trying to scare off a postman.

'All clear,' I said after a brief inspection.

'How about the rest of me? What are people saying about the gown?'

Apart from dressing up in my mum's when I was younger, I had no interest in wedding dresses. Like the wolf that dresses up as Grandma in *Little Red Riding Hood*, something didn't look right. Underneath it all, Christina was still the swollen-faced woman putting on a charming act. For want of a better turn of phrase, you can't polish a turd.

'They all said that the dress looks *amayzing*,' I gushed, heaping praise on the apparel and not her. 'It was a good choice to go with the feathery shoulders. Really classy.'

'Super! Make sure people take photos during the first dance. I've only got this dress for one day. Your mum is taking it back to the shop while I'm on honeymoon, while *we're* on honeymoon, so I want to get as much wear out of it as possible.'

'Yeah, I'm helping her with that.'

Judging by Christina's next line, the happy face I had painted on must have been less convincing than I thought.

'Don't worry, I'm sure it'll be your turn soon,' she said without conviction. 'Remember to take lots of photos. Ciao!'

Christina hoisted up her dress a few inches and trotted off to find Roy. Cue my time to leave. I reached a fire exit just as the opening bars of Savage Garden's 'Truly, Madly, Deeply' kicked in. Watch my little brother and his new wife do a slow dance? I'd rather get front row tickets for a Justin Bieber concert and have to endure it without ear plugs or eyelids. The rest of my family seemed content enough to watch the dancing, but it all seemed a bit incestuous for my liking. I took in a breath of the clean, summer air and followed the night lights round to the hotel's huge rear grounds – although Christina would have described it as a standard back garden. On one of the benches by the fountain, I could see the silhouettes of two other people who had chosen to bypass the cringe fest. As my eyes adjusted to the darkness, the two shadowy forms became more recognisable. My cousin and his girlfriend were cuddling and kissing. So that I wouldn't look like a deviant if seen, I fast-walked through the open back doors, with the intention of heading up to my room and enjoying the delights of the mini-bar.

'Sorry!' I said as I narrowly avoided a collision with Martin.

'Where are you disappearing to in such a hurry?' he asked.

'I was just going to my room... to freshen up,' I said, pointing in the direction of a corridor – the one that led away from the function room and towards the stairs.

Please don't drag me back in.

'I don't blame you for wanting to get away from what's going on in there,' Martin said.

I smiled and looked down at the parquet flooring. I'd been rumbled.

'Come up to my room and watch a film,' he suggested. 'They won't notice if we're not around for a bit.'

I pondered his offer. Although I'd initially rated him as the less attractive of the two brothers, Martin had grown on me throughout the day. Wine goggles certainly are a useful piece of kit, and so much cheaper than a prescription pair.

Sensing that I wasn't completely averse to the idea, Martin upped his game by getting the key card to his room out of his pocket. 'Take this and I'll meet you up there. Room two-twelve on the second floor. I'll just get us a bottle to share. White OK for you?'

He had sealed the deal.

I got up close to him and said, 'You read my mind.' I snatched the card from his fingers and started walking towards the stairs. 'See you in a bit!'

This is a turn-up for the books. And I've got my pulling pants on...should anything happen. That's what I call a result!

My pulling pants were still waiting to make their bedroom debut. I called them my pulling pants, but I'd never pulled in them. They weren't strictly pants, either; they were tight boxers. But they had set me back fifteen quid, so I gave them a suitable name and pride of place in my underwear drawer. Despite having bought them two years previously, it was the fifth time I'd worn them. Yet the only other person outside of Taiwan to have touched these undies was my mum when she washed them.

I inserted Martin's key card into the slit by the door

handle and entered the room. There, lying naked on one of the twin beds, was Christina's other brother, Graham. I wouldn't have minded, but in the cowboy position on top of him was Clare, riding away as if on a bucking bronco. I stood there aghast at what was taking place, but I couldn't tear my eyes away. I wasn't perving; I was dumbstruck. The temporary curls that Clare had tonged into her long blonde hair bounced up and down in time with her motion. Graham saw me, and his body froze. Clare's hair flicked round as she turned to see why Graham had gone stiff. All in one swift movement, she performed a Frankie Dettori-style dismount and clambered off the far side of the bed, while Graham flapped about as he covered his genitals with a pillow. The senses that had been rendered useless suddenly regained activity. My mouth must have been open the whole time, because I had to close it before I could gulp. I covered my eyes and reversed out of the room. As I did so, my bum pressed up against something. With a start, I turned to see what the obstacle was. Standing before me was Martin, who had purposely been blocking my exit. His face bore a devious grin, and there was no bottle of wine to be seen.

'I told you I didn't want to be disturbed!' Graham shouted as I barged my way past Martin and hurried down the corridor.

'It's my room too,' I faintly heard Martin reply.

Without forethought of where I was heading, I ended up at the bar. Though I tried not to, I couldn't resist looking in the direction of the dance floor. As well as the married couple taking centre stage in a romantic clinch, my parents had also taken to the floor and were swaying as if it was a school disco. I felt as though I was *at* the school disco, watching from the sidelines as others coupled up and had fun. I'd now graduated to being a gooseberry amongst my own family, in addition to being one when out with my decreasing circle of friends. Everyone was partnered up.

They might as well have dangled normality in front of me and sang, 'This is what you can't have, you can't have, you can't have. This is what you can't have, because you are a freak.'

'On second thoughts, make it a double,' I said to the woman serving. I passed over Martin's key card that I still had in my hand. 'Charge it to room two-twelve.'

She placed the drink on the bar and gave me a knowing smile. 'In my experience, the best bottles stay on the shelf.'

I took heed of the woman's intimation and, after downing my beverage, procured a bottle of white wine and a bottle of champagne from the shelf. I left the bar and took a different flight of stairs to get to the wedding suite, digging Martin's key card deep into the soil of a potted yucca on my way. When checking in, we were told that there was a forty-pound fine for losing a key card. Clumsy, clumsy Martin. I placed the champagne by the threshold that Roy would no doubt be carrying Christina over in a few hours' time. When I reached the room that I was sharing with Clare, I homed in on the mini-bar and took out the bars of chocolate I'd put in there earlier. I poured myself a coffee-mug of wine, sat on my bed, rested my head against the wall and had a tipsy think.

How could she? With someone called Graham? I'd never sleep with someone called Graham. And I certainly wouldn't sleep with someone who was related to Christina. Cheers for saving me from Martin, God. I wouldn't have done anything, just watched telly and had a drink. Nothing else, honest. Do you not want me to find a boyfriend? Is it my destiny to stay single for ever? To sit on the shelf and... Bitch! Rewind to earlier, that barmaid meant me when she was talking about good bottles being on the shelf! Maybe it was intended as a compliment. It probably wasn't, but I'm going to take it as one. Perhaps I have an 'eternal singleton' look about me. I'm going to end up stuck in a drawer alongside my pulling pants. I'm only twenty-eight!

After polishing off the last of the wine, I brushed my teeth, climbed into bed and turned off the light. It must have been a good couple of hours later when I woke. Clare had managed to enter the room without me stirring. She knew I was a light sleeper and had been creeping about so as not to disturb me. It had been a sterling effort but, like so many an unseated rider, she hit the ground with a thud. She had fallen at the final hurdle. I turned on the lights.

'Are you alright?' I asked, squinting.

'I think so,' Clare said, getting back to her feet. 'I take it this empty wine bottle I slipped on is yours?'

'Oops. Sorry,' I said, pulling my bed sheet over my mouth so she wouldn't see me suppressing a giggle.

Clare got into bed, and I hastily turned out the light.

'I'm still bruised from the last time I hit the floor.'

My giggle couldn't be contained, and I burst out laughing – mainly out of relief that the ice had been broken. Clare followed suit. I recalled her earlier comedy dismount and the look of terror on her face that had accompanied it. I hated the idea of a man coming between us. The day would inevitably arrive when she found a partner and moved on, but I wasn't ready for that to happen just yet. My initial upset was more to do with jealousy; I struggled to attract men's interest, whereas Clare's less desperate approach worked wonders. Oh, to be carefree... I'd have to try that approach in my next job – one that the people at my table seemed to have chosen for me. Come Monday, I'd be applying for a role at Regal Post.

3

I didn't have many male friends – not even ones who were after a bit of no-strings sex – but I hoped working at the male-dominated mail centre would rectify that. The fact there weren't any gay bars within a ten mile radius of Crockham wasn't doing me any favours. The nearest decent gay bar was an effort away in Guildford – half an hour by train and a bit of walking – not that my best friend Jay and I had minded. Before Jay moved to Brighton, we would be on the pull at that bar every weekend without fail. But I didn't feel like heading over there once my partner in crime had left town. Excluding family members, I spent very little time with men, and that went some way towards explaining why I practically pounced upon anyone remotely masculine. Just as some women chase after gay guys, I chased after straight guys – 'proper' blokes that liked beer and football. I'd already settled for a type and knew what I was looking for: a humorous, considerate, well-presented, sporty man. A gay straight man would have been ideal.

Becoming a postie was almost the final straw as far as jobs went. I'd already tried my hand at just about every unskilled profession under the sun and wasted over ten years of my life as a result, but none of the positions had been right for me. My ultimate goal was to join a company that closed at weekends and paid its employees monthly. Rich people were paid monthly; crappy jobs paid wages weekly. The longest I'd stayed in one job was fourteen months, back when I was a teenager working at the local pizzeria. Being someone who gets bored easily didn't help, and nor did trying to unzip the boss's fly at the Christmas party. (I only attempted that once. It's good to aim high in life.) Major qualifications were needed for all the jobs I wanted to do but, disregarding GCSEs, the sole certificate I had that bore my name commended me on my level of gymnastics. That and an A5 piece of card I received for passing Pizza Den's 'food management' course. A sports physiotherapist would have been the perfect job for me, so I could massage rugby players' bodies and take sneaky peaks under the towels covering their beefy arses. But that was pure fantasy. Instead, I became involved with mail packages rather than male packages. Lame, I know.

*

Living in a house with just the one upstairs bathroom brought with it some major drawbacks in the mornings. Only so many times could I walk into said bathroom and be faced with my dad's ballbags floating on the surface of the bubble-free bathwater before it started to look as though I was doing it on purpose. Maybe I was doing it on purpose, as it had been quite a while since I'd seen genitals I wasn't in some way related to. Our local GP quite regularly stuck a finger up my dad's bum hole – for prostate reasons, or so he said – so being seen in the bath wasn't going to affect his dignity. Thanks to my early starts, though, these occurrences were a thing of the past.

The delivery office I was due to start work at was in my small home town of Crockham, so I didn't have far to drive in my little green Peugeot. The quickest route to the office took me straight through the high street, past all of the shops, banks and eateries I'd previously worked at. Cycling in was a possibility, but it was late-November and mightily cold at five o'clock in the morning. Also, I didn't think sweat patches, dishevelled hair and insects stuck to my oily forehead was the most attractive of looks to have on a first day. Four minutes after I left home, I arrived at work.

The building itself was situated near Crockham train station and, before an extensive makeover in the 1970s, had been used as a primary school. I parked in the car park – which would have been the playground – at the rear of the delivery office and walked in through the staff entrance. In a self-assured manner, I strode towards the manager's office, passing a few workers and smiling at them to show I was composed. I knew where the manager's office was, as I'd already had a look round the place before my interview. It had been virtually empty and quiet then, but the forty-odd staff, the volumes of mail and the office radio put an end to that.

'That smile won't last long,' I heard one man say.

From what I saw of my new colleagues, I was one of the youngest – if not the youngest. I preferred it that way. It made a refreshing change from the role model tag I'd been burdened with at home. Mercifully, there were only five women in the office, so I stood a much greater chance of snaring a man when there was scant competition for my fellow workers' affections. With the odds more in my favour than at previous jobs, surely one of my new colleagues would fit the bill… or could at least be swayed to the dark side for a night.

I had difficulty taking the manager seriously. He was a mere five foot five, and his sandy hair had receded in such a way that an island of it had formed at the front of his head. I detected a slight Welsh accent, which became more pronounced when he used words containing the letter 'U'. There was a framed photo on his desk of two young children. Men always appeared more attractive when I found out they were dads. However, I stopped seeing my new manager in a sexual guise when I found out he drove the same model of car my gran had once owned. Sharing a cramped back seat with a wet mutt and a pair of Wellington boots with dog turd on the soles is enough to turn anyone off a Nissan Micra.

The manager – or 'the boss' as he was known within the office – handed me my uniform, which consisted of a royal blue polo shirt, a pair of charcoal trousers, a royal blue fleece, a pair of black trainers, fluorescent waterproofs and a cycle helmet. I hoped the items were new and not an ex-employee's cast-offs. The boss gestured towards a comfy woman in her early fifties who had streaks of red through her short grey hair and wore red-framed spectacles to match. She was standing halfway down an aisle that had two-metre tall mail frames along either side, each of them looking upon the postperson in front of it as they reached forward – from side to side, head height to waist height – to feed it letters. As I joined the woman at her mail frame, she put down the letters she had been slotting and introduced herself. Comfy Kath started my postal education by showing me how to read an address on a letter. I gritted my teeth and let her carry on speaking to me in her condescending – albeit well-intended – manner. She had been in the job almost thirty years, but the rules and regulations were fresh in her head.

While others were getting ready to leave the office and start delivering, Kath and I were still standing at her 'bench'. I presumed the mail frames were given this nickname because – when the twenty-minute meal relief was called – some workers liked to sit on the waist-high ledge in front of their mail frame and eat sandwiches or read a paper. I looked on as Kath took the mail we had sequenced out of the frame and put rubber bands around each bundle. It was stuffy in the office, and I held my breath every time someone near me sneezed. The horizontal windows that ran along the top of every wall were fixed shut, so the only air entering the building came from the heating system.

'I hope I don't catch anyone's germs,' I said to Kath in an attempt to bond with her. 'It would defeat the purpose of me being hired as a Christmas relief postie if I was off sick at Christmas.'

Kath glossed over my comment. 'We put the short rubber band on first, then the long one.'

I must have missed the section on rubber band usage at the two-day induction course. I know, two full days to learn about the inner workings of being a postie. Whatever next? An intensive week-long course for fruit pickers?

'Any parcels you want me to take, Kath?' a burly chap came over and asked. He looked like the sort of bloke who would have given me a wedgie at school.

'Not today, thanks,' Kath replied. 'But I'm glad you're here, Dean. This is Louis, and he'll be on this round over Christmas.'

Dean gave me a nod. 'Alright?'

'Yeah, I think so,' I said.

'Any parcels bigger than a shoebox, give them to Dean and he'll deliver them,' Kath said.

The office had four vans, and Dean drove one of them. According to Kath, Dean had only recently been promoted to the role of a driver, having joined Regal Post five years ago. He must have been educated (if at all) outside of Crockham, as he appeared roughly my age.

Kath and I finally made it out of the office at eight-thirty. I took in a deep breath of the cool fresh air and hoped it would nuke any germs that were potentially forming. Something else I'd not been taught at the induction course was bicycle usage. Having been assigned a bike, I heeded Kath's advice and took it for a spin. No problems. Trying to cycle off with a 16kg bag of mail in the 'basket' on the front, however, was a different task altogether. Thankfully, Kath was the only one around to see me looking like a unicyclist with tender external haemorrhoids.

I bet even Chris Hoy would have trouble getting this contraption round a velodrome.

Complete with helmet, I followed Kath and her doughy derriere as she cycled through the high street traffic and off into the outskirts of Crockham – to where the 'affordable' housing was. It was the only place in Crockham where you would find any flats; even semi-detached houses were few and far between. A lot of my friends had been priced out of the area, preferring to move a few miles further afield to get more for their money. The local 'affordable' housing wasn't affordable to young couples starting out in life.

*

The journey to our start point took twelve minutes, yet from looking at me you would be mistaken for thinking it had taken a lot longer and occurred during the height of summer. Kath, on the other hand, wasn't even puffing. The old bird was deceptively fit. I wasn't one for exercise. I did press-ups and sit-ups in my bedroom to keep me in shape, but that was evidently no substitute for a hardcore workout.

'Are you OK, Louis?' Kath asked when we got off our bikes. 'Was I going too fast?'

'No... you were going at... just the right speed,' I panted, fighting my knees' desire to give way. 'I think I've got... too many layers on.'

In case I didn't know what somebody posting letters looked like, Kath told me to shadow her for ten minutes. During this period, I was given the lowdown on the area and informed which properties had dangerous dogs or uneven paths. Following this enlightening experience, I started delivering... under Kath's supervision. It was pretty straightforward; the intense training seemed a tad extreme. Having made light work of what I'd been given, I was entrusted with two bundles, which I cracked on with while Kath pedalled off to complete another part of the delivery. I'd been left in charge of a cul-de-sac, so I could see my finishing point. All I had to do was walk to it while posting mail. Simple. I upped my speed so that I could be on the corner before Kath returned. It was cold, and I didn't want to keep her waiting.

SMASH!

Shit!

In my haste, I'd accidentally kicked a milk bottle off a customer's doorstep. I looked around to see if anyone had witnessed my mishap. The only thing looking in my direction was a tabby cat. Before I could grab the cat and place it at the scene of the crime, Dean pulled up in his van and wound down his window.

'You've only been here five minutes and you're already causing havoc,' he joked.

'It wasn't me,' I said in a panic. 'Some cat knocked it off the doorstep. I think I must've scared it.'

'Best go and get them another pint, then.'

'Erm... I don't have any money on me. Could you lend me some? I'll pay you back tomorrow, I promise. How much will it be? Fifteen pence? Twenty pence?'

Unless it had a price tag, I didn't have a clue how much things cost. My rent was forty pounds a week, and I assumed that amount covered my living expenses, as my parents rarely increased it. Included in that total, I had my clothes laundered and ironed, my dinners cooked and my food shopping done. To me it seemed a fair deal.

Dean reached into his pocket and pulled out a pound coin. 'I'd give you a lift to the newsagents, but I've got to get these parcels done.'

'Yeah, totally. Thanks for this.'

'No worries. Can't let the new boy get in trouble on his first day.'

As Dean drove off, the front door of the semi-detached cottage opened. An elderly man dressed in pyjamas, dressing gown and slippers appeared.

'I knew I heard something,' the man said as he looked down at the smashed glass. 'I'm not going mad.'

'Bloody cats,' I said.

Lying is wholly unacceptable. Telling a tall story to get oneself out of a spot of bother, however, is permissible.

'I needed that to put on my All Bran,' he said, gesturing towards the milk that was slowly trickling down his driveway.

'There's a newsagents a couple of roads over. I could go and get some for you?'

'That's very kind. I don't get about as easily as I used to.'

Kath was only in the next road, so I stopped by and spouted the same story I'd given Dean.

'...so I'm heading up to the newsagents now, and I'll finish delivering what you gave me when I get back.'

'Take your time, Louis. I'm happy to carry on while you help old Ron out.'

'Thanks, Kath, you're a star. I won't be long.'

Some good did come of my untruths. Kath, who hadn't particularly warmed to me, now considered me to be a decent chap. I was a decent chap, but it was tough to get that across to the others I worked with.

*

Aside from Kath and Dean, hardly anyone found the time to speak to me while I was at work. To everyone else, I was merely the Christmas casual; it wasn't worth their time getting to know me, as I would only be there for six weeks. Even the old fart who delivered to my house kept his distance – no Christmas tip for him this year, then. The pressures of the Christmas post clearly affected people. I must admit, being in a courier job at Christmas was more taxing than I'd imagined. The cards and packages that turned up at the office every morning throughout December seemed to never end. I ranked it as my worst job ever.

'How do you fancy turning your Christmas contract into a permanent one?' the boss asked me on Christmas Eve.

'Umm....'

'We've a couple of staff leaving at the beginning of next year,' he continued. 'One on medical grounds and one retirement. And it makes sense to replace one of them with somebody who knows what they're doing.'

'That does make sense, yeah,' I stalled.

'And the customers like you.'

'Do they?'

'We've had no complaints. You must be doing something right.'

I had no intention of returning but, to avoid giving a definite answer, I said I'd think about it over Christmas and get back to him.

'Coming out later?' Dean asked me as I was leaving the office. 'We're having drinks down the Social. I'll even buy you a pint, if you're lucky.'

Suddenly, the offer of extending my employment seemed too good to turn down.

4

Getting interest from a bloke always had a strange effect on me, so deciding to stay on as a postie simply because Dean asked me to the office party was in no way out of character. Being snubbed by a bloke had a similar effect. The reason I quit my A-Levels after eight months was down to Jonny Thomas from my French class not responding well to my advances. Admittedly, I shouldn't have tried to kiss him while he was having a wee, but it was the only time I could do it without him being able to run away. He called me names, so I blew a raspberry in his face and galloped off, never to return to education.

Following Dean's invite, I left work and drove straight to Guildford to buy myself a new outfit. Crowds or no crowds, I *needed* something new for the office party. Crockham had such limited choice – being a small town – so its inhabitants were often seen wearing the same items, especially on a night out. Not that they cared; they saw it as a sign of excellent taste and a good way to start up a conversation. I ended up buying a fitted red shirt – to let everyone know I was feeling festive... and up for it. I looked shorter in red, so hopefully the four inches height advantage I had on Dean wouldn't be as noticeable. Men don't like to reach up for a snog.

After a stressful few weeks, and an even more stressful few hours of shopping, I was ready to let my hair down. At eight o'clock, with Kath tagging along behind me, I made my entrance into Crockham Social Club. Kath hadn't planned on going, but I managed to twist her arm by telling her I wanted to buy her a drink as a thank-you for helping me on my first day. I had to walk into the place with somebody, and the older and less of a threat they were the better. Inside, the Club was dimly lit, as if someone had recently turned the lights on in a room that used energy-saving bulbs. I scanned the half-full room and saw our colleagues tucked away in a corner, though Dean wasn't among them. My shoulders dropped. After I'd bought her a drink, Kath wandered over to the group. I reluctantly followed, but stayed on the periphery and chatted solely to Kath. I didn't get on with the older men in our office, only because they didn't get on with me. I got the impression they liked their posties to be a little more traditional. They never strayed from the correct uniform and invariably wore pressed trousers and shirts – complete with non-compulsory tie – and flatly refused to wear the polo shirts that Regal Post had recently brought in.

The event itself was less of a 'party' and more of a 'do'. The heating was turned up to the max, and the faint smell of stale sick filled my nostrils. I didn't dare touch the finger food. Contracting food poisoning and puking up on Dean wasn't quite what I'd had in mind when I was getting ready. My outfit deserved a better debut than this. I'd anticipated being the star attraction, but I could have arrived wearing something from a decade ago and still stolen the show.

Dean's appearance was timed to perfection, as far as I was concerned. Kath only stuck around for fifteen minutes, because her son and his family were coming to stay over Christmas. I tried to claw on to her so I wouldn't be left with just the others for company, but then Dean showed up and I relaxed my grip on Kath. I might have been wrong, but it seemed as though it was Dean's arrival that prompted her to make a move. Before she left, I gave Kath a kiss on the cheek and wished her a happy Christmas. I hoped Dean was watching, so that he would think to do the same to me later on. The top two buttons of Dean's smart black shirt were undone. The bare skin, together with the scent of musky aftershave stemming from it, was extremely inviting.

'Let the drinking commence!' Dean announced as he breezed over.

A few of the men greeted Dean's arrival with a blokey cheer. I merely gave him a smile.

'I'm going to the bar. What can I get you?' I asked him.

Without even looking at me, Dean said, 'A pint'll do me.'

The lack of a 'please' or 'thank you' hadn't bothered me. In fact, I relished the opportunity to leave the group. Dean fitted in with them much better than I did, even though he was only seven months older than me. There were a couple of factors working in his favour, though: Dean played football, despite being more of a rugby player build – one of the shorter, stockier players that get stuck in with the scrum. He also had a girlfriend. Yet until I saw her with my own eyes, I chose not to dwell on it.

'Need a hand?' Dean asked as he joined me at the bar.

I was struggling to get served due to the barmaid taking an instant dislike to me. She could clearly see that I thought I was too good for the place.

I nodded. 'If you wouldn't mind.'

Dean swiped the ten pound note out of my hand and slipped it into the back pocket of my skinny jeans. 'I'm buying Steve a pint, so I might as well get this round.'

My perineum tingled. Nobody had touched my arse in ages, albeit clothed. It was a step in the right direction, though. He could have easily handed the note back to me, or added his drink to my order and let me pay for them.

'What are you drinking?' he asked.

In most other circumstances, I'd have replied with 'double vodka and coke', because I could quaff it like a Russian fish and it often made my clothes fall off. But as the rest of the Club's clientele were drinking pints, I felt pressured to act like a bloke and do the same.

'I'll have a lager shandy, please.'

'Sure. No probs,' Dean said, turning his head so he could catch the eye of the woman who hadn't served me.

As Dean leant on the bar, I studied his profile. His average-looking face was growing on me, but his hair was in need of a serious restyle. Dark brown, mid-length hair with a fringe gelled up into spikes was so last century. But I could work on that, given the chance. The small chickenpox scar that adorned Dean's temple was the only blemish on the right side of his face. From where I was sitting, his nose looked more like a beak – the total opposite of my button nose. Whatever leftover material God had from making Dean's full-size nose was probably used to make mine, as if the runty bits of dough left after cutting mince pie circles had been squidged together to form a small, misshapen pie – the one that usually gets fed to a dog or an unwelcome guest.

Pint number one was plonked down on the bar. The noise woke me from my mini trance and reminded me there were other people in the room. Shakin' Stevens' 'Merry Christmas Everyone' was coming to an end – the only song that got me dancing at an end-of-term school disco. Those days of innocence had long gone. That track was a festive favourite, so I was rather miffed that I'd been away with the fairies for the duration. Why couldn't I have zoned out during that depressing Mud song instead? As I watched my drink being prepared, I caught Dean staring in the reflection of the mirror behind the bar. He flicked his eyes away from the reverse of my face and onto the barmaid, but he had been too slow to do so without me seeing.

'Won't be long now,' Dean turned and said to me.

'There's no hurry,' I replied a little sheepishly.

I lowered my head, took out my phone and pretended to

text. It was then I noticed how near to my knee Dean's crotch was. His shirt was tucked inside his dark jeans, and he had a big, thick belt holding them up. My legs were crossed, and I thought about slowly running my right foot up the inside of his leg, finishing at his impressive bulge. It might have been the zip on his jeans creating this illusion, but I hoped to soon find out.

'One lager avec lemonade for the lady. Would you like an umbrella and a cherry to go with that?' Dean said sarcastically as he handed me my drink.

'I'll accept the drink, thank you, but that doesn't mean I'll accept the droll remarks,' I said, swivelling my bum off the bar stool.

'Cheer up. It's Christmas!'

Dean walked over to the group and left Steve's pint on the table. Steve was outside having a cigarette and chatting up a blonde, so Dean knocked on the window and pointed towards the drink. Steve gave him the thumbs up and carried on smoking. Had Dean not worked in our office, I would have settled for Steve. He exuded the same fatherly allure as our boss did. His hairy chest added to the appeal, though only the top of it could be seen. Tease.

With Steve not around, Dean chose to keep me company rather than spend his evening with the older folk. As Steve was in his late-thirties, the average age of their group rose significantly without him there. Dean and I stood opposite each other, and as he took the odd swig from his glass, I took frequent small sips from mine. The noise emitted by the group made the silence between the two of us more noticeable.

'So, how are you finding the job?' Dean asked.

'It's really good, yeah,' I replied, trying hard not to look at his open shirt.

'Getting used to the early mornings is hard to start with, but just go to bed in the afternoon if you get tired,' he suggested.

He's dropping hints about sleeping with me!

'And are you ready for Christmas?' Dean asked, before gulping down some lager. I expect he wanted to get away from me and back to the bar as quickly as he could. He had exchanged more words with the barmaid when ordering than he had done with me. 'No last minute wrapping?'

'It's all done,' I replied. 'I like to have it all finished by the end of November.'

'That's very organised of you.'

I knew I should have gone to the trendy wine bar in town with my girl friends. At least in their presence I could be myself and have a laugh. I didn't invite them along to my office 'party' because a couple of them were irritatingly attractive, and I couldn't risk being upstaged by them. Without them there, though, capturing Dean's focus had all been too easy. Sometimes it's good to have a bit of competition, just to know what league you are in.

'I don't mind if you join the others,' I said, hoping that he would.

'Nah, it's cool. I know they're not your sort of people,' Dean astutely picked up.

I scoured my surroundings, looking for a much-needed discussion topic. At the far end of the room I spotted a dartboard, so I asked Dean if he fancied a game.

'*You* play darts?' he scoffed.

'And what's wrong with that?'

'Nothing! You just surprise me, that's all.'

Dean set off towards the bar. 'You're not going to hustle me, are you?' he asked, flashing a grin on his way past.

'Don't worry, I'll go easy on you,' I called after him, ogling his buns while he walked away unsuspectingly.

By having his shirt tucked in, there was more of Dean's bubble butt to leer at. His shirt was always hanging out at work, so now was the chance to study its shape while it was all on show.

The last time I'd played darts had been in my early teens against my dad. He'd had to make do with playing against me until Roy was a bit older. With fingers crossed, I hoped my rusty skills would help me in my hour of need. I sat on a stool near the oche – well, a scuffed line on the floor – and Dean came back from the bar with two drinks, a bag of peanuts hanging from his mouth and three darts poking from his back pocket. As he stooped over the table to place our drinks down, I reached around him and slipped the darts out. Dean opened the peanuts and tipped out three halves onto my palm. I guess it was better than not sharing them at all. After Dean had thrown a few arrows, it was clear he had never played before. I was no expert, but even a complete novice could see how shite he was. No doubt he only agreed to play to put an end to us looking like two ill at ease thirteen-year-olds on a blind date.

'The outer ring is worth double,' I instructed. 'It's the inner circle you want to aim for if you want to score highly. The red spot in the middle—'

'—is the bull's-eye,' Dean interrupted. 'What do I get if I hit that?'

'It's not easy to hit, but it's worth going for,' I said suggestively, gliding a finger around the rim of my glass as I spoke.

I never knew darts was so sexual. Whether Dean was picking up on these subliminal messages was a different matter. To help with his action, I told him it was all in the wrist and that he should pretend he was a camp man waving a hanky. It was quite refreshing for the stereotypical roles to be reversed; a gay man was teaching a straight man how to throw a better arrow. My dad would have been proud.

After being soundly beaten by Dean during a game of Round the Clock and taught a lesson in hustling, I called it a night. Dean insisted on walking me home, but not before saying his goodbyes to our colleagues.

'He's had more pricks than that dartboard,' one of Steve's group muttered, though loud enough for me to hear.

I glanced across and saw Steve laughing along with the rest of the imbeciles, one of which I would soon be replacing at the office.

'Give him a break,' I heard Dean say. 'Lou's alright.'

I put the taunt down to drunkenness, but they clearly weren't happy that I'd taken Dean away from their group. I carried on past them all and waited outside the entrance.

Annoyingly, I lived a mere six minutes from the Social Club, and it was two main roads away; there weren't any dark alleys or quiet wooded areas en route. No bark rash for my back that evening. Being forced – albeit willingly – against a cold tree and feeling Dean hit my bull's-eye was all I wanted for Christmas that year.

'So, where are you staying the night?' I asked Dean as we walked.

It was a leading question, one which I was hoping would be answered with the two small words 'at' and 'yours'. I knew Dean lived in the neighbouring town of Northwood, and he wasn't sober enough to drive.

'I'm at my parents' place. They only live a couple of minutes from town,' was the disappointing reply.

Now that it was just the two of us, Dean's true speaking voice revealed itself. It was the first time I'd heard him talk without sounding like a Londoner. Through the medium of chat, I learnt that Dean had been brought up in Guildford, so where the Cockney accent came from was a puzzle. I admit, I sometimes toned down my middle-class accent so as not to be mocked. But I spent my early years in East London, so I was merely going back to my roots.

'I've had a really good night tonight,' I said. In fact, it had been the nearest thing I'd had to a date all year.

As we reached my house, Dean and I faced each other, replicating the awkward pre-darts scenario. Having seen almost every rom-com in my vast collection several times over, I knew what was supposed to happen next. I hoped Dean did too.

'Looks as though someone's been waiting up for you,' he said, gesturing towards the living room window.

The fairy lights on our Christmas tree had lit up my mum's face as she craned her neck around it to look outside. I smiled at her through clenched teeth, then turned back to face Dean.

'There's nothing like embarrassment for warming a person up,' I said.

Dean grinned. 'Have a good one,' he said, the vapour from his breath reaching my face. 'See you at work after it's all over.'

'OK, yeah,' I said, annoyed that our evening together wouldn't be lasting any longer. I wasn't going to get my kiss goodbye because of my nosey mother. 'Thanks for a good night.'

Dean set off on his way, leaving me to go into my house alone.

'Who was that outside?' my mum quizzed. 'He looked nice.'

'Just someone from work who walked me home,' I said.

What I really wanted to say was that it had been my boyfriend. My mother's constant prying remarks about my relationships were taking their toll on our own relationship. I reckon she was more desperate for me to get a partner than I was. She had looked devastated when I'd told her that Jay and I were just friends.

Despite both being adults, Clare and I continued to hang a stocking every year. It was a small effort to make in return for some nuts, a bag of chocolate money and an orange from the fruit bowl. I sellotaped my stocking to the ledge above the fireplace and headed up to bed shortly after midnight. I took off my pulling pants and put on my pyjama bottoms. Wearing my pulling pants proved to be tempting fate once more, and they remained unseen for another year – although they didn't have long to wait for their next outing.

5

Eleven o'clock on a Christmas morning was usually the best time of the year, as it was the longest amount of time before I next went to church... unless there was a wedding or funeral, of course. It always came as a pleasant surprise when I didn't burst into flames as I entered the building, what with being a 'sinner', and all. Alas, there was little reason to celebrate following this year's service. After having my head split open by the resonance of a bellowing organ and a congregation of warbling women, I drove my parents and Clare the fifteen-minute journey to Roy and Christina's house in Worfield for turkey lunch. Rather than take Gran out of the nursing home for a day and squash her in with the six of us, Dad had made the earlier decision to visit her on Boxing Day. Clare's boyfriend, Graham – who Clare had been dating since the wedding – was also missing from proceedings, choosing to spend the day with his brother and mum. I still saw him as an add-on and not a proper member of the family, so his absence suited me fine.

From the outside, Roy and Christina's semi looked the same as it normally did, but inside was a different picture. There was silver tinsel running up the banister, paper chains in the hallway, balloons hanging from each corner of the living-cum-dining room ceiling and a five-foot Christmas tree by the patio doors.

'It looks good, don't you think?' Christina said to anyone that was listening. 'It's better to be understated than go over the top, like some of our neighbours have done. It looks so tacky.'

'The balloons are a nice touch,' Clare said.

'Roy did them. I didn't want balloons, but Roy said we had to have some.'

According to Christina, Roy felt left out of family life, although we only had her word for that. The first time I met her, she took me to one side.

'It wouldn't hurt to include your brother more,' she cautioned. 'He's always the last one to know what's going on. Talk to him more.'

Who are you to tell me that? I knew him first.

'OK,' I cowered.

Christina rapidly established herself as a figure of authority. Maybe that's what youngest siblings like in a partner. Yet from where I was sitting, it wasn't a redeeming quality. Roy was quiet and kept himself to himself, so it was unlikely he bemoaned his outsider status. It was her; she was the nosey one who wanted to know what was going on. I can see why Roy could have felt excluded, but it was his own fault if he did. He *chose* not to rejoin the family unit after finishing university. And the two of them were hardly ever invited over because he *chose* to have a domineering partner who made underhand comments, such as the state of our back garden and its lack of flowers. It was more of an allotment than a garden, that's why. If you want to be welcomed back, never criticise the garden of a retiree.

Don't get me wrong, I did love my little brother, but that was tarnished when he became part of 'Roy and Christina'. I wanted things to go back to how they used to be when he was just plain Roy. OK, be married to her and spend time with her, but stop bringing her along to family occasions. I think that's a fair compromise. Now that Roy had settled down, though, he was happy to play the role of youngest child once more. Still, anyone would think he was the eldest of the three siblings; I should have been the one getting

36

married, living in my own place and inviting family over for Christmas dinner.

Quite apart from my feelings about Roy's new life, celebrating Christmas away from home for the first time and without Gran made the day seem less special. Clare and I couldn't partake in our tradition of standing on the patio and catching the Asti cork Dad popped; the gravy tasted different, which tainted the taste of everything I'd already poured it on; and there was no money in the Christmas pudding. Nevertheless, we did have crackers – although we didn't get to pull them simultaneously in a circle, as was the tradition at home.

'One at a time!' Christina ordered. Because of her job, keeping people in order had become second nature. 'I don't want a flailing limb knocking over one of the candles and setting fire to the tablecloth.'

The four guests looked at one another and then looked at Roy. He rolled his eyes, but didn't dare say anything. Dad and he were quite similar. They were both slim six-footers, and Roy had followed Dad – who had taken early retirement – into a techy, computery job. I didn't know exactly what they did, but it sounded important. Roy tried hard to dispel his geeky nature, but there was no getting away from it. Every birthday and Christmas list he had written between the ages of five and twenty-one had a *Star Wars*-related product on it. He also wore those awful jumpers patterned with argyle diamonds – a sure-fire sign that he was aiming to reach middle-age in record time. It's highly likely he was *advised* to wear them, so it wasn't him I held responsible. I knew Dad enjoyed Roy's company, because he was far more talkative when Roy was around. Dad felt outnumbered at home. He had nobody to converse with about intellectual subjects, and he was forced to endure Aussie soap opera *Sunny Bay* while eating his dinner. He had no such worries today, though.

After everyone's crackers had been pulled, Roy read out his joke. 'What do you call a camel with three humps?'

'Put your hats on, everyone,' Christina instructed. 'I'll be taking photos later, and I want people to know we had a fun Christmas.'

'Edward Woodward,' Clare replied.

'You can swap cracker presents, if you like,' Christina said over the laughter. 'What did you all get?'

'That's the answer to an entirely different joke!' Dad corrected. 'A three-humped camel is called Humphrey. That joke is older than I am!'

'I got a fabulous ring,' I gushed, suppressing what I truly thought about the quality of Christina's crackers.

'Let's see what it looks like when it's on,' she commanded.

I hated wearing jewellery, real or plastic. Rings especially drew notice to my bony knuckles. If I managed to get them over the joint, they would then be too loose to wear properly. I didn't even wear watches or chains. They looked funny on me, like a giraffe wearing a necklace.

I did as Christina said and wedged the ring over my knuckle.

'It doesn't really look right,' she said. 'Perhaps it's a sign.'

I'll give you a sign, love, and it won't be with my ring finger.

'What are your family up to today, Christina?' Mum put forward as a topic of conversation, getting in quick before I said something improper.

After the meal, our family waited in turn for the downstairs loo to become free. We weren't keen on using the upstairs bathroom because it was situated directly above the dining table. Dad made the mistake of having a rather noisy wee in there once, and those of us below could hear every splash. His prostate problem had evidently worsened, as every time it sounded as though he had finished, another dribble could be heard. The look on

38

Christina's face had been a picture. Sour was not the word. I did an accidental purp in their bathroom once and opened a window to help the smell escape – using the pine air freshener would have given the game away completely – only to be confronted about it later in the day.

'If you *must* use our toilet for number twos, can you remember to close the window afterwards,' Christina scolded. 'It was absolutely freezing when I went in there. I had to put a layer of Triple Velvet on the seat. That's how cold it was.'

She scared me. I didn't have the nerve to tell her I'd only farted.

At Christina's request, we lifted the dining table into the corner of the room to give us more space for the present opening. Having the table out the way made it look as if they had another room. No doubt the photos Christina was taking would be posted online before the end of the day, then her lucky friends who hadn't visited their house would think it spacious.

'Just to let you know, so as not to embarrass you in the pics, you might want to turn your crown around,' Christina advised, pointing in the direction of my yellow paper hat.

'Have I got food on it? I can be so clumsy sometimes,' I said, acting like an airhead. I found it easier to take on that role when in a one-on-one situation with her.

'No, it's not grease from the food. Rather it's from your forehead.'

I unstuck the hat from my forehead and slipped it off. There were no excuses at all. I placed it back atop my head as lightly as possible, with the damp patch at the rear. It was good to be forewarned of the greasy area ahead of the photos being taken, but I wished it hadn't been Christina who told me.

The Lawrence family's grand present-opening ceremony always began straight after the Queen's speech. As a child, it

39

was a struggle to hold out for so long. Yes, we had the stockings first thing, but showing the other children at church our soft fruit and sack of gold coins when they had brought in their main presents was humiliating. The opening of gifts gradually became my least favourite thing about the day – until Christina joined the family, that is. She was more noxious than sprout wind. I hated being watched while I opened presents, just in case I didn't convey the reaction that the giver was hoping for. This Christmas, however, nobody was looking at me.

'I told you *I* was buying me a set of cake forks,' Christina grumbled at my poor brother after unwrapping one of the few presents he had gone to a shop and bought. 'There's another set *exactly* like this still under the tree.'

'That's what happens when you buy things for yourself before Christmas,' a plucky Roy replied. 'Good job I kept the receipt.'

I'd never heard Roy speak to her like that before. Christina had clearly pushed the wrong button. I shot a glance over to Clare. She was already looking at me. A fleeting glance had to suffice... until we slagged Christina off on the drive home.

'I hope this isn't all you've got me,' I heard her moan under her breath.

'Clare, find some more presents for everyone,' Mum jumped in. 'I put some from us around the back of the tree.'

'Thanks for my thermal gloves,' I said to Roy in a bid to lift his self-esteem. 'These'll come in really handy.'

'I've got the receipt if you want to change them,' Roy said.

Christina tutted. 'Why don't you stick the receipts onto the presents next year? Then you won't have to keep mentioning them.'

Though not written in stone, our Christmas Days adhered to the same routine every year. So, once the torture of presents was finally over, the natural progression of the day's events meant it was time for games. The previous year's game of I Want To Be A Millionaire caused a lively debate, with Christina adamant that the amount of BAFTA awards Titanic won was D) 10. As we had been playing in three teams of two – with me pulling her name out the hat – I put forward the idea that she was mistaking BAFTAs for Oscars. Heaven help the person who ever challenges something Christina says. Even though I am competitive when it comes to playing games, I deferred to her greater knowledge to keep the peace. I felt I had to because she was eighteen months senior, which made her six years older than Roy. Christina's introduction into our family meant I was no longer the eldest of this generation; I'd been replaced. When the answer was revealed to be A) Zero, I had to try hard not to transfer my internal grin into an external one, even though we had lost over £75,000 of paper money. It was worth it to see Christina scrambling to get her phone out of her bag and checking the answer. 'It was *nominated* for ten. I knew I was close.' Priceless.

This Christmas, we stuck to the traditional Charades. There were no teams and no points to be scored, therefore no arguments. I liked the guessing part of Charades, same as I preferred the guessing part of Pictionary, rather than the drawing. (Whenever a straight line was drawn, I'd shout out, 'It's a stick!' just to annoy.) I couldn't act and I couldn't draw, but I was a brilliant guesser. Dad found a small amount of floor space to act out his Charade.

'Film... Three words... First word,' everyone said in unison.

'Standing... Breathing... Thinking... Frustration... Man with hands on hips... Angry,' I said, describing *everything* Dad was conveying. I knew it was winding him up, but it made the rest of us laugh. 'Twelve Angry Men!'

Dad's phone rang.

'Answering a phone call... Listening... Sticking finger in ear,' I carried on, forcing Dad to leave the room and close the door behind him.

A minute or two later he came back in.

'That was the nursing home. Gran's been taken to hospital.'

6

I must have been the only person in the country looking forward to going back to work after the Christmas break. Thankfully, the fall Gran sustained wasn't serious, and we were able to ease our guilt by spending some quality time with her at hospital on Boxing Day. After Gran was released from hospital on December 30th, I walked to her nursing home almost every day, hoping that Dean would drive past in his van and stop for a chat. My permanent contract started in late January, and all I could think about until then was being reunited with Dean. The fact I hated the job hadn't entered my thoughts. But I'd managed to survive being a postie at Christmas, so the rest of the year should be a breeze.

Nothing at work seemed to have changed when I eventually became a full-time employee: I was on the same delivery, it was freezing cold outside and there was a lot of mail to deal with. January signalled the start of chunky holiday magazines, stacks of *Reader's Digest* material and endless leaflets advertising cut price sales. One thing that had changed, though, was Dean's appearance: he was wearing shorts. I had always been a sucker for a decent pair of legs, and that was down to a sports teacher at my secondary school. His fit, tanned, hairy legs set the standard for other legs to match up to. Those legs had been unrivalled up until now, but there was a new contender in town. I fell in lust with Dean the moment I set eyes on his brawny stilts. There's something safe and sturdy about a man with thickset legs, like a lighthouse or a mighty oak tree. The beefiness of his calves made me want to sink my teeth into them. I must have looked like a salivating coma victim when he came over and spoke to me.

'Hello, mate. Good to see you again,' Dean said.

'What's with the shorts? It's January, not July!'

Improvised and *witty. Bravo to me!*

'One of my mates was killed in a car accident on New Year's Eve. He used to wear shorts to football training, even through winter, so I thought I'd do the same,' he said, causing my inane grin to fade. 'Any parcels for me today?'

'No, nothing from me,' I said, subtly kicking the two biggish parcels under my bench out of view. I didn't want Dean to hate me for giving him more work to do, so I struggled out to my delivery with them on my bike.

For the next few days, my conversations with Dean were as short as his shorts. Christmas Eve now seemed like yonks ago. Perhaps Dean had been ribbed by Steve and the others for not spending time with them at the office party, then leaving with the office homo. By this point, a few of the men, including Steve, were now starting to let me join in with their light-hearted office banter. Dean had proved that it was safe to talk to me, and they duly followed suit. To be fair to Steve, he was a hard worker. Any overtime that needed doing, Steve was the one to do it. Not because he liked the job, but because he was divorced and had three kids to support.

*

A couple of weeks later and my relationship with Dean still hadn't blossomed, so I thought I'd give it a nudge in the right direction. One morning in particular, I arose fifteen minutes earlier than usual so I could tart myself up a bit. I hair-straightened my fringe, concealed even the tiniest of

44

blemishes and wriggled into my pulling pants – I always felt more confident when I had them hugging my balls. On delivery that morning, I reviewed my mental timetable of Dean's whereabouts, put my mailbag over my shoulder and started delivering. When I saw his blue van approaching, I popped a minty Tic Tac in and waved my arms as if in distress. The van drew level with me, and the driver's window wound down.

'What's up?' Dean asked.

'I cycled over a broken headlight and got a puncture,' I said pitifully.

'That was rather dopey.'

'It would have to happen on a day when I'm meeting a friend for lunch,' I sighed.

'I've got a few more parcels to deliver, but I can come give you a hand after, if you like?'

'That would be ace. I'm never going to finish in time otherwise,' I said, regretting that I'd used the word 'ace'. That wasn't in the conversation I'd been rehearsing all morning. And neither was Dean's next comment.

'You do know you've got a snail on your forehead?'

I quickly wiped my hand across my brow, knocking a tiny snail to the ground in the process. And then – and I'm not proud of it – I let out a feeble scream.

The snail must have been there for about an hour, as I'd cycled through a wet, low-hanging branch on the way out to my delivery. Nobody had been about to see that branch incident, though, so I downgraded it on my long list of embarrassing moments. Why hadn't old Ron – or anybody else I'd already stopped to chat to – told me about the snail? I could understand if I'd had a smattering of bird poo on my shoulder, but a posh slug on my forehead?

Te-rrific. Now Dean will for ever know me as Snail Head. This is not good.

Dean checked his mirrors and sped away, tyres

screeching. He was showing off for my benefit, of course.

Fifteen minutes later, I was struggling to lift my cannily injured bike into the back of Dean's van.

'Right, Heath Way will be tricky to deliver in a van. So, if you walk up one side and down the other, I'll crack on with the cul-de-sacs,' Dean ordered, effortlessly lifting my bike and throwing it into the back of his van.

'Yeah, OK. I'll meet you back here.'

'Unless I finish first, then I'll come find you.'

We delivered our sections and, true to his word, Dean tracked me down. It wasn't hard to miss him, because he flashed his headlights as he drove towards me. In the most covert manner possible, I wiped my nose on my fingerless glove to get rid of the dew drop that was forming. Despite the temperature being in single digits, Dean had sweat on his brow when he pulled up alongside me. He had obviously been dashing between houses, no doubt trying to impress me with how quick he was. I mean, what's not to like about someone who has had a mollusc on his forehead?

When I finished delivering my section, I hopped into the van and Dean drove us back to the office. I couldn't resist taking sly glances at his legs. Because he was seated, Dean's shorts had inched up and uncovered his mighty thighs. I felt the urge to reach over and place my hand on his left leg. It wasn't the same type of urge that made me want to chomp into a window sill – you know, the juicy bit that overhangs the wall – but it was an urge, nonetheless. There were no health and safety issues stopping me from this urge, though. I didn't have much of a conscience when it came to men, and the little piece I did have liked to sit in the sun and drink cocktails, not to be disturbed. I was about to reach over and brush an imaginary insect off Dean's leg, when he spoke. Dean, that is, not the imaginary insect.

'I don't suppose you play football?' he asked.

'No, no, I don't,' I replied, forcing my eyes from his

meaty quads. 'Why do you ask?'

'Well, my mate Coxy that died at New Year, me and the lads from football are organising a five-a-side memorial competition for him. The four delivery offices in the area are putting in teams, and I'm in charge of getting a Crockham team together.'

As Dean spoke, my eyes wandered back to his legs. I found myself sitting on my hands, as if the masculine part of my brain was subconsciously telling me they would be better there than on Dean's thigh.

'Three of our team are over fifty,' Dean continued, 'If you played, I could put one of them on the subs' bench. It might only be a friendly competition, but I still want to win.'

'If you want to win, you don't want me on your team. Believe me, I'm terrible at football.'

'Come along and support us. We've pencilled it in for the last Saturday in March.'

'Yeah, I'm up for that.'

Being forced to play football – be it at school or with Roy in the back garden – had put me off the sport, though I'd recently started watching highlights of matches. I didn't fully understand the rules, and I didn't particularly enjoy the games. Yet I thought it was about time I looked beyond the fit players and their WAGs and took an interest in the sport itself, especially if I wanted something to chat to blokes about.

We passed Steve on our way back to the office, and Dean stopped to give him a lift. Steve put his bike in the back alongside mine, jumped in next to me and warmed his hands up in front of an air vent. This turned out to be a stroke of luck, as it meant I had to shuffle nearer to Dean to make room for Steve. The consequence being that Dean lightly grazed my leg whenever he changed gear. I made no attempt to move my right leg away from the gear stick, even though the baggy leather that encompassed the gear stick's base conjured up images of my dad's floating scrotum. Now that Steve was present, Dean's faux-Cockney accent picked up again.

'Did that bloke on your round get you that discount phone you wanted?' Dean asked Steve.

'Yup,' Steve said, getting the phone in question out and handing it to me. 'It's worth three hundred new, but I only paid one-fifty for it. My old SIM card works in it too.'

As Steve started to list its technical qualities, I flicked through his list of contacts. All my friends were getting touchscreen phones, but I was determined not to appear a copycat and vowed against purchasing one, preferring to stick with my trusted flip-open phone. It was so old it had gone past the uncool phase and was heading towards retro style status. I liked to feel the buttons as I texted. Texting blind – while my phone was out of sight, under the dinner table or steering wheel, say – was much easier on a non-touchscreen phone, and it left my screen free of unsightly fingerprints.

'Hey, isn't that the bird you were chatting up at Christmas, Stevo?' Dean said as we drove through Crockham high street.

'Beep the horn at her!'

Neither of them heard the twinkly noise coming from my pocket.

I'd added quite a few numbers to my phone over the years, but none of them created the high I felt from being in possession of the eleven digits that formed Dean's number. The best thing of all, he didn't know I had it. On a couple of drunken occasions that February, I called Dean from a phone box outside the local pub in the early hours. I didn't speak; I just listened to him while he answered, hopefully from his bed. I couldn't be suspected of doing it, because I didn't have his number... or so he thought. I'd had stalker-like tendencies before, but not to this degree.

48

7

The five women I worked with were too old or too scatterbrained (or both) to be considered serious competition. The only attractive woman to spend a considerable amount of time in our office was Debbie from Regal Post's health insurance department. Every month, without fail, she signed up new members, updated existing members on their policies or persuaded them to increase their payment in return for a super-duper policy. The five minutes that the men in the office got to spend alone with Debbie must have been worth the extra two quid a week that was deducted from their pay. To them, coming into contact with a pretty woman was a rare treat, like a Turkish Delight. I liked it when Debbie came in, as it was the only day of the month when the older men managed to hold in their farts.

'Morning, Louis,' Kath said as I walked over to my bench one chilly March morning. 'This is Amy. It's her first day, and I've been put in charge of "mentoring" her. It's no longer called training, apparently.'

'Oh... Hello,' I said.

'Hi,' Amy replied, beaming a lovely big grin.

Health insurance Debbie had been toppled from her perch. There were going to be a lot of fart-free days from now on, I could tell.

Amy was undersized, and her long dark hair was tied back, which placed the emphasis on a mouth that was too large for her face. She did, however, have great boobs. I was doomed. I could compete with women on most fronts – sense of humour, peachy bum, killer legs, winning smile – but this was one department where I didn't stand a chance. The blue polo shirt Amy later changed into was a snug fit, complementing her hefty bosom. Even I found it tough maintaining eye contact.

I've been told that straight blokes see any hole as a goal, but a nice pair of boobs would make luring men towards mine a whole lot easier. I wouldn't swap my cock and balls for anything, but a pair of breasts would be advantageous. Supposedly, personality is the trait that overrides all others when a man lists what he is searching for in a woman. Bollocks! It's big tits! When asked, men frequently say, 'I want someone I can watch the footy with, have a laugh with over a pint down my local and who won't mind when I burp and fart.' If that's the case, they should try dating other men. Tits aside, another bothersome thing about Amy was that she was rather likeable, which I had hoped she wouldn't be.

The office was quieter than usual. Dean was away on holiday with his girlfriend for the week to celebrate his thirtieth birthday. Before long, Kath was rattling off to Amy the same guff she had lectured me with four months previously. The two of them were at the bench that faced mine, so Amy and Kath were working directly behind me. With a slight turn of the head, I could listen to what Amy had to say without actually having to speak to her. Amongst other things, I heard Amy tell Kath she lived in Crockham with her family and that she was only on a six-month contract, which suited her perfectly because she was hoping to start university in September. She said she had finished her A-Levels the previous summer and was taking a year out of education to raise funds for her studies. Kath had only asked for her name, not her bloody life story. Amy shadowed Kath – who knew most of the deliveries in the

50

office and a lot of the customers on them – for a day, before being left to manage on her own.

*

I knew what it was like being the youngest in an office full of fogies so, on her second day, I felt obliged to talk to Amy. I was still a relative newcomer myself. Plus, I needed someone younger to talk to within the office. The topics of conversation didn't vary much. Other than work-related issues, there were four staple subject matters: fishing, ailments, favourite dinners and the glory days of West Ham United. There were only so many things people could say about them before they started to repeat themselves.

'What are you hoping to study at uni?' I probed while showing Amy the canteen. It was more of a small room that housed four plastic patio chairs and three vending machines, but everyone still called it a canteen.

'I'd like to do environmental science up at Leeds,' she replied.

'That's a bit of a trek.'

'It's about three hours by train, but I want to get my licence this year so I can drive up. My parents said they'd buy me a car if I passed my test. They told me they'd try to help out when they can, because my uni fees are going to be, like, astronomical.'

'How come you've ended up here? You're way too qualified for this job.'

Amy slotted some coins into the vending machine for snacks. 'It's easy money. And I can walk here because I live round the corner. I was working at the bank in town up until Christmas.'

I couldn't repress a groan. 'They're all knob heads in there. And the manager hasn't got a clue how to manage. I hated working there so much that I walked out.'

'My dad's the manager.'

I choked on my Red Bull.

'Must be a different manager,' I said, trying to redeem myself. I coughed hard a few times to make it look as though my reddening face had been caused by the fizz going down the wrong pipe. 'It was ages ago that I worked there.'

'It's OK. He *is* a bit of a prat. It's the reason I left.'

'My dad's a prat too. Living at home sucks.'

'Join the club. I can't wait to get away.'

I knew I sounded like an old person trying to be young and cool, but I just wanted Amy to feel at ease knowing we had things in common. As it turned out, we were more alike than I realised.

Because Amy's start point was two roads before mine, we cycled out together. The newer entrants were always given the bogey rounds, though I'd grown to know and like the one I was on. It was the long cycle out that put my senior colleagues off claiming the delivery for themselves. After I'd posted to my last house, I rode over to Amy's patch and gave her a hand, cycling back to the office when we had finished. To thank me, Amy bought me a Mars Bar from the canteen, so I carried on helping her for the rest of that week.

*

Now, you would think that receiving help five days on the trot would be enough. I know that if the roles were reversed, I'd have declined more help for fear of becoming a burden. I certainly wouldn't risk doing an Oliver Twist by asking for more. But I wasn't Amy, and I agreed to her pleas of help on the following Monday. The fact it was Dean's first day back after his holiday had nothing to do with my decision. OK, it was *partly* to do with that. Actually, my extended benevolence had a *lot* to do with Dean's reappearance. Befriending Amy had nettled a few of the salivating old men, as if I was stepping on their toes, or something. Like they ever stood a chance.

'Miss me while I was away?' Dean asked as he perched himself on my bench.

'Not really,' I replied. 'It's been nice and quiet.'

'Yeah, whatever.'

'Where did you go? You're not very brown.'

'Liverpool.'

'Oh... Nice.'

'It was, actually,' a defensive Dean said. 'Holidays abroad are such a rip-off. We refuse to go out of principle. Anyway, I got to look round Anfield and watch the derby game against Everton.'

'Didn't Everton win that match?'

Dean ignored me and nodded in Amy's direction. 'Who's the new girl?' he asked, reducing his customary loud voice to a whisper.

I turned to look over my shoulder, even though I knew who he was talking about. 'Oh, that's Amy. She's only temporary. I've been giving her a hand the last few days because she's a bit slow. She bought me a Mars Bar, though, so it's not all bad.'

'Give her a chance. You weren't exactly perfect when you first started,' Dean argued. Without pausing to let me respond, he carried on, raising his voice so those nearby could hear. 'Lou, don't forget it's the football tournament next weekend. I know how much you're looking forward to eyeing up the men in their shorts and getting in the showers with them afterwards.'

The office's male contingent let out pathetic cheers. 'You can tell Dean's back!' one of them called out.

'OK, *Dean*. But there's no need to shout, I'm standing right next to you,' I said in the same tone and volume Dean had used.

Kath, who worked at the bench to the right of mine, giggled. Dean pretended not to hear us. As comebacks go, mine was pretty poor, but it was the best I could do at that time of the morning. Several wittier ones came to me on delivery when I reviewed the scenario.

'With me playing,' Dean boasted, 'we're gonna do loads better than the game at them.'

'Talk in riddles much?' was my response.

Although I'd been studying psychology before I walked out of college, it didn't need a graduate to fathom that his jumbled words were down to a lack of concentration. Dean might have been talking to me, but he was already thinking about impressing the new girl.

8

A couple of days later, there was a near-naked man on my bench when I arrived at work. Bronzed skin, rippling abs, bulging biceps, chunky thighs: the man on the postcard had the lot.

'OK, so which of you comedians put this here?' I asked. 'For your information, I'm not into muscle men.'

'It's addressed to you, Lou-Lou,' Steve said from his bench, which was situated next to Amy's.

I turned the postcard over. 'You've had a good read, then?'

'Being nosey is all part of the job.'

Hi Lou-Lou!
Saw this in a shop and thought you'd like it. He's a hottie! Hope the paperboy job is going well. Make sure you come down and visit me soon.
Jay-Jay x

The guy on the postcard may well have been what Jay deemed sexy, but I preferred my men less preened and more masculine. I hadn't been to Brighton since New Year, so I was due another trip. In fact, Jay and I had talked about me searching for work down there and finding a flat together, but then I was offered the full-time postie job. Had it not been for Dean, I would have requested a transfer to the Brighton office.

'What you got there?' Dean asked, swiping the postcard

out of my hand. 'You don't seriously like this sort of thing, do you?'

'What's not to like? He looks pretty fit to me.'

'And to me,' Kath chipped in.

Dean tossed the postcard onto my bench. 'It's all done on computers. That six-pack has been airbrushed on.'

'Jealousy is an illness,' I said, leaning the postcard against the top of my bench for all to see. 'Get well soon.'

'I'm not surprised you're single if that's the sort of guy you chase after. You've got no chance.'

'Louis is allowed to dream if he wants,' Kath said. 'It's not doing any harm.'

While we had been talking, Amy had quietly turned up at her bench... ten minutes late. Her excuse being that the early starts were beginning to catch up with her.

'I've got no energy this morning,' Amy said, taking off her excessively long knitted scarf.

'I'll get you a coffee,' Dean said. 'That'll wake you up.'

'Cheers, Deano. Black with two sugars.'

Deano? That's rather over-friendly for someone she's only just met.

'Cheers for offering to get me one, Deano,' I mocked as he walked off towards the canteen.

A few minutes later, Dean reappeared. He gave Amy her coffee and placed a can of Red Bull on my bench.

'I know you drink this instead of coffee,' Dean said.

He noticed!

'Thank you.'

'Would you be able to help me out today, Lou?' Dean asked. 'Could you take some of your own parcels? I've got loads of them today and I need to get done early.'

'Yeah, course. Anything to help out a mate.'

Every morning, before we were let loose on the public, us posties had to queue up at the secure area to be given our Crucial Delivery items – items that contained valuables and were insured against loss or damage. After I'd collected mine, I walked outside and saw Dean getting into his van. There was nothing unusual about this. What was unusual was that he was accompanied by Amy. I couldn't stop myself running over to the van.

'What about your Crucials?' I asked Amy.

'Dean sneaked in earlier and got them for me,' she replied.

'Are we not cycling out together, then?' I carried on at her.

'No, I offered to give her a lift,' Dean butted in. 'She's on a hard delivery. It takes her ten minutes just to cycle out.'

'I manage it fine,' I said, getting worked up.

'But you do it every day,' Amy disputed. 'Your body's used to it.'

'That's not the point. Why do I not get a lift?'

'There's only room for one,' Dean stated.

'Me and Steve managed to fit in there together,' I argued.

'The van was empty that time. I haven't got room for two bikes *and* parcels.'

'You could've given me a lift out before.'

'You never asked,' he snapped back. 'And Amy's prettier than you.'

They laughed as Dean drove off, causing my brain to boil over at the unfairness of it all. I bet *she* didn't have to let air out of her front tyre to get Dean's help. The motive behind him asking me to take my own parcels was now evident, and it wasn't that he wanted a free Mars Bar.

*

We were all working on the morning of the football tournament. The early finishes in the week were the best thing about the job, but the downside to that was having to work Saturdays to make up the full forty-hour week. Most of us finished before noon, so it wasn't a complete waste of a Saturday – although it meant that Friday nights were no longer drinking nights.

'You'll never guess who me and my husband saw eating lunch at Pizza Den yesterday,' an excited Kath said to me that Saturday morning.

'I don't know,' I grumpily replied.

I didn't have time for idle chatter. I wanted to be in the office for the least amount of time possible, deliver as quickly as I could and get home for a power nap before heading to the football.

'That's why it's called guessing. Just have a guess!' Kath challenged, jiggling up and down like a demented squirrel.

'Kate and Wills.'

'In Pizza Den? In Crockham? Don't be stupid.'

'You're the one acting stupid, not me,' I said irritably. If there was one insult over any other that raised my hackles, it was being called stupid.

'There's no need to be like that.'

I apologised without meaning it. 'Who did you see?'

'Dean and Amy!'

'Maybe they were just delivering there and stopped off for a snack.'

'No, they were having a full lunch.'

I slowed my work rate so I could pay full attention to what Kath had to say.

'There's definitely something going on with them,' an animated Kath continued. 'According to Steve, Dean picks her up and drops her home every day.'

'But she only lives a few minutes away.'

'That's not all. Steve said that Dean's been helping Amy with her driving. When they finish work, he drives them over to the Pizza Den car park in the van, then they swap seats and Amy practises her manoeuvres.'

'I bet she does.'

'Amy looked so shameful when she saw me, like a dog that's been caught pooing in a slipper.'

She is a dog.

'Dean wouldn't do anything with her,' I assured myself. 'Have you forgotten that he's supposed to be in a relationship?'

'Maybe this will help him decide whether getting married is the right thing for him. Perhaps that's what I needed before I jumped into my first marriage.'

'Who said anything about marriage? I think you're getting a bit carried away, Kath.'

Not that she needed an excuse to talk about her own life.

'Dean's getting married. Didn't you know?'

I turned to look at Kath. 'He's...getting married?'

'Yes. He proposed on Christmas Day.'

The day after our date? He must've been thinking about her the whole time he was with me. All future Christmases have now been ruined.

'But... But he doesn't wear an engagement ring,' I said.

'Well, maybe he—'

'Good morning,' Amy chimed in, rocking up for work ten minutes late again.

'Ooh, hello,' Kath said with a start, a look of guilt plastered all over her face.

'And what are you two gossiping about?' Amy asked as she hung her jacket and scarf on the side of her bench.

'Dogs,' I said bluntly. 'And how dangerous they can be when they're let off the lead to have a sniff around.'

'That's a pretty *random* conversation,' Amy stated, emphasising local students' favourite word. Surely they can conjure up less annoying adjectives?

'Don't you agree that dogs need to be taught right from wrong? Otherwise they'll think they can have whatever they want,' I said, carrying on with my allegory.

'Yeah, I guess,' Amy responded.

'And if we're not careful, these dogs will be free to chase after postmen. Do you hear what I'm saying?' I asked with rancour.

'Seriously, Lou. You need a hobby.'

Amy was right. I had nothing better to do than to warn a girl off a boy. In case there wasn't enough tension in the air, the boy showed his face, as he so often did when the girl turned up.

'Morning all,' Dean chirped, echoing the gaiety of Amy's entrance. Kath and I stayed quiet and carried on with our work.

'Hi, Deano,' Amy responded. 'Is that for me?'

I desperately wanted to turn around and see what Amy was talking about, but I didn't wish to look like someone who desperately wanted to turn around and see; I couldn't let Dean think I was in any way interested. I remained facing my bench and waited for the conversation to pan out.

'Yup. Black with two sugars. Just how you like it.'

'Man, I really need this today,' Amy said without thanking Dean. 'Took me ages to get out of bed this morning.'

I looked over at Kath, who had also turned to look at me. I bet it *had* taken her ages... to get her knickers back on and wipe the cum off her breasts.

'Will your *fiancée* be at the footy tournament later?' I asked Dean, glancing at Amy to see if she twitched. She didn't.

'Not sure. She might.'

Dean stuck around for the next half an hour and helped Amy gain lost time by giving her a hand to prep her mail. They kept their voices low, but I heard some of their in-jokes, which were all followed by an unnatural guffaw.

'Because we need to get done early,' Dean suggested to Amy, 'how about we team up and deliver your round, then you can come and help me deliver parcels? You can be my runner.'

'Are you losing your stamina in your old age?' Amy teased.

'Cheeky cow! I turned thirty, not sixty!'

'You drive like a sixty-year-old.'

'And *you* drive like a six-year-old!'

'Keep it down,' I called over to them. 'Some of us are trying to work.'

'Sorry, Lou,' Dean said. 'Are we making you jealous?'

'Hardly. I just don't see why those of us who come in on time should get penalised by those who come in late.'

'Someone's obviously not getting any,' Dean said to Amy, causing her to giggle again.

Dean clearly had time to spare before setting out to deliver parcels, and he could have put it to much better use. Before Amy joined the workforce, Dean would go out early and leave parcels on doorsteps, as the majority of customers were still in bed. Parcels weren't allowed to be left unattended, and nothing was allowed to be delivered before seven o'clock, but that didn't stop Dean in his quest to finish earlier. He signed for customers' Crucial Deliveries, and all recognition of the parcel needing a signature was peeled off so the recipients were none the wiser. It was against the rules and a sackable offence, but there were never any complaints. None of this troubled me when we were chummy, but now that Dean was chummy with someone else, his rule-breaking bugged me a lot. I expect he taught Amy to do the same when they were out delivering together. Shortcuts, yes, I took a few – cutting across gardens if I knew the owner was out, cycling up driveways and leaning my bike against garages – but nothing that would get me the sack. Maybe a trip to the boss's office was called for. In just the first two weeks of knowing each other, Amy and Dean's friendship had well and truly put my and Dean's in the shade. My hopes to snare Dean had taken a huge knock. Still, if there's one thing us gay men do well, it's a good old bitch fight. And if things carried on as they were, I was prepared to get my claws out.

9

I'd been eagerly anticipating the football tournament because it involved my two favourite people: me and Dean. But it had now been tainted by Amy's arrival. Thanks to Kath's dire timekeeping, the two of us turned up at the school venue in Northwood a tad late. We could hear that matches were underway as we made our way across the school playground towards the playing field. To make the occasion look more credible as a charity event, there was a St. John Ambulance tent nearby and a few tables with players' wives and mothers selling homemade produce. Kath deposited her offering on one of the tables, then we walked over to the action.

'Stop mincing!' Kath joked as she struggled to keep up with me. 'We're going to a football match, not a George Michael concert.'

'For your information, this is a fast-paced walk, not a mince,' I corrected her. 'And George Michael stopped being relevant *years* ago.'

The playing field was still quite boggy from overnight rain, so I slowed when we reached it to prevent any mud splashing onto my jeans. Two of the pitches looked suitable for purpose, with professional corner flags and five-a-side goal nets. The third pitch, however, was roughly marked out, with the school's javelins doubling up as goal posts and traffic cones instead of corner flags. It was clear the event had been organised by men. Dean's Crockham team was in action on the shoddy pitch, so Kath and I made our way over. Benches from the school gymnasium had been positioned along each side of the pitch to indicate the field of play. They also made handy seats, though there wasn't any room for two latecomers to perch.

'I can't believe I paid two pounds to get in and there's nowhere to sit.'

'Sorry, Louis,' Kath said. 'If I hadn't been so busy making my blueberry muffins, we'd have got here earlier.'

'It's fine.'

It was far from fine. Our job involved being on our feet six days a week, and I certainly didn't want to be doing the same for three hours of my leisure time. Although I'd gone to bed after work, my over-active brain prevented me from getting any sleep. It would be fair to say that I was in an irritable mood long before I'd picked Kath up from her cottage in Crockham.

'Why haven't they put any chairs out?' I moaned.

'People don't usually sit on chairs when they come to these sorts of matches. The legs would sink into the ground,' Kath quite sensibly said.

'They could've put more benches out, though.'

'Don't be so woolly, Louis. Standing never killed anyone.'

'I think the people in the Hillsborough disaster might disagree with you,' I said. I was determined not to be outsmarted by Kath, who duly ignored my comment.

On the far side of the pitch were the Crockham supporters, who I'd spotted early on thanks to Amy's horsey mouth. She was down the end near one of the 'corner flags'. It took me less than a second to realise why she was there: Dean was in goal. Amy and I acknowledged each other with a smile, though neither of us meant it. I didn't want to stand too near my spectator rival, but I wanted a decent enough view to keep a beady eye on her. As Kath and I neared our colleagues' group, she pointed out a few faces that she recognised.

'Those three kids belong to Steve,' Kath said. 'He only sees them on weekends now, poor thing. And the woman with the hat on is Liz, Dean's fiancée.'

Great. Now I know her name. Liz. Liz. Liz. Say it enough times and it loses all meaning. What is a Liz? Liz likes her jizz with a bit of fizz.

To describe Dean's fiancée as a fiancée would be making her sound attractive. Prospective spouse sounded more dowdy and suited her better. The reality was confirmed and there was no hiding from the fact: Dean genuinely did have a partner. It had been an intentional move to not question Dean about his relationship status, because the less I knew, the less guilty I would feel about pursuing him. There was a huge chunk of his life I knew nothing about, and I suddenly felt as though I didn't know the real Dean at all. I'd not given this woman serious thought thus far. I hadn't credited her with being an actual person, one who had feelings for Dean just as I did. To her credit, she was displaying matching colours: her hair, skin and teeth were all beige. Even the straw hat she was wearing to keep the weak sun off her beige face and neck was beige. From what I could see, there was nothing special about Liz, so it was no surprise that Dean was tempted to stray.

'Kath! Here, take my seat,' one of our colleagues said, performing an uncharacteristically selfless gesture.

'Thanks, love,' Kath replied. 'My feet could do with a rest.'

So much for 'standing never killed anyone'. I'd accompanied her to the event, so the least she could do was stand with me and stop me from looking like a loner. It was the only reason I'd offered her a lift.

A few spectators moved out the way so Kath could get to the newly vacated seat on the bench. The gap in the crowd swiftly sealed, preventing me from following Kath through. As it was, I ended up standing behind a seated Liz, who didn't appear interested in the match at all. She was too busy reading her magazine to realise she was taking up valuable seating space. I pondered tapping her on the shoulder and telling the naïve sow what Dean was really like, mentioning the flirting, the driving lessons and the meal at Pizza Den. Dean would either thank me for getting him out of his relationship and thereby paving the way clear for him and Amy to get together, or he would hate me for poking my nose into his business and trying to stir things up between him and his prospective spouse. Once she was out the way, I'd then only have Amy to deal with.

During lulls in the game, I peered over Liz's shoulder and tried to read some of the articles in her magazine. I was nosey like that. As she read, Liz moved her finger along the line she was on. I could have understood her actions if she was reading braille, but it seemed an odd thing for an adult to do. When Liz reached the magazine's spring horoscope feature, my eyes followed her finger along the line of Pisces. Pisceans: like to avoid ill-feeling; don't like to experiment; are sexually undemanding; are over-possessive; have an inclination to physical laziness; are greedy; are dependable, like a pair of old slippers. A typical Piscean would work well as a farmer. Being a Piscean, a trout farmer would be highly appropriate. I was too far away to read it clearly, but my predictions were probably more accurate than the ones she was reading. I bet it didn't say anything about keeping an eye out for a love rival.

The supporters around me let out a collective sigh as Dean picked up the ball from the back of his net. He had already let in two goals before Kath and I arrived. Liz looked up briefly, but then it was eyes down for another read.

'Keep going, Deano!' I heard Amy call out.

Aside from using them as a reading guide, there was something else that puzzled me about Liz's fingers: there was no engagement ring. I knew Dean didn't wear one – for a reason I'd yet to fathom – but women love engagement rings almost as much as the man they're engaged to, so the ring was noticeable by its absence.

They can't be officially engaged if neither of them has a ring. Dean probably asked for it back. I bet he only proposed because he felt he had to. He didn't think it through, and now he's changed his mind about getting married. I know I would if I'd proposed to a Liz-type person.

A whistle blew to signify the end of Crockham's first of four group matches. There were ten teams in total, and the top two from both groups would qualify for the semi-finals, with a final scheduled for six o'clock. With all matches lasting fifteen minutes, it was going to be a long afternoon. As our team trudged off the pitch for their towels and refreshments, our supporters flocked around the players and congratulated them on a valiant, but losing, performance.

'That team recruited lads from outside the area,' Dean said. 'We didn't stand a chance.'

'Yeah, they had... an unfair advantage,' Steve added, puffing heavily. 'I'd go and complain... but I can't be arsed.'

Sounds like sore loser talk to me.

The crowd gradually dispersed during the five-minute interval, and it gave Dean a chance to introduce his freckle-faced fiancée to a few people. Despite being more or less the same age, Liz and Dean looked so wrong together. How was it that she had a partner and me not? If anyone had spinster potential it was her. Selfish cow, keeping a fit bloke all to herself. Whatever happened to free love? I studied her as she spoke to Kath. Only the bottom set of Liz's teeth was visible, which made her mouth look evil and triangular, like a beige Darth Vader. To help me remain calm before Dean ushered Liz in my direction, I started to mentally list all the things that her thin upper lip could have been hiding.

False teeth, no teeth, little teeth, more beige teeth, decaying teeth, braces, a high gum line, a low gum line, ulcers... Will anyone notice if I run away?

After briefly acquainting Amy with his prospective spouse, Dean moved her on towards me. I didn't want to kiss her, so I shook her hand. It was like grasping a soggy Ryvita. She would need a firmer wrist than that if she wanted to keep a man happy. I grinned a big grin – showing her that it was wholly acceptable to bare one's upper teeth.

'...and this is Lou, the office gay. The one you're always talking about,' a twitchy Dean said.

Liz's naturally sombre face came to life. She let go of my hand and threw her arms around me. Talk about scaring the sweet bejesus out of someone.

'I love gay guys!' she trilled.

'Whenever I talk work, Liz asks about you,' Dean revealed.

Liz relaxed her grip, but I was far from relaxed. I stood rigid while she and Dean continued to chatter. It appeared that Liz's thin upper lip was hiding a beautiful smile. How disappointing.

'*He's* the one who keeps talking about you,' the-woman-formerly-known-as-the-fiancée-but-is-now-called-Liz said. 'Lucky I'm not the jealous type!'

'Yeah,' I said, followed by a short exhaled sniff-laugh to let her think I found her funny.

Little did the dollop know that it was Amy she should have been watching out for.

10

Crockham's second and third matches took place on the professionally set-out pitches, so our supporters, even Kath, had to stand for a time. Not that I needed her for company now, as Liz hadn't let me out of her sight. Out on the gay circuit she would be labelled a 'fruit fly'. Like a straight man driving a MINI, a Crockham goal was seldom seen. When Crockham did manage to find the back of the opposition's net, Liz clapped her soggy Ryvita hands together and let out a shriek. She was the one acting like a gay man, not me. It was highly irritating, and even Dean looked ashamed by his fiancée's actions. I had been looking forward to seeing some nice guys in shorts, but they were few and far between. Naturally, my eyes were focused on Dean most of the time, but his shorts were long and his socks were pulled up to his knees. Spoil sport. There were one or two fit players on the other teams, though, and it was an excitable Liz who pointed them out to me. Perhaps she did consider me to be a threat and wanted to swerve my eyes away from Dean and onto someone else.

As soon as we found out Crockham's final match was taking place on the shoddy pitch, Liz darted over to reserve us some bottom space near the goal. I let out a sigh as I sat down, then realised I must have sounded like someone twice my age. I'd been on my feet for the best part of a day, so that's how I justified taking someone else's spot on the bench. Amy loitered around her original position by the traffic cone in the corner. Much to Amy's displeasure, Dean

69

stood by me and Liz until he was called onto the field of play. While Liz rambled on about her wedding plans, I wondered if Dean had known any of the details or was learning about them at the same time I was. Flashbacks of the one-sided conversations Christina had bored me with were forming.

'When is the big event?' I enquired, my eyes close to glazing over.

Liz and Dean looked at each other.

'We had planned on getting married in May,' Liz said. 'But money's been a bit tight. That's why I've not got a ring yet.'

There was a tinge of sadness in her voice. Although I knew what a ringless finger looked like, she showed me her bare digit for added impact.

'I told you at Christmas,' Dean said firmly. 'I'll get you a classy one when I've saved up.'

'Have you had to cancel the wedding?' I asked a bit too keenly.

'We've, erm, just put things on hold for a bit,' Liz said.

'Put on hold? You make it sound like you're on the phone to the bank.'

Liz let out a roar of laughter. 'Gay people are so witty!'

'It wasn't even funny,' Dean rightly stated, conscious that his mates had turned to look at the source of the commotion.

'We've definitely got to swap numbers,' Liz said. 'And maybe we could go out for a drink one night this week?'

'Oh... I go to bed about half eight because of work,' I lied. Bedtime for me was usually midnight.

'How about an afternoon? My hours are flexible because I work from home. I'm my own boss.'

Bugger.

'I'll make us some lunch,' Liz ploughed on. 'Then I can run some wedding ideas past your queer eye.'

'I'm not much of an expert on wedding stuff,' I said.

'Don't be daft. You're the perfect person to ask. With you I get a girl's and a boy's opinion for the price of one. It's ideal!'

My Maths teacher at secondary school once told me – in front of the whole class – that I was crap at equations because I listened too much to my 'feminine brain'. He saw it as a disadvantage; I saw having 'two brains' as a positive. I passed my exams, so who was the winner here?

'I didn't help with any of the planning for my brother's wedding last September,' I said.

'Even better!' Liz shrieked. 'You'll have to bring the photos along. I want as much info about weddings as possible so I can pick up tips. I'm glued to that *Dream Weddings* show. I record it as well in case I see something I like.'

'Players for Crockham and Worfield to the pitch, please!' the man who was refereeing the match politely shouted.

Dean put his gloved hand on Liz's shoulder, stepped over the bench and jogged to his goal. Dean's arse didn't half look munchable in his shorts. I detested polyester, though I could see its advantages.

'Good luck!' I called after him.

'Aaah, you're lovely,' Liz said, resting her head on my upper arm. 'Why are the best ones always gay?'

Are they?

I bit my tongue to stop myself from lecturing her on the statistics of gay men in the population. There were thousands of sexy straight men out there, and I'd pined after a fair few of them. She was engaged to one of them.

'Can you tell which are the gay ones?' Liz asked. 'I mean, I thought you were straight when I first saw you.'

'My god, how dare you!' I joked, playing on the stereotype. 'If only you'd seen how long it took me to get ready. I'm surprised my stylish attire and groomed hair

71

didn't give me away.'

Following a game of 'Celebrities in the Closet', we adapted the rules and cast the net a little closer to home.

'OK... The guy over there with the jacket and stubble,' Liz said, nodding towards the benches on the other side of the pitch. 'Gay or straight?'

'The beardy guy in the cagoule? I wouldn't be interested even if he *was* gay,' I sniffed.

'Oooh, I like this game! Right, what about the guy with the tan standing directly opposite us? He looks fit.'

He did indeed. Tall, dark blond and handsome: near perfection if you are into that classic look – I wasn't particularly, but its appeal was growing on me. His brooding eyebrows would rival those of any Hollywood hunk, and his features were so defined that they could have been sculpted by Michelangelo. The hotness also stood out because he was the only spectator to have a golden tan, despite it being March. There was an older guy to his right and a pretty young woman on his left. I hoped she was a fruit fly, like Liz. I must have been so engrossed in the match – in Dean, at least – that I'd failed to spot him. How was that possible?

'He's staring right at you!' Liz squealed, grabbing hold of my arm.

'No, I think he's looking at you,' I said bashfully.

I wriggled my arm free of Liz's grasp. I didn't want the guy to think Liz and I were together. If Liz thought I looked straight, how many others thought the same? How many potential boyfriends had I missed out on?

'I wonder who he is,' Liz said. 'He's watched all of Crockham's matches so far. I'll ask Dean if he knows him.'

'No, don't. That girl is probably his partnAARGH!'

'Lou!'

The ball smacked me on the forehead with enough power that it knocked me backwards off the bench. Whoever was standing behind me at the time moved out of the way so, instead of being caught, I fell back onto the muddy grass. A potentially minor incident was made to look a whole lot worse because my legs were in the air. Shame Liz wasn't still holding on to my arm, because I could have taken her down with me.

'Lou! Are you OK?!' Liz asked.

I tried to get up swiftly and save any remaining dignity by pretending I was fine, but I couldn't.

'No,' I winced. 'I think I've done something to my wrist.

Liz helped me back onto the bench. There was no need to make a scene purely for my benefit. Nevertheless, the match came to a halt and people were gathering around me. This was easily trumping the forehead snail for Most Embarrassing Moment.

Dean rushed over. 'I'm so sorry, Lou! I sliced the goal kick. I did call out.'

'Don't worry about it,' I assured him.

'Get my towel out the bag,' Dean instructed Liz. 'Help get that big circle of mud off Lou's forehead.'

Liz emptied out Dean's kit bag and proceeded to wipe my face with his sweaty towel.

'Hold his arm up in the air,' Kath advised. 'That's what they do on telly.'

'Can you please just carry on with the match and stop fussing,' I growled, batting the towel away with my good hand.

'Only if you go and get checked over by one of the St John's,' Dean said.

'Fine,' I huffed, getting to my feet.

'I'll come with you,' Liz said. 'Just in case you start feeling faint.'

I grudgingly agreed.

'Right, lads. Game on!' Dean ordered.

Liz and I weren't going to miss much by getting my wrist checked out. Even before Crockham's final match, there was no chance of us qualifying for the semi-finals. Dean had already let in seventeen goals – which he blamed on his leaky defence – and only four goals had been scored. The average age of our squad was forty-five, so they had done well to take to the pitch for the last game.

After being sat in the St. John Ambulance tent with Liz for twenty minutes, I exited with my right arm in a sling across my chest, looking like a muddied Admiral Nelson. He had gone back to work half an hour after getting his right arm amputated, whereas I'd be off work for at least a week with my mild wrist sprain. He was hard; I was precious.

'I feel awful,' Liz fretted as we left the tent. 'If I hadn't distracted you, none of this would've happened.'

'Don't be silly,' I said, although I was of the same opinion.

It would have come as no surprise if Dean had kicked the ball askew on purpose to stop Liz and me ogling the talent. The two of us walked over to Dean and Kath. By the looks of things, they had been waiting in near silence.

'Oh Louis!' Kath gasped.

'It looks worse than it is,' I said. 'They said the ligaments had been stretched, not torn. If it's still swollen after forty-eight hours, I'll have to see a doctor.'

'PRICE!' Liz exclaimed. 'Protect. Rest. Ice. Compress. Elevate. It's a useful word to remember.'

'If I'd known how well you could head the ball, Lou, I'd have begged you to play,' Dean quipped.

'How many goals was it you let in?' I ribbed.

'The main thing is that you all helped raise lots of money for charity,' a chirpy Liz interjected. Meeting me had totally transformed her.

'Louis, I gave my husband a call to come and pick us up,' Kath said. 'You looked in a lot of pain earlier and didn't think you'd be able to drive.'

'Thanks, Kath,' I said. 'I'll have to get my mum and sister to drive over and pick my car up.'

'We could've dropped you home,' Liz said. 'Didn't Dean offer?'

All three of us stared at Dean. 'Can we hurry this up?' he said, trying to drag Liz back to the football. 'The final's about to start.'

'You go,' Liz said. 'I'll catch you up in a bit.'

After thanking us both for coming, and apologising for my injury, Dean turned and jogged towards the playing field. Kath's husband drove onto the playground and flashed his lights, so Kath said goodbye to Liz and walked over to meet him.

'It's been lovely getting to know you,' I said as Liz gently embraced me.

'I'll call you tomorrow to see how your wrist is,' she said. 'All being well, we can meet up and chat weddings later in the week.'

I was in no position to decline.

11

Using Liz's directions, I arrived outside a row of terraced houses in Northwood the Thursday after the football tournament. It was the first day since my accident that I'd woken and not felt pain in my wrist, yet I was still advised to wear a wrist support for another week. My heart rate increased as I walked up the cracked concrete path towards Dean's home.

'Hiya!' Liz trilled when she came to the door. 'Come in! Come in!'

No sooner had I stepped inside than Liz was giving me a hug.

'It's so good to get out,' I said. 'My parents hardly leave the house now they're both retired. They're starting to do my brain in.'

'How was it driving over? Did your wrist give you any problems?'

'None at all. I don't use my right hand much when I'm driving.'

Liz sighed. 'I wish I could drive. Dean says he'll teach me one day, but he never has the time. He's been doing loads of overtime recently, because of the wedding, and he's always shattered when he gets home.'

I bet he is.

'He's probably doing some of my round,' I said.

'I was hoping he'd be back in time for lunch, but he texted and said to start without him.'

Liz walked through the living room towards the kitchen.

So as not to tread dirt on the carpet, I took off my shoes before following. The living room walls, curtains and carpet were all a version of magnolia. Most of the colour came from the dark brown leather sofa and two matching chairs. On the window sill were three lit vanilla-scented candles and several framed photos, which were of Liz and Dean looking happy on various holidays. Sadly, Dean's top was on in all of them.

'No way!' I called out. 'Dean used to have a centre parting just like I did!'

'He absolutely hates that photo! But it was taken on our first date, so I told him it's staying up.'

'I've brought the photos you wanted to look at,' I said, raising the carrier bag I was holding.

'Leave them by the coffee table for now. You'll have to excuse the mess on it, I'm in the middle of a job.'

Liz's 'job' involved making greetings cards, using ribbons, prints, stencils and buttons – which is probably what she ended up selling them for. Dean was the one bringing home the bacon, whereas lazy Liz's craft hobby didn't contribute much at all to the kitty. No wonder they were struggling financially.

Lunch was basically an indoor picnic: shop-bought sandwiches, carrot sticks, cherry tomatoes and a bowl of mini rice cakes, followed by a slice of low-fat fruit cake.

Someone has started to eat healthily so she'll look slim on her wedding day, methinks.

'I should be back at work sometime next week,' I said, lifting my glass of lemonade as Liz advanced towards it with a doily. 'My boss said I can take this time off as annual leave so I don't ruin my hundred per cent no-sickness record. As you probably know, we get fifty quid in shopping vouchers if we go for a year without calling in sick.'

'No, I didn't know that. In the five years we've been together, Dean's longest stretch without taking a sickie is about three months. Most of them have been because I asked him to. Some days it's just nice to have a day together in bed.'

That's what Sundays are for, love.

'I've given myself some time off to go and visit my mum in a couple of weeks,' Liz continued.

'Where does she live?' I asked, before biting into a tuna sandwich.

The damp bread clung to the roof of my mouth. While my tongue fought to un-suction it, I covered up the motion by nodding in agreement as Liz spoke.

'Spain. She moved out there a few weeks ago with her new boyfriend. It'll be the first time Dean and I have been apart for more than a day since we got together. He's saving up what's left of his annual leave for our honeymoon... when we eventually go.'

Dean still hadn't turned up by the end of lunch. His 'overtime' must have been exceptionally demanding.

After looking at Roy and Christina's wedding photos and watching two episodes of *Dream Weddings*, Liz switched on her laptop. She clicked on a link in her 'favourites' list that took us to a bespoke bridal wear website.

'I've narrowed it down to three,' Liz said, detailing why she had picked each one when it appeared on screen.

I sucked air through my teeth as I looked at the prices. 'Have you thought about renting? My brother's wife rented hers. I'll look up the address, if you like?'

'I'll be renting the bridesmaids' dresses and shoes, but I want to keep my dress. I don't like the thought of somebody else wearing the exact same dress as me.'

'No wonder Dean's been doing so much overtime.'

'I'm paying for it myself,' she said proudly.

Liz had opened a savings account when she was twenty, putting money into it whenever she could. She swore she wouldn't touch the money until she got married, as she had always wanted a big wedding. In those ten intervening years, Liz had saved over nine thousand pounds.

'It's not as much as I'd have liked,' Liz said, 'but it'll easily pay for all the outfits. By the way, Dean knows nothing about the account. I told him my mum's paying for them all.'

'If money's not a problem, I'd go for the third dress,' I said.

'The ivory duchess satin one with the beaded Chantilly waist?'

'Yeah, that one.'

'I *knew* you were lying when you said you didn't know much about weddings. You've picked the one I had my eye on right from the start!'

'Queer eye, and all that,' I said.

'I hope they can make the dress look as good on me as it does on the model.'

'You'd look stunning in any of those dresses. Dean's not going to want to leave your side for a second.'

Liz turned to me and gave me a hug. 'Thanks, Lou.'

There was no need to thank me. I hadn't done anything more than read Liz's body language and listen to her tone of voice when each of the dresses appeared on screen.

'I'm starting to get worried about Dean,' Liz said, checking her watch. 'He's never been this late back from work before. I'll give him a quick call.'

'While you do that, I'm going to nip to the loo.'

'OK. It's straight ahead of you at the top of the stairs.'

With Liz out of the way, I was free to have a good nose, as she hadn't given me a guided tour. Aside from the bathroom, there were only two upstairs rooms. One had a single bed, ironing board and exercise bike in, and the other was the main bedroom. My heart rate picked up pace again as I neared Dean's lair. I was mindful of their room being directly above the living room, so I only poked my head around the door. The room looked clean – as did the rest of the house – but with Liz spending most of her time at home, it wasn't a shock. Pastel colours were the main theme upstairs. It was rather a bland colour scheme for someone so creative. I assumed they were renting and weren't allowed to change the décor.

The mint green toilet seat was the most colourful thing in the whole house. After putting it back down and washing my hands, I poked about in the bathroom cabinet. A packet of Wind-eze tablets fell onto the floor – they were probably Liz's. I visualised Dean using the bath, then wondered how many times he had dragged Liz in for a long romantic soak or a bit of bubbly sex. In the corner of the room was their basket for dirty clothes. As one does when presented with such an opportunity, I opened it and peered inside. There was very little in there; Liz evidently liked to keep up to date with the washing. One of Dean's work shirts was on top, so I took it out and had a sniff. All the men who I'd ever been close to were clean and tidy, and it wasn't a turn on. I much preferred the dirt, sweat and uncleanliness of a proper man. I put the shirt back in the basket and had a snoop in the airing cupboard. A few pairs of boxer shorts were in there, so I picked up the blue and red striped pair and held the waistband against my waist – as if I was in a shop, trying them on for size. They were far too big for me, but I liked how close I felt to Dean when his boxers were pressed up against my crotch.

'Hi, Lou!' Dean yelled up the stairs.

I almost needed a clean pair of my own after nearly cacking myself. In a panic, I made a split-second decision. Instead of putting the boxers back where I'd found them, I followed through with the urge I had to stuff them down my trousers. My perineum went into overdrive.

'What took you so...' I started as I re-entered the living room.

Dean was down on one knee, placing a ring on Liz's finger.

'It's beautiful!' Liz cried, trying to fan away tears with her right hand.

'You've already seen it,' Dean said. 'It's the one you pointed out in the shop.'

'I know, but... Oh, I love it!'

Dean got to his feet and Liz flung her arms around him. Neither of them knew there was a burglar in the house – one with an impressive newly formed bulge, at that.

'Sorry I couldn't make lunch,' Dean said, trying to bring me into the conversation. 'Now that we've set a date for the wedding, I thought it was about time I bought the ring. I'll have to start saving for the wedding ring now.'

'You've set a date?'

'Yeah, didn't Liz tell you?'

'I was waiting until Dean arrived so we could tell you together,' Liz said, taking hold of Dean's hand.

'September the fourteenth,' Dean announced.

'It's a Saturday,' Liz added.

'This September?'

'We've been together long enough, so there's no point hanging about,' Dean said, underplaying the significance of the moment.

It didn't matter when it was, as I would make sure I was busy doing something else. There was no way I was going to this wedding.

12

Having had the best part of two weeks off work, I was itching to get back. On that Friday, I stood at my bench and prepped my mail. Kath was the only person to ask how my wrist was, and I told her it felt fine. While Kath was filling me in on the gossip I'd missed, Dean crept up behind me, wrapped his arms around my waist and lifted me off the ground. Amy had turned to watch, so I presumed Dean's sudden show of machismo was for her benefit.

'Put me down!' I said loudly, trying hard not to sound like a girl.

'You're no fun,' Dean said, allowing my feet to touch the floor.

'Being picked up isn't fun.'

'Not even by a buff guy with big muscles?'

'If a buff guy with big muscles *had* picked me up, I wouldn't have complained.'

'Oooh, you can be such a bitch sometimes,' Dean said with affected campness. 'But it's still good to have you back.'

Kath agreed. 'I forgot to say, I found this in the bin while you were away,' she said, handing me Jay's postcard that had been torn in two. 'I don't know who did it, but I kept hold of it in case you wanted to tape it back together.'

'That's just evil,' I said. 'But thanks for keeping it, Kath.'

'The temp guy who's been covering your delivery obviously didn't like it,' Dean said.

I went to the office with my Brighton postcard and used

the boss's Sellotape to stick the two halves together. To show the culprit their actions weren't going to scare me, I put the postcard back atop my bench and carried on with my work.

A few minutes later, an envelope addressed to me turned up in the mail I was prepping. There was no stamp on it, so it must have been from an internal source. I opened the envelope and took out the handmade card. Small glittery hearts fell out of it and onto my bench.

Louis and partner,

Mr. and Mrs. Jeremy Knight
request the pleasure of your company
at the marriage of their daughter
Elizabeth Victoria
to
Mr. Dean Andrew Greening
at St. Mary's Church, Guildford,
on Saturday 14th September,
at 14.30
and afterwards at
The Tudor Hotel

'What do you reckon?' Dean said. He had been peering over my shoulder.

'Erm...' I gulped. I hadn't yet thought up my excuse.

'Liz was up late last night finishing this off. It's only a practice one. She asked me to find out what you thought.'

'Oh, I see. Well, the wording is good, and I like the purple and pink theme...'

'Liz said you'd like the colours. She got the idea from looking at your brother's wedding photos.'

'I'm not too keen on the confetti hearts, though,' I continued. 'But that's just a matter of personal taste.'

'I thought they were tacky too.'

'I didn't say tacky! Don't tell Liz I said they were tacky!'

'OK, best not. She'd probably take you off the wedding list if I told her that.'

Here's hoping, otherwise it's another September ruined by a Saturday wedding.

＊

When I returned to the office after my delivery that day, I noticed two undelivered bags of mail underneath Amy's bench. It gave me the incentive I needed. I had plenty of ammunition, and the time had come to use it. If I caught Amy out, it might put a stop to her and Dean's blossoming relationship. So, after a trip to the loos to un-flatten my cycle-helmet hair, I went and spoke to the boss, real name Colin. I didn't question why he had insisted on being known as 'the boss' rather than have us use his real name – although I suppose it must be difficult as a manager to convey an air of authority when your staff members call you Colin. That said, he wasn't an imposing character even with his butch moniker. There's no escaping a name like Colin.

Having been a regular postman for ten years, Colin had worked his way up to the position of manager. The lack of exercise had caught up with him, though, and had seemingly exceeded forty both in age *and* waist size. Colin rarely ventured out of his office, not that his staff needed managing; we all knew what had to be done each day and simply got on with it. Besides, there was no need for him to leave his office, because he had brought in a kettle, a small fridge and a microwave. No doubt company funds were dipped into to purchase these items, so they should have been in the canteen, but nobody said anything about it.

'You'll have to speak to Amy about her timekeeping,' I said to Colin, who had his back towards me.

Colin hastily turned off his computer screen, then swivelled his chair round and growled, 'Have you not heard of knocking?'

'You said you like an open door policy,' I disputed.

'Damn that rule.'

'And if that was porn you were watching, this isn't exactly the best place for it.'

'I never get the chance at home,' Colin said, freely admitting what he had been up to. 'The wife and kids are always in the way. They keep wanting to do stuff as a family.'

I could imagine Dean saying the exact same thing ten years in the future. It was up to me to make sure that didn't happen.

'What did you want again?' Colin said, changing the subject by bringing up the initial subject.

'Amy. She turns up late every morning.'

'Does she? I'll have a word with her. Is that all?'

After getting my pre-gripe out the way, I informed Colin about the bags of mail under Amy's bench. Someone had to tell him, as he wasn't likely to notice them. My smug grin faded when Colin filled me in. Apparently, Amy had left early to catch a train to Brighton as she was looking to apply for a place at university down there. And the two bags of mail were waiting to be delivered by Steve on overtime.

'Brighton?' I said. 'But she told me she was hoping to go to Leeds.'

'No, it's definitely Brighton. She showed me the paperwork. Perhaps she heard what Leeds is like and had second thoughts.'

As nothing seemed to be sticking to Amy, I changed tack.

'Did you know that Dean's been wasting company petrol by teaching Amy how to drive in one of the vans?' I pressed on.

'That's not all he's teaching her, so I've heard,' Colin said

85

unprofessionally.

I shook my head. 'Dean wouldn't go with her. She's got a big horse mouth.'

'It's probably why he likes her. She can cram it all in, balls included!'

Colin let out a dreadful crow of laughter. His testosterone levels must still have been high from the porn-watching.

'Doesn't it bother you that they're finishing late and claiming overtime for it?' I carried on ranting.

'I don't really care, it's not my money. As long as I don't get any customer complaints, Dean and Amy can do whatever they like,' Colin responded, growing tiresome. 'Would you close the door on your way out? I don't want to be interrupted again.'

Seeing that I was fighting a losing battle, I left. I wasn't going to get anywhere, not when the two of them had the boss on their side. The injustice of it all stuck right in my craw. Why couldn't anybody see what was going on? It wasn't solely Amy's prospective move to Brighton that stopped me from moving there. Jay had found himself a boyfriend and moved him in. That hadn't taken him long. So much for the flat-share idea. I went back to my bench, took down my taped-up postcard and threw it in the bin.

*

Coincidentally, both Amy and Dean called in sick the following morning. I didn't want to make presumptions, but all I could think of was the two of them shacked up at a hotel somewhere. Conclusions were jumped to when I received a text from Dean later that day. I didn't even know he had my number.

Hi Lou. Hope your having fun at work.

86

>I only know where the gay bars are,
and I doubt you want to go to one of
those. Why do you want to know?

(No reply)

I glossed over Dean's poor grammar and showed Steve the text.

'Dean's rash is still "checking out the university" down in Brighton,' Steve informed me. 'They're probably shagging.'

'What makes you think that?' I asked, not wanting to hear the answer.

'Well, on my way home the other day, I see one of our vans parked up in Alderney Road. When I drive past, I only went and saw Amy and Dean sneaking into a house together.'

'Did they see you?'

'They were too engrossed in each other to notice anyone else,' Steve said. 'Good for him, I say. Because once he's married, that's it. No more fun on the sly.'

'He shouldn't even be doing it now!'

'I don't expect you know much about the fairer sex,' Steve lectured, 'but there are two types of women in this world: the type you marry and the type you don't. My ex fell into the second category, though I didn't realise it at the time.'

'And which category does Amy fall into?'

'I think you already know the answer to that one, Lou.'

Even though she was still young, I could tell that Amy wasn't the marrying kind. She was the sort who used men and then ditched them when she got bored. We were very much alike. The only difference being that I rarely had the opportunity to do it.

I put two and two together and presumed Dean had persuaded one of his mates to let him borrow their house for an hour or so. I imagined Dean's mate handing over the house keys and saying, 'Get in there, my son! Take all the time you need!' and then giving Dean a macho pat on the back as he left. What was wrong with these people to make them think having an affair was acceptable? Where were their morals? In the same place mine usually were, that's where. I bet they would have had something to say if Dean had been seeing me, though.

'It wouldn't surprise me if him and Amy do it in the back of his van,' Steve said.

She's such a tramp. I bet it's her way of thanking Dean for giving her driving lessons. It's all so easy for her: pulls into a lay-by, pulls her knickers to one side and reverse parks onto Dean's cock.

I had a hazy brain for the rest of that day. I thought about nothing other than Amy and Dean enjoying a dirty weekend in Brighton. It was pleasing in a way, because it proved that Dean's relationship with Liz wasn't impregnable, giving me a chance. And, even though I knew he was soon to be married, I still wanted a chance. Just one chance to continue what we had started at Christmas.

13

Early starts were categorically the worst part of my job. And because I had two sleeps a day, it felt as if it was always time to get up. After securing three winks of the quoted forty for the third night in a row, I struggled to make it to work on time that Monday.

'Morning!' Kath trilled. She had an annoyingly chirpy voice for someone who rose at four every morning. 'You're a bit late.'

'Hi, Kath,' I replied as I tossed my car keys and banana onto my bench. 'I had the rolling news on while I ate breakfast, and I forgot the time.'

As well as commenting on my tardiness, Kath also picked up on my persistent yawning while we worked. Instead of giving me a lecture, she gave me some advice. Her recommendation for getting a good night's sleep was to have a nibble of blue cheese shortly before going to bed. No matter how sleep-deprived I was, there was more chance of a snowman surviving in Hell than there was of me putting any blue cheese near my lips. Although I'm not averse to trying new things, crossing my lips with a food that resembles old people's legs and smells like the contents of one of their colostomy bags is one thing I'm not willing to try. Kath then progressed to the subject of dreams, though I was close to drifting off just listening to her. As a consequence, I was all the more startled when Amy's replacement showed up.

Because Amy's extra time off had been unforeseen and

not booked in advance, the boss was struggling to cover her delivery, so an extra staff member was brought in as relief. And what a relief he was: it was the guy Liz and I had been checking out at the football match. He was exactly what my weary eyes needed. Kath was still talking and hadn't noticed the new guy's entrance. I looked around me, but nobody else had batted an eyelid. Was I imagining this vision? I knew I was tired, but I didn't think I was dreaming.

I stopped what I was doing and sat on my bench to finish off my can of Red Bull. The new guy had his back towards me as he put his bag down and removed his jacket. The short sleeves on his polo shirt gripped his defined biceps as he reached up to hang the jacket off the top corner of Amy's bench. When Kath finally realised I was no longer listening to her, she looked round to see what I was staring at. We gave each other a look, raised our eyebrows in approval and tittered like silly schoolgirls. I looked at the ground when the new guy passed me, then it was eyes up again as I watched him walk towards the staff register, which we all had to sign upon entering or exiting the building.

'He was on your round when you were off,' Kath divulged.

'I can't believe you didn't tell me sooner! What's his name?'

'Oliver. He's ever such a nice young man.'

Before I could quiz Kath further, Dean strode over. For a moment I'd forgotten he existed.

'Morning,' he said.

'No Amy again?' I asked.

'Guess not.'

I wanted my next comment to sound off-the-cuff, even though I'd been thinking about the topic all weekend. I threw it out there and hoped for the best.

'So, did you two have fun in Brighton on Saturday?'

'Shhhh!' Dean warned. He came close to me and carried

on. 'Anyone could be listening! I was meant to be off sick, remember?'

'Sorry, I forgot.'

'But yes, we did have a good morning in Brighton,' Dean said casually. 'We had lunch on the pier before I dropped her at Gatwick. She says it's thirty degrees in Alicante.'

I suddenly remembered Liz's trip to Spain to see her mum. My heart rate calmed back down again.

'Hello, mate,' Dean said to Oliver when he returned to Amy's bench. 'Back here again, I see.'

'Yeah,' he replied. 'I'm always getting called in to help you lot out of trouble. Do any of you know this round?'

Oliver's green eyes looked at us in a pleading way. I was about to answer in the negative, but Kath opened her mouth first.

'Louis does,' she blurted.

'I've only done a bit of it,' I said, starting to swing my legs to and fro.

'If it's a hand you're after, I'm your man,' Dean said, muscling in.

Give me a frigging chance!

'Cool,' Oliver said.

A smug Dean stood in front of me with his arms folded. He knew I'd been enjoying the view, so he was doing his best to put a stop to it – just as he had almost certainly done at the football tournament. It was time for my revenge.

'What's up, face ache?' Dean asked me.

'Nothing,' I said, swinging one leg with more exuberance and kicking him in the balls with it.

'AAARGH!' Dean wailed, hands clasped to his groin. 'Why would you *do* that?!'

'Sorry, it was a reflex action. My knee had a spasm.'

'You *are* a bloody spasm!'

Oliver looked at me and smiled. Although I had plenty of work of my own I needed to be getting on with, I bypassed an immobilised Dean – who subsequently shuffled off – and joined the temp at his bench. This was too good an opportunity to miss out on, even if it led to me finishing my own round when the kids were coming out of school.

'Thanks for this,' Oliver said. He looked younger than Roy, so I put him at about twenty-three. 'It's always a struggle getting the hang of a new delivery, especially when you don't know where you're going.'

'That's OK. I like to help out the new starters when I get a chance,' I said, picking up some letters and slotting them in with him.

'You were at that charity football thingy last month, weren't you?' he asked.

He recognises me! I've made an impression on a fit man!

'How's your head?'

Oh yeah. That's why he remembers me.

'Fine. No lasting damage.' I swiftly changed the subject. 'I hear you did my delivery last week?'

'Yeah, it's not a bad round. It's nice to be on the same delivery for more than a couple of days. I'm a part-timer, so I get shunted off to wherever I'm needed.'

'That sucks. Can't you get a full-time contract?'

'No. I can only work a few weeks at a time because of my other job.'

'And what's that?'

'I'm an amateur golfer. I play on the PGA EuroGo tour.'

'Isn't that a computer game?'

He sniggered. 'No, it's a tour for promising golfers. Some of our matches are covered on Channel Six.'

'Wow!' My interest in golf was instantly piqued. 'What are you doing working with us minions, then?'

Oliver explained that he wanted a job that gave him time in the afternoons to practise. From what he told me, it sounded as though he was well on his way to becoming a successful golfer, as he was looking to play some tournaments in South Africa later in the year. His ultimate goal was to be competing in the major tournaments within the next five years.

'That's amazing!' I overstated. 'What's your name? Then I can tell everyone to look out for you.'

'Oliver Johnson. You might have heard of my dad. He used to be manager of Preston North End,' he boasted. 'He also played for Norwich back in the eighties.'

'In the days when they were rubbish,' I added cheekily.

'Yeah, they were a bit!'

As we carried on slotting mail, we did our best to dodge each other's arms as they reached out. I liked it when he had letters to slot in the top row, as I caught a whiff of whatever he used on his underarms. It smelt classy. No cheapy Lynx products for Oliver Johnson.

'I was out in Spain a couple of months ago playing in a Pro-Am golf tournament,' Oliver said in a bid to carry on his showing off. 'I was partnered with Jamie Redknapp.'

'And he was the professional?'

'No, I was the pro. Jamie was the amateur.'

'But I thought you said you were an amateur golfer?'

'Not compared to Jamie I'm not.'

Oliver was a beautiful looking young man and would have given Jamie Redknapp a run for his money during his pin-up years. Yet Oliver's head seriously needed to be removed from his backside. I was doing little to stop his ego from swelling, fawning over everything he said. But I knew it would wind up Dean and give him a taste of his own medicine, so I carried on.

'I can't believe you know Jamie Redknapp!' I gushed.

'My dad knows David Beckham,' Oliver crowed. 'He captured Becks on a loan spell from Man United before he got really famous. You could say he helped kick off the transformation into the Beckham we know today.'

'No way!'

'It's true. Dad came to the football tournament with me, and people were asking him for his autograph. We're off to another match this evening. He still has friends in the business, so he gets given loads of free tickets. Tonight it's Spurs against Wigan.'

Working alongside someone who had a goal in life made a pleasant change. When I got home from work, I typed 'Oliver Johnson' into a search engine. He had a profile on his golf club's website, and I memorised his stats. Oliver had recently turned twenty-one. He played right-handed, weighed 175 pounds and was 193 centimetres tall. His hobbies included gym, rugby and football. According to the profile, he hadn't qualified for the latter stages of a single tournament. Still, there was plenty of time for that to change. The internet is so handy: it makes stalking someone you have just met a whole lot easier.

14

My legs were my best feature. They were the only decent body parts inherited from my mother. As the weather was starting to warm up – and as I had someone else to impress – I wore shorts to work the next day.

'Morning, all,' I chirped as I showed my face.

'Hi,' Oliver said.

'How was the delivery yesterday?' I asked, joining Oliver at his bench. 'Any problems?'

'No, it was fine.'

'And what abOWWW!' I yelped.

I turned around and saw Dean holding a few of my leg hairs between his index finger and thumb.

'What did you do that for?!'

'Dunno,' he responded. 'I just felt like it.'

'Weirdo!'

'*You're* calling *me* a weirdo?'

'You're the one holding another man's leg hairs, not me.'

'You can have them back, if you want?'

I reached over to Dean's hand and smacked it. I didn't quite know what else to do. Tickling him was an option, but it wasn't something grown men did in the company of others. Dean's free hand grabbed my smacking hand and pulled me close to him.

'Fancy a wrestle?' he asked.

I did, but not in these circumstances.

'I'm a lover, not a fighter,' I said smartly, trying to nudge him away.

Dean grabbed my other hand, letting go of my pinched leg hairs in the process. Whatever this charade was about, it certainly wasn't about the leg hairs anymore. He put his arm around my neck and tried to force me down to my knees.

'Let go of the poor lad, Dean!' Kath ordered. 'His face is going red!'

My reddening face was now deliciously close to Dean's crotch. I didn't know what he was trying to do, and I don't think Dean did either.

'Come on, Dean! Take him down!' Steve cheered.

'If you want me to nosh you off, you only need to ask,' I strained to say.

Dean promptly released his hold on me. 'There's no need to be vulgar. We were just having a friendly wrestle.'

'You do that to all your friends, do you?' a maddened Kath asked. It was good to know I had someone on my side. 'Worse than schoolchildren, some of you.'

I folded the collar back down on my polo shirt and walked to my bench, while Dean took my place next to Oliver. If I'd known my legs were going to have such an effect on Dean, I'd have worn shorts to the Christmas party. Nevertheless, I stored the image of us wrestling, though in my version we were alone and had removed our clothes. You can tell I wasn't getting it often.

Dean proceeded to help Oliver in the same way I'd done twenty-four hours earlier. Everything Oliver said was followed by forced laughter from Dean.

'Louis, I looked up that dream you told me about,' Kath said, peering at me over the top of her glasses.

'Which dream?'

'The one where your teeth fell out after eating candy floss, remember?'

'Oh, *that* one,' I said, recalling our soporific chat the previous morning.

'My book says that dreaming about your teeth falling out means you have a fear of losing your looks.'

Dean and Oliver sniggered, turning my mood into a more prickly one.

'You don't need to be Einstein to work that one out,' I said in my most sarcastic tone. 'And all along I thought it meant I didn't like men with beards.'

'I was only repeating what I read in my book,' Kath said, slightly affronted.

'Anyway, you can't lose your looks if you don't have them to start off with,' Dean butted in, causing general amusement.

In an attempt to put a stop to the mirth, I talked over it and asked Oliver the question I'd failed to finish earlier on.

'Did you enjoy the football last night?'

'Yeah, it was good,' was Oliver's understated response.

'I saw on the news that Spurs won five-nil,' I persisted.

'It ended five-one,' he corrected.

Oliver had watched his football team win at a canter and all he'd had to say was that it had been 'good'. Dean made up for Oliver's lack of enthusiasm by going totally over the top.

'It was a brilliant match!' Dean proclaimed. 'That second goal will be up for goal of the season.'

'I didn't think it was being televised?' I questioned Dean.

'It wasn't,' he replied. 'I went along with my pal Olly.'

Dean reached across Oliver's back and gave the arm furthest from him a manly squeeze, which in turn forced the two lads closer together. My throat became tight, as it often did whenever I felt frustrated or hard done-by.

'I'd just like to say cheers again for taking me to the match,' Dean said in an unashamedly sycophantic manner. 'I really appreciate your kindness.'

BLEURGH!

An observer might have said Dean spouted that garbage

so Oliver would remember him the next time free tickets were being dished out. Yet Dean had unquestionably been waiting for an audience before making his speech, and that could only mean he was trying to rile me. It worked.

'I'm glad you both enjoyed it,' I said through gritted teeth. I could not let Dean bathe in the satisfaction of getting one-up on me.

'We had a top evening,' Dean bragged. 'Olly bought me a pint afterwards.'

'That was nice of you, *Oliver*,' I said, becoming irked at Dean's use of the name Olly. It sounded so unclassy; not the name a future top golfer would use.

'All his mates were calling him Olly last night,' Dean said, picking up on my correction. 'It's OK to call you Olly, isn't it?'

'I don't really mind,' Oliver said.

Grow some balls and stick up for me!

It was lovely that Oliver was making new friends and settling in. Lovely for him, not for me; I wanted him to be extra friendly to me. Dean had already tainted my friendship with Amy, and I didn't want him poaching another potential friend. But with Dean prowling, I decided to fight for my man. Dean may have won the battle, but there was no chance I was going to let him win the war.

*

Later that day, when Dean finally left the office to deliver some parcels, I turned to see how Oliver was getting on. He was sitting on his bench and ready to go, so he pulled an apple out of his man bag and started to eat it. Not big, manly bites; just nibbles. He probably didn't want to pull out a gleaming tooth. I still had a bit of work left to do, but Oliver just sat and watched.

'Thanks for your help,' I called over to him sarcastically.

'I didn't think you'd need any,' he responded, hopping off his bench and walking over to mine. 'You're an expert.'

'And don't you forget it,' I said with a smile that I hoped was seen as cute.

'What time do you think you'll be done today?'

'Being the expert that I am, probably about half ten.'

Why did I say half ten? I never finish at half ten.

'Half past *ten*? If you're done that early, you can come and give me a hand.'

'OK. I'll call you when I've finished to find out where you are. What's your number?' I asked, grasping at the slightest of opportunities.

'My battery is running low,' Oliver said, using one of the oldest excuses in the history of mobile phone usage. 'It might've died by then.'

'Unless you can find two yoghurt pots and a length of string, it looks like I won't be coming to help you.'

'Yoghurt pots and string?' he questioned.

'Yeah, to make a communication device,' I said, trying my best to sound quirky and winsome.

Oliver retained his blank look.

'You link the pots with the string and talk through each end, like walkie-talkies,' I prattled on.

'Is that something they did back in your day?' he joked.

I punched him lightly on the arm. 'You haven't lived until you've made something out of old yoghurt pots or washing-up liquid bottles.'

'We use a dishwasher,' Oliver said bluntly.

That killed the conversation. I didn't have any stories about dishwashers.

'Take my number in case. I'll put my phone on silent to save some battery,' he said. 'But if my phone does die, you'll just have to track me down.'

Oliver took my phone, flipped it open and added his number to it. He said he had owned the same phone five years ago, so he knew how to use it. I'd chosen my phone because it resembled the communications device the characters in *Star Trek* spoke into when they wanting 'beaming up'. If God ever decides to grant us all our own special power, I'd hope for teleportation. Too much is made of invisibility. Can invisibility get you the other side of the door when you are locked out? Can invisibility take you to a desert island during your lunch hour? The merits of teleportation totally outrank invisibility, and then some. It would also help in my efforts to finish my delivery by half ten. Oliver added himself to my phone under 'Oliver Johnson'. I didn't have any other Olivers in there, so it seemed rather pretentious – although I suppose being a minor celebrity qualified him to be a tad conceited.

'I detect a sexual rapport!' Kath chirped when Oliver was out of earshot.

'Really?' I said, trying to sound apathetic.

'I saw the way he was looking at you, and he certainly doesn't look at me or any of the other women in here like that.'

That comes as no surprise.

'But he plays golf, Kath. I mean, who ever heard of a gay golfer? Apart from the lesbian ones, of course.'

'All the classic signs are there,' Kath said. 'He's well-mannered and well-presented, and I've not heard him mention a girlfriend.'

'And he smells ruddy gorgeous!'

Kath may have been a nosey cow, but if there was one thing she knew about, it was people. She chatted to her customers at length, and she had amassed well over £400 in tips the previous Christmas, along with wine, chocolates and other gifts. Thus, there must have been substance in what she was saying.

'You two would make such a good couple,' Kath said.

'Do you think so?' I asked, though I fully agreed with her

100

statement.

'Absolutely. You with your brains and him with his good looks. You're a perfect match.'

'That's a backhanded compliment if ever I heard one.'

'I didn't mean it to sound like that,' she said. 'I just meant that you two go well together, like Jack Sprat and his wife.'

'Who?'

All of a sudden I became the uneducated, much like Oliver had been during our earlier exchange of words.

'Jack Sprat couldn't eat fatty meats and his wife couldn't eat lean meats, so between them they always finished their dinners,' Kath elaborated, no doubt wishing she hadn't opened her gob in the first place.

'That was a good story,' I said drily. 'Why didn't they just eat vegetables?'

'Perhaps they did in the second verse. I can't remember. I think he ended up trying to drown her.

I know how he feels.

The moral of the story wasn't lost on me, though: in a relationship, both halves of a couple compensate for what the other half lacks. Basically, it was Kath's underhanded way of saying I was punching above my weight by chasing after Oliver. I had his phone number, so what did she know? By Kath's theory, her husband must have had many strings to his bow. Yet from what I could see, Oliver and I were a well-matched couple. And if Oliver didn't agree, then I'd have to convince him otherwise.

15

Same as it always rained when I went to an open-air concert, mishaps always slowed me down when I needed to finish my delivery early. I'd made a rod for my own back by saying I could be finished by half ten. That time was achievable if I dashed round, but it was nigh impossible after the weather intervened. April had thus far been a warm and sunny month, but the fine weather took a nosedive the moment I put shorts on. To compensate for having no trousers, I pulled my eye-catching purple socks as far up to my shivering purple knees as they would go. I deemed the socks to be stylish, but I have been known to be delusional. The stares I received were probably not from admirers but from people thinking I looked like a total goon. As I hotfooted it round my delivery, not pausing to shelter from fleeting downpours that hadn't been forecast, I stepped through two elastic bands to help keep my socks up. My waterproof clothing was in the boot of my car.

'Would you like a cup of tea?' Ron called out to me from his front door. It looked warm and dry where he was.

'No, thanks. I don't drink it,' I said as I jogged past his driveway.

'Do you have any mail for me?'

'Nothing today.'

'I'm expecting a letter from my daughter. Are you sure there's nothing for me?'

'Yes, I'm sure,' I said with irritation, before muttering under my breath, 'That's why I'm heading away from your house and not towards it.'

Cold-hearted so-and-so. Ron had probably been relying on me to provide him with his only contact with the outside world that day, and I'd brushed him off as if he was one of the cobwebs I frequently encountered on delivery. On any other day, I'd have stopped and fingered through my bundle to put his mind at rest. Five seconds that would have taken me, but I couldn't even spare him that. Not today.

Having a letterbox with a draught excluder is all well and good, but trying to feed soggy mail through one is time-consuming. The letters must have resembled papier-mâché when they appeared on the other side that morning. Letters in that state are of no use to anybody, so a day off when it rained would have been ideal. Thoroughly soaked, I finished delivering at a quarter past eleven and immediately gave Oliver a call.

'The person you are trying to call cannot be reached at the moment. Please try again later,' said an automated voice.

I jumped on my bike and cycled to Oliver's delivery, scanning each of his roads as I passed them. Luckily, I caught sight of him down the end of a cul-de-sac. Before he caught sight of me, I took off my helmet, ruffled up my flattened hair and blew my drippy nose. I then got my phone out and took a selfie to see if I looked presentable, double-checking that no wet tissue residue had been left under my nostrils.

'Not as good as you think you are,' Oliver said as I pedalled up to him. Though he must have had at least three layers on, I could see two small lumps where his nipples had thrust through. In spite of the bad weather, not a hair on Oliver's head was out of place. He was evidently a fan of hairspray.

'I've been cycling around for ages... trying to find you,' I said, breathing heavily to support my story. 'If you'd had your phone on... I could have found you a lot quicker.'

'The battery died,' Oliver said. 'Anyway, I've just got this bit to do and then I'm done.'

'Oh, OK. See you back at the office, yeah?'

'You could try the flats in Bramley Place again. I couldn't get into them earlier. Pressed all the buzzers, but nobody seemed to be in. I guess everyone's at work.'

Oliver took the mail, which included a parcel, out of the bag he had over his shoulder and tossed it into my 'basket'. I freewheeled down to the block of stylish studio flats and pressed all the door buzzers on the wall outside. No luck. A few moments later, Oliver pulled up alongside the flats in his car. I say car, but it was the size of a caravan. He parked half his vehicle on the kerb. He needed to for other regular-sized cars to pass.

'No wonder you're almost done,' I said, gesturing towards Oliver's car. 'That's cheating!'

'It kept me nice and dry when it rained, though,' he responded as he joined me at the flats' entrance. 'I sat in there for a few minutes with the radio on until the showers passed.'

'...while I bravely soldiered on,' I added. My hair dropped a bead of rain onto my face, and it trickled down the side of my nose before I wiped it away.

'Hey, there's a window open on the second floor,' Oliver pointed out. 'You try throwing the parcel in and I'll lob up the bundle.'

'I'm not very good at throwing,' I said, thinking the idea was a bad one.

'Launch it like a shot putt, or pretend you're playing basketball.'

'What if it lands on something and breaks it?'

'The window is directly above the entrance, so it's probably a stairwell,' Oliver deduced. 'The mail will be inside, that's the main thing. I'm sure the residents will understand.'

Jay once said that if I wanted a bloke to remember me, make an impression. I'd already made one impression on Oliver, and it hadn't been a good one. Time to erase that one and replace it with a better one.

'OK,' I said. 'Let's go for it.'

We both launched our missiles. Both missed. As I stood gawping up at the parcel, I was so focused on catching it that I didn't see the falling bundle of mail. It smacked me directly on the forehead.

'OWWW!' I yelled, bending over and clutching my face. It hardly hurt at all; I was totally over-acting.

Oliver put his hand on my back. 'Are you alright?' he asked.

I paused for dramatic effect, before straightening up. 'I think so.'

'Good, because that was hilarious!' he said, creasing up. I presumed that's what he was doing, as there was no sound of laughter emanating from his mouth, only faint vapour from the cold. It looked as if he was the one in pain.

'You could've broken my nose, or something,' I said, trying to convey irritation.

'It's not my fault you failed to see a large object heading straight for your face,' he quite rightly said. 'That's the second time I've seen that happen to you now.'

Blasted forehead! Why do you keep ridiculing me?

'Someone as freakishly tall as you shouldn't have missed that,' I teased. 'How about you reverse your portaloo a bit nearer and stand on the bonnet? You could practically slam dunk the mail inside.'

'My sponsors wouldn't be too happy if I damaged their car.'

My eyes lit up. 'You have sponsors?'

'Yeah. They bought that car for me so I can drive myself to tournaments with all my golf stuff. They also pay for me to see a sports psychologist.'

'That must be a tough job, trying to find something inside your head.'

Oliver tried hard to suppress a grin, before we turned our attention back to the job. One of the elastic bands holding the bundle together had snapped, causing the mail to come loose.

'Here,' I said, taking off one of my rubber band garters.

'Proper little cub scout, you,' Oliver said, putting the bundle in order. 'If I hold it, you put the rubber on.'

'OK,' I said coyly, pretending the sexual undertone of Oliver's comment had gone unnoticed.

As I looked down at what I was doing, I could sense Oliver staring at me. All I had to do was look up into his eyes and we would have had a romantic moment. Our faces were barely a foot apart. I wondered if his reactions were quick enough to dodge a kiss if I tried to plant one on him. Carrying out his instructions, I sensually fed the rubber band over Oliver's tightly held bundle, imagining the situation he had alluded to. I hoped we would soon be looking back and laughing at this incident while enjoying unrestrained sexual intercourse.

'Nice job,' Oliver said once I was done. He then hurled the bundle through the open window. 'Your turn.'

'Actually, I'm starting to feel a bit light-headed,' I exaggerated. 'Can you do it?'

Oliver threw the parcel up with ease.

'You shouldn't be cycling if you're feeling faint,' he said. 'How about I give you a lift back?'

I'd rather you gave me mouth-to-mouth... and then mouth-to-willy.

In case I had delayed whiplash or shock, I agreed. After all, it would have been silly to jeopardise my safety. It would also have been silly to turn down the chance to spend more time with Oliver. I watched as he lifted my bike into his 'car'. I made myself look a complete mule by trying to slide the side door shut after me, but it only shut automatically with a plip of the driver's key. Oliver must have been gay: there was a strawberry air freshener dangling from his rear-view mirror. Strawberries don't exude an air of heterosexuality.

The traffic lights weren't being particularly helpful on our journey back. It was the first time I'd been in a vehicle and wanted the lights to change to red on approaching them. Although I found it difficult talking to fit men face-to-face when alone, talking while staring out of the front windscreen – whether as a driver or passenger – was fine. Disappointingly, there were no detours to Pizza Den for an early lunch. We did pass Crockham's trendy new bar, though, prompting Oliver to (sort of) ask me out.

'I'm a demon on the dance floor,' he said. 'We'll have to go there for a drink one night so I can show you my moves.'

I looked forward to seeing his hip action.

16

For the first time in ages, I had a spring in my step as I got ready for work. I wore my favoured yellow and green striped socks, and I squirted a smidge of my most expensive aftershave on my neck. The only times I used it were on special occasions; I'd worn it six times in two years. Instead of going to my bench when I arrived at work, I made a beeline for Oliver's. There was nobody there. I said a brief hello to Kath, then texted Oliver.

>Hiya! It's your morning wake up call!
Do you want me to start getting your
delivery ready for when you get in?

(No reply)

I presumed he was driving and couldn't reply, or had forgotten to turn his phone on. Instead of getting on with my own work, I collected the mail for Oliver's delivery and started prepping it, hoping that he would come in and be ever so grateful for the help.

'You must really like him,' Kath said to me. 'You'd never do that for anyone else in here.'

'I'm helping because he's new, same as I helped Amy when she started.'

Not that helping Amy had done me much good. I hoped for a better outcome this time around. Yet my dreams were shattered by an untimely loophole.

'Morning, everyone,' Amy said. 'Thanks for starting my round off for me, Lou.'

I spun round on the spot. 'You're back!'

'What's with the random surprised look? I've only been away five days.'

'But... I thought you...'

Just as I was about to put down Amy's mail and make a start on my own, Dean bounded over.

'Awww, were you expecting Olly to be in today?' Dean said, sticking out his bottom lip.

I ignored the fool and walked over to my bench. My phone vibrated.

> Hi Lou. I'm at the Worfield office today.
> Sad face. Thanks for helping me out
> yesterday. You're a top bloke.<

'Who wants a doughnut?' Amy called out, opening a tub of twenty jam-filled treats.

'You're too good to us,' Dean said, tucking in.

'I know,' Amy chirped, before a devious grin spread across her face.

Steve and the other men in the office who weren't fussed about their waistlines swarmed around Amy like vultures. A pretty girl with doughnuts: most men's dream woman. Even the boss was treated to one. It wasn't hard to figure out Amy's motives. For having unauthorised leave, Amy should have received an official warning. However, by enticing the boss with food, she escaped any form of punishment. Sharing the doughnuts with the rest of the staff was a nice touch, though, and helped keep them on side. When the rabble had departed, I went over for mine.

'Sorry, Lou, they've all gone,' she said, closing the lid. 'You should've been a bit quicker. I'll make sure you're first in line next time.'

That's about right. Fatten us all up to make yourself look thinner.

'You mean, the next time you come back from *Leeds*?'

Amy was lost for words. I looked askance at her. She had a panicked expression on her face, akin to the one Kath had described after seeing Amy and Dean in Pizza Den. Amy had been caught out... again.

*

Whichever way you looked at it, Amy's return was bad news and had a damaging effect on my friendships with Oliver and Dean. I desperately needed to see Oliver so I could follow up on the initial spark we had, before the fuse got snuffed out and he forgot who I was. However, one male friendship was set to become a lot stronger following an unexpected text the Saturday after Amy's return. At the time, I was rather disappointed it was from Dean and not Oliver.

Hi. Staying at my parents house in crockham tonight while liz is away. Fancy going for a drink in town?<

>Are you meeting anybody else from work while you're out?

No. It will just be the two of us. Are you up for it?<

>Sure am. What time will you be ready? Where shall I meet you?

I will be waiting for you at the plough at 8. See you there.<

Oliver's arrival seemed to have ignited the jealousy flame in Dean. Playing hard to get was definitely a winning strategy. I didn't want to jinx the evening, so I wore my third-favourite shirt and left my pulling pants in the drawer. If I went along to this date without any expectation, I couldn't be disappointed. Calling it a 'date' and taking two hours to get ready wasn't exactly helping, though.

During my three-minute walk to The Plough, I pondered over subtle questions I could ask Dean that would help me unearth the nature of his relationship with Amy. As I entered the pub, the landlord nodded at me from behind the bar, and I duly returned the gesture. Our relationship had been frosty ever since he turned me down for a job in his pub, my local. I was twenty-three at the time, and it was the first occasion where I'd been to an interview and not been offered the job. Coincidentally, it was the only interview I'd been to where I'd taken my mum along for moral support.

I scanned the room and saw Dean sitting at a table in the corner near the unlit fireplace. It wasn't surprising he had arrived first, seeing as I was ten minutes late. I walked across the solid wood floor and took a seat opposite Dean. Judging by what he was wearing, he had been to watch a football match that afternoon and not bothered to change. I instantly felt as though I'd made way too much effort. After Dean had bought me a drink and we had got the chit-chat out of the way, talk turned to the inevitable.

'How come Amy was away for so long?' I baited. 'It doesn't take five days to check out a university.'

'She's *your* friend,' Dean said. 'You tell me.'

'You're the one who spends the most time with her,' I said, trying to remain calm.

'Only because we both need the overtime,' he explained. 'It gets done quicker when there's two of us.'

I started to fiddle with a beer mat, picking at one of its

corners and exposing its layers. I knew how it felt.

'Were you delivering to Alderney Road the other day? I saw you both get out of your van there.' I realised I was starting to sound like a stalker, so I swiftly added, 'I just happened to be driving past on my way home.'

'That's where my parents live. Amy helped me lift some of their old furniture into the van. They wanted it taken to the charity shop in the high street.'

Steve had set me up. He must have known Dean's parents lived there. I felt a bit better hearing Dean's explanation, but why did he have to do everything with Amy? Why couldn't he team up with Steve?

'I asked Amy if she had a boyfriend,' Dean said nonchalantly, shaking some of his dry roasted peanuts into my hand. He must have remembered I liked them.

'And what did she say?' I pried.

'She said she was single,' he replied. 'What do you reckon?'

It dawned on me that I'd been invited out to spill the beans. Perhaps the peanuts he treated me to were given as a sort of bribe. But if that was the case, Dean would be wasting his time and money, because I didn't know anything about Amy's private life.

'If she says she hasn't, then she hasn't,' I said, eating the nuts from my palm. 'Why does it matter?'

'No reason,' he said. 'It'd just be good to know.'

'Because you don't want to be knocked back if you make a move,' I joked.

My cheeks started to tremble because of the smile I'd forced onto my face. I covered the nervous grin by finishing my shandy, despite there being a generous quantity remaining. The few precious seconds of drinking enabled me to compose myself.

'Look, I'm getting married in a few months. I'm hardly likely to do anything stupid,' he professed, as if Liz was listening in. 'Actually, there's something I've been meaning to ask you.'

'And what might that be?' I enquired, a flirty smile forming.

I leaned in towards him so I wouldn't miss what he had to say. As if being a few inches closer was going to make any difference at all.

Dean put glass to mouth and stalled for a few seconds. Whatever it was he wanted to ask me was making him act a bit twitchy.

'Come on. Out with it,' I demanded.

'OK, here it is,' Dean started confidently. 'I know this is going to sound strange, but will you... Do you want to...' he stammered, finding something rather scratchworthy on the back of his neck. 'At my wedding, could you greet people and show them to their seats... at the church?'

'Me?!' I said, utterly bowled over by his out of the blue proposal.

'Yes, you,' he said.

'What about Steve?'

'Steve's agreed to be my best man.'

'And you want me to be a sort of usher?'

Now that Dean had come clean, he relaxed. 'Yeah. I've already roped in two of my mates from football to help, but Liz said we needed someone with a more welcoming face at the door.'

'And you thought of me?'

'You're one of the nicest people I know. Nobody has a bad word to say about you.'

I knew Dean's latter statement was hokum, but I believed the former to be true. However, I got the impression that choosing me to help at the wedding had been Liz's idea. Inviting me out for a drink to ask me was probably her idea too; Dean's way would have been to text me.

'Thank you,' I said bashfully, before lamely adding,

'You're nice too. But maybe you should give up the peanuts if you want to get into your suit.'

'But you eat peanuts and you're fit.'

Swoon!

'So, are you going to do this usher thing for me or not? I would've asked Coxy, but he, y'know, died.'

What a way to lay a guilt trip on someone. I'd done my best to change the subject and give myself a bit more time to think, but I'd now been put directly on the spot.

'Yes, OK. Yes, I'll do it!' I said, feeling slightly giddy after only one pint.

'Cool!' Dean said excitedly. 'And I don't suppose you could help me with my speech? You've always got something smart to say.'

'Yeah, alright!'

It must have meant a lot to him, because my reply had made him leave the comfort of his chair and come towards me. Expecting the handshake method of thanking someone, I stood up and held out a hand. Dean went for the firm hug option, complete with manly pat on the back. With my hand squashed between us, I patted the side of his belly with my elbow. It was worth my saying yes solely for the embrace. After all the positive things he had said about me, I couldn't turn him down. Maybe that had been his aim. I wouldn't have to do much as an usher anyway.

'Hello! Here's an Order of Service. Here's a seat. Here comes the beige... I mean bride,' I imagined myself saying on the day. But then thoughts from somewhere else emerged and made me imagine another line. It said to me, *'Here's where you sabotage the wedding.'*

17

I'd gone about trying to win Dean over in completely the wrong way. Dean wanted me as a mate, hence the trip to the pub, the usher request and the play-fighting. It was a start. As long as I ended up with the result I wanted, I'd take whatever route necessary. I'd recently read an article in *Scandal!* magazine that explained how men are highly likely to fall for an amiable work colleague, because that's who they spend the majority of their time with. They then take their friendship one stage further than mere team bonding and get it on during a spot of after-hours socialising, usually when pissed. I needed to take Amy's lead – the dog reference is purely coincidental – and be more like her if I wanted to get closer to Dean.

*

So much for distancing myself from the wedding. Being at the nuptials of the man I wanted to be with and watching him wed someone else, someone he wasn't suited to, would be sheer lunacy. I was in way over my head. Added to that, I was turning into a gay cliché by becoming some kind of personal wedding planner for Liz. Something had to be said, so I gave her a call when she was back from Spain. Following a detailed description of Liz's mum's apartment, her mum's boyfriend, her mum's day-to-day life and the flights, I managed to bring the conversation round to my role in her wedding.

'And I bet Dean's pleased to have you home,' I said, fifteen minutes after I'd made the call.

'I tell you, even though I spoke to him every day, it's not the same as having somebody there to cuddle,' Liz said. 'I felt so lonely in bed without him.'

'Mmmm,' I agreed. 'Anyway, I was just ringing to speak to you about the usher thing. I'm not sure—'

'I'm thrilled he chose you for that!' Liz said.

'With a bit of help from you, yes?'

'I had no say in it.'

'He told me you wanted someone with a welcoming face.'

'Yes, I did say that. But I wanted him to feel as though he was being involved in the preparations, so I gave him the job of picking the ushers... and the best man, of course. If he hadn't picked you, I would've made you usher number four.'

Curiouser and curiouser. I knew at the time that Dean felt uncomfortable when asking me to be an usher, so perhaps using Liz's demands as an excuse had made it easier for him. After all, he still had a masculine image to uphold.

'That reminds me,' Liz said. 'Are you free to come over after work one day? I've got you something from Spain.'

'You didn't need to do that,' I said, in the way people do when they're given a gift they don't want.

'I'll see you in the week, and then we can have a proper chat.'

What does she think we've been doing for the last twenty minutes?

∗

I was coming to the end of a tiring week at work, and instead of driving home for my afternoon nap on the Friday, I took a detour to Northwood. I don't think I could have tolerated Liz any sooner than that. She was like ice cream: fine in small portions, but too much and it brought on a headache. And neither of them responded favourably to heat.

'...I don't think I could've stayed there any longer,' Liz droned on as we sat on her leather sofa. It was a struggle to keep my head from lolling. 'The heat was so uncomfortable. It's not the best place for someone with fair skin to go.'

'Won't Dean be home soon?' I cut in, suppressing a yawn.

'Ooh, I almost forgot! I'd better fetch those things for you before he gets back.'

Liz put down her mug of tea and skipped to the kitchen. She came back into the living room on tiptoes, carrying a plastic bag. Before I had a chance to take it from her, she opened it and pulled out two rolls of shimmery fabric.

'It's organza,' Liz said. 'One magenta and one lilac.'

'Right... And this is for me, is it?'

'Sort of. As gay people are known for their creative qualities, I want you to help me make some wedding favours.'

There wasn't a gay man in the land who was less creative than me; I was a disgrace to my kind. Along with my Charades and Pictionary flaws, I couldn't dance, I was tone deaf, I knew nothing about musicals and, more important to the task in hand, I had trouble cutting in straight lines and I couldn't sew. Apart from that, I was the perfect man for the job.

'You can buy those things already made,' I hinted.

'I know, but I like the personal touch. It also saved me a bit of money buying the material in bulk. A Euro per metre, or something like that. It must be made in Spain, considering how cheap it was. Organza sounds Spanish, don't you think? Or-*gan*-za!'

It sounds Italian to me.

'How many do you want made? Have you got a guest list yet?'

'I'm hoping to get the invitations finished this weekend

so I can post them on Monday. I'll let you know when I finalise the numbers.'

'And what's going inside them?'

'Pink and purple sugared almonds, but we don't have to do that until nearer the time. All I wanted to show you was how to make a bag, and then you can do the rest at home. There's no hurry to do them, I just want the material out the house so Dean doesn't stumble across it. I don't want him to see *anything* until the day itself.'

Liz unravelled some of the fabric across the floor and started to cut it, while I tried my best to remain alert.

'What about your other friends?' I asked with purpose. 'Are they helping with any of the preparations?'

'I've got a hairdresser friend who's been trying out different styles on me. She's coming round again tonight, actually. But most of my friends are too busy with careers or children or both. I know I don't have to worry about those things with you.'

Coming from someone who also had diddly of either, that comment hurt.

Liz dropped the scissors and squealed. 'I haven't told you about my hen party, have I?'

'I thought you'd chopped your finger off!' I said, clutching my chest.

'We're going to hit some gay bars! You *have* to come so you can tell us which ones to go to.'

The token gay. I'll probably be made to wear pink for everyone else's amusement. Ugh!

'Try and stop me!' I said, deliriously tired.

'There's loads of them up in Blackpool, apparently.'

'Blackpool?'

'It's going to be so much fun! And it's far enough away for people to think we're going abroad. Road trip!'

'Beep beep!'

Liz picked up the scissors again and nattered as she

snipped. 'I've already booked a fifteen-seater minibus. We're aiming to leave early on a Saturday morning to give us more time. Tired people can sleep on the way.'

I let out a dramatic sigh. 'That is *such* a shame. I work Saturday mornings.'

'Dean pointed that out, which is why I decided to have the hen party on the August Bank Holiday weekend. That way, you can join us for the big party night on the Sunday.'

'You don't have to change the date on my behalf,' I objected. I should have made my response sound more like a protest.

'I didn't do it just for you. Dean and his friends from football are coming. And because they play on a Sunday morning, they're driving up Sunday afternoon.'

'They're all going on your hen night?'

'Don't be a noddy, course they're not!' Liz scoffed. 'Dean's having his stag do up in Blackpool on the same weekend. Then we only have to pay for the one hotel room. So, will you be coming?'

'Yaaaay!' I whooped, mimicking Liz's excitement. 'I'm defo up for that!'

'I realise you won't know anyone on the hen night, so feel free to bring a few gay friends. Or how about that girl you work with. Emily? She seemed nice.'

'Amy? Yes... I'll see what she says.'

'The minibus was dead cheap, only four hundred pounds to hire it for three days. After petrol costs, I worked out that it'll be about thirty pounds a head. It might be less than that, because petrol is cheaper up north. Everything is cheaper up there. It's part of the reason we're going.'

The cost of getting everyone to Blackpool and back – not to mention hotel prices – far out-weighed any savings that would be made. Driving two hundred and fifty miles to get cheap petrol was the sort of thing Dean would suggest. It wasn't *that* much cheaper up there. If they were strapped

119

for cash, a night out in Guildford and a taxi home would have saved them even more.

'...then you tie the ribbon around the top... And there it is. Done,' Liz said after finishing her first and last wedding favour. It had taken her ten minutes.

'It all looks very straightforward,' I lied.

'Like I said, I'll let you know numbers so you know how many to make. I'm inviting a hundred and thirty-three people, so it won't be any more than that.'

One hundred and thirty-three... people invited to tea... Marvellous!

'I've just realised,' Liz sat up and said. 'Tomorrow it'll be exactly a hundred and thirty-three days until the wedding! It's fate!'

I'd come over to Liz's with the intention of telling her I wanted to take on a lesser role in proceedings, but I'd ended up taking on another task *and* agreed to go on the hen weekend. It was all too much; a time out was required. The Gay Best Friend needed to speak to his own GBF.

18

It was my best friend Jay who introduced me to gay life, taking me to bars and clubs and explaining why some of the condoms in vending machines were flavoured. Jason 'Jay' Parkin and I had been immediately magnetised to each other when I started working alongside him at Pizza Den after I quit college. He could see I was a younger version of him, and he swiftly took me under his wing. I believed Jay to be seven or eight years older than me. It was pure guesswork, as he never divulged his exact age. Jay was the first friend-boy I'd ever had. Before him, the only boy I'd spent moderate amounts of time with was Roy, but he didn't like spending time with me because I didn't like *Star Wars*. Jay left Pizza Den before I did, and my zest disappeared with him. I didn't see him as much after that because he moved town whenever he grew tired of the one he was living in. He had lived in many parts of southern England, before choosing to settle in Brighton to be among other men of the skinny-wristed variety. I fully understood why he left Crockham. The gayest place in Crockham was its macchiato-selling coffee shop. Jay and I hadn't seen each other since a messy night out on New Year's Eve, so it was high time we had a catch-up sesh, and the Early May Bank Holiday was the day we agreed to meet.

The drive to Brighton was a tedious one, and it seemed to get longer each time I did it. Ninety minutes and a couple of Beyoncé albums later, I was in the gay capital of Britain. There wasn't ample parking outside Jay's block of flats, so I left my car at a multi storey in town and walked for ten minutes.

'Hello, sexy!' Jay bellowed from a window as I approached. 'Come on up!'

After passing a rusty oven and manky sofa on the ground floor and a line of washing and a retching cat on the first floor, I reached a spotless second floor and knocked on Jay's door. At least, I thought it was Jay's.

'Sorry, I'm... I must have the wrong flat,' I said to the bruiser who answered the door.

'Marc,' the guy said flatly, holding out a hand.

'Oh... Of course you are. I'm Louis... Or Lou, if you prefer.'

Following a firm handshake, Marc turned his back on me and walked off. As he had left the front door open, I presumed he was allowing me access to the flat. The bolt through Marc's nasal septum didn't bother me. I didn't even look thrice at the green strip of hair atop his skinhead. What I was bamboozled by, though, was that Jay's three-room flat was looking immaculate. The last time I'd visited, the place had resembled the stairwells on the bottom two floors – I knew I'd seen that manky sofa before.

'Drink?' Marc asked.

'A glass of water will be fine, thanks. Do you have any bottled?'

'No.'

'OK... I think I'll leave it. Thanks all the same.'

An awkward silence was endured before Jay eventually appeared. He was looking thin, much thinner than when I'd last seen him. His dyed black hair intensified his gaunt countenance.

'It's so good to see you!' Jay said, grabbing me and giving me a hug. 'I had to change my trousers quickly because you're wearing the *exact* ones that I had on.'

I didn't believe him for a second. Jay was never ready on time, and it was inconceivable he would ever wear jeans that were two seasons out of date, as he always had a well-manicured finger on the button of fashion.

'Thanks again for agreeing to help me with the wedding favours,' I said.

'Don't thank me,' Jay said. 'Marc's the one who'll be making them.'

I turned to Marc. The tattoo of a naked lady on his forearm looked more animated than he did.

'This is really good of you, Marc,' I said, handing him the bag of organza. 'There's one already done in there, but I can show you what you need to do.'

'No need,' Marc said. 'I made stuff like this all the time in prison.'

I gulped. 'I'll pay you, of course. Is ten quid OK?'

Marc raised an eyebrow.

'I meant twenty... Twenty quid.'

'Lou, don't be daft,' Jay said. 'Marc's got loads of time on his hands. Nobody's willing to employ someone with a criminal record... even though the drugs were planted on him... But, on the plus side, that stint inside taught him a thing or two.'

'Like how to keep his living space clean,' I joked.

Jay and I carried on our chatting as we walked towards the seafront, leaving Marc in the flat. According to Jay, Marc designed his own tattoos and cut his own hair. From what I could gather, spending hours on their hair was one of the few things they had in common. Marc must have been a demon in the sack.

'I'm due behind the bar at six, so we can't be too long,' Jay said.

'How about we grab a bite to eat and then hit the shops?'

'I don't eat on Mondays.'

'Come again?'

'I never get time these days.'

'You've got time today, so let me buy you lunch.'

'OK, but nothing big.'

Jay had clearly taken on more than he could handle. Brighton was unquestionably the best place for him, but it was so expensive. Sacrifices had been made, and it looked as though eating and sleeping were no longer a priority, though purchasing designer clothes was. Marc wasn't paying rent, so Jay had to provide for them both. However, were Jay to reduce his monthly clothing budget by a quarter, hundreds of pounds would be immediately saved.

I bought two hotdogs when Jay and I reached the pier, then we sat on a bench to eat them. It was typical bank holiday weather: overcast with rainclouds looming.

'You said on the phone you were thinking about getting *another* job,' Jay said. 'Anything to do with that bloke you work with?'

'Why do you say that?'

'Whenever you're narked off with your job, there's always a man at the bottom of it.'

'You can talk! There's always a man at your bottom,' I retaliated.

'Better that than stay celibate until the right guy comes along,' Jay barbed.

'The right guy *has* come along.'

'He's getting married, Lou!' Jay spluttered, spraying bits of white roll that the seagulls duly pecked at.

'But he's been flirting with me for ages.'

'There's a difference between flirting and teasing, and this Dean twat sounds like a proper prick tease,' Jay said in his usual no-nonsense way. 'Straight men are wankers. At least with gay men you know where you stand.'

'Legs apart with your face pressed against a cubicle door?'

To stop an argument breaking out, I went back to the hotdog kiosk and took a couple of ketchup sachets. I knew Jay had been hurt by a couple of bad experiences with straight men, but that didn't give him the right to generalise. He didn't know Dean like I did.

'All I was trying to get at was that I think you should steer clear of Dean and all the blokes like him that you always fall for,' Jay said when I returned.

It was good advice, but about ten years too late.

'I'll just give up and spend my life with someone I don't fancy, shall I?' I huffed, squirting the contents of a sachet onto my hotdog.

'Beggars can't be choosers,' Jay said tritely, cramming some hotdog down his throat. Ironically, he was the one who looked like a beggar. 'But if you *must* pursue a straight bloke, the best time to do it is when he's been married for a few years. That's when they're at their most vulnerable.'

'You seem to know a lot about it.'

'Blokes are all the same, whether they're gay, het or bi. Bloke gets tied down. Bloke gets comfy and puts on a bit of weight. Bloke feels insecure. Bloke gets bored. Bloke cheats. That's why you'll never catch me walking down the aisle.'

Settling for second best was something I'd done many times before, and it never ended well. Most of them were one-nighters – gay men I'd slept with to help get the straight men I was lusting after out of my system. I'd had ten one-night stands, and on every occasion I'd been woken in the early hours by the snoring of a man who had looked so much better before I'd put head to pillow. The snoring was quite convenient and acted as an alarm clock for me to gather my things and leave. The sex was never magical – or alcohol-free – so I didn't see the point in seeing them again. Making my way home wearing clothes that had sat wrinkled on the floor was bearable, as there weren't many people up and about between four o'clock and six o'clock on a Sunday morning – which was when I did my walks (or taxis) of shame. Despite being excellent at avoiding the squeaky floorboards and reaching the safety of my own room without disturbing anyone, my mum must have known what I'd been up to by there being a foreign smell in the laundry basket the next day.

'Can we head to the shops in a bit?' I suggested. 'This sea breeze is starting to annoy. I'm surprised you can tolerate it.'

'I've got used to it. And half a can of hairspray a day helps,' he said, standing up and letting the wind take his napkin.

'You might want to sort that ketchup stain out first,' I said, pointing at a small splodge of it on Jay's shirt.

'For the sake of fuck!' he yelled, as if a seagull had shat on him. 'Do you mind if we go back to my place so I can change into another one? I can't go into town like this.'

So that Jay's reputation wasn't ruined, we walked to the Lanes via his flat. I brought up the subject of Liz's hen weekend and asked Jay if he wanted to come with me. He didn't seem that eager to start with, but he soon warmed to the idea when I told him how inexpensive the trip would be. I'd be driving up, so that was most of his travelling costs sorted. And he would save a bit more if he agreed to share a room. Other than that, it was just money for food and drinks.

'Come on,' I begged. 'It'll be like New Year's Eve all over again.'

'I'll ask my manager tonight,' Jay said. 'I've worked every bank holiday this year, so I might be able to wangle it. I'm due a break.'

'And you'll be giving him plenty of time to arrange some cover for you.'

'Her. My manager is a she.'

'Then suck up to *her*, keep out of trouble and I'm sure it won't be a problem. And don't worry if you can't go. I can make up an excuse to get out of it should I need to.'

'Do you reckon I'll be able to bring Marc along?'

126

'I don't think so, no,' I said, thinking on my feet. 'Liz told me she wanted her hens to feel relaxed so they can properly let their hair down, and she thinks they won't do that if there are too many strangers in the group. It was hard enough convincing her to bring you along.'

'It's probably a good thing,' Jay agreed. 'I can't afford to pay for both of us.'

'Sounds like you've made up your mind.'

'Yeah, it's been ages since you and me went away together. And if my manager says I can't have the time off, I'll call in sick.'

'Sweet! Blackpool, here we come!'

19

God must have wanted Liz and Dean's wedding to go ahead without any interruptions from me. Kath was rushed to hospital during her delivery one morning in early June, and the first question I thought to ask Colin after hearing this news regarded Oliver. I felt rather ashamed of myself when I found out Kath had a ruptured appendix and would need emergency surgery. God didn't have to go *that* far just to shift my focus off Dean and onto Oliver again; a simple broken arm would have sufficed. A card was passed round the office for everyone to sign. People had written the standard 'Get well soon' platitude or merely scribed their names. I stopped in a card shop after delivery for inspiration and jotted down some prose from the inside of another card. 'Under repair, so handle with care' was the only appropriate wording I spotted. Plus, it was a bit witty, so it would hopefully bring a smile to Kath's wrinkly face. Her loss (of appendix) was my gain, though. As Kath was out of action for the foreseeable future, Oliver had a more regular role within our office.

I wanted to arrive at work before Oliver on his first day back, because then he could walk up to me with his tail between his legs and apologise for not responding to any of the eleven texts I'd sent over the past seven weeks and five days. But I knew my plan had been thwarted when I drove into the car park and saw Oliver's over-sized car in one of the van bays. Styling, restyling and re-restyling my hair is what cost me the time. Jay would have been proud. Being

Kath's replacement meant Oliver would be working next to me, but I was reluctant to strike up a conversation with him. I wanted Oliver to know I was ignoring him, so I intended to saunter past and speak loudly to someone nearby.

'How's it going?' Oliver asked when he saw me approach. I snapped out of my mood.

'Hiya! I didn't know you were coming back,' I replied.

'I would've texted you, but the phone that's got your number in died and I couldn't find the charger anywhere,' he explained. It sounded plausible. 'My sponsors bought me this new one.

Oliver revealed a sleek black phone three times the size of mine. His missing battery charger story must have been valid, unless he had gone to great lengths and bought a new phone simply to give himself a reason for why he hadn't replied to my texts. That's the sort of thing I would do.

'It's dead smart,' I said. 'It's a smart smartphone.'

Oliver glossed over my droll remark and passed me his phone so I could have a look at it in more detail. During the handover, I grabbed the opportunity to glide my hand against his. It's the little things in life that bring a smile to the face of a singleton. I'd been living off similar cheap thrills for years.

'If you write your number down, I'll add it in when I get the chance,' he said.

As I copied my number onto a piece of scrap paper, I knew it would 'accidentally' fall off his bench and into the bin as soon as I was out of view. It was just another excuse to not have me as a contact. Perhaps he didn't want all the hangers-on from his past getting in touch once he had made his fortune as a professional golfer.

'It's got loads of games and apps on it,' Oliver boasted. 'But I've no idea how to work it properly. It's got a GPS thing on it so my sponsors know exactly where I am, which means they can see if I've gone up to London with friends instead of practising.'

'So turn it off. Then you can sneak off to London and pretend the battery ran out.'

'It has to be on in case I'm needed to play in a tournament,' he explained. 'I'm on standby if someone pulls out with an injury.'

'Like falling out of a golf cart, or stubbing a toe on a fir cone?' I scoffed.

'Shows what *you* know,' he said defensively. 'I was called up for a tournament two weeks ago because a guy had damaged the tendons in his shoulder.'

'You can't have done very well in it if you're back here doing this.'

'Have you heard of a player called Tom Graham?' Oliver asked, seemingly disregarding my facetious comment.

'Is he really bad at golf too?'

'Tom's my inspiration,' he carried on. 'A few years ago he was working in a cake factory. Last year he was at the top of the Masters leaderboard after hitting a first round sixty-five.'

'Did he celebrate by having some cake?'

'He's probably sick of the sight of them,' Oliver said, warming to my humour.

Thankfully, the spark I'd worked hard to create during Oliver's previous stint in our office remained, meaning we didn't have to start our friendship from scratch.

'So, when are the two of you getting married?' Dean butted in.

I hadn't heard the clumping of Dean's elephant feet or felt the floor shake; I'd been totally in the moment with Oliver.

'Why? Do you want to be bridesmaid?' I replied with a wry smile, before turning my back on him and heading to my bench.

Not content with me having the last laugh, Dean called over, 'You've been pestering the boss to get Olly back since he was last here. Looks like you got what you wanted.'

'No I haven't!' I said heatedly.

'Actually, your boss said the same thing when he called me to ask if I'd work,' Oliver interjected, joining forces with Dean to make me look even more like a desperate stalker.

'Nice one!' Dean lauded, holding his hand up so Oliver would high-five him. Oliver duly obliged, then grinned at me to show that he could give as good as he got.

'Oh, so you gave the boss your new number, but you didn't give it to me,' I said huffily.

'No, he called me on my home phone.'

'Ha! In your face!' Dean taunted, jabbing his index fingers in my direction.

I took no notice of Dean's attempt to act street, so I began my daily routine by putting down my things, hanging up my jacket and going to the canteen to buy my Red Bull. It was a task keeping track of who I was using to make the other jealous. Game-playing was hard work, but they were making their playing of me look easy. I couldn't be truthful with either of them just yet, because boys get scared off when honesty and feelings are mentioned. As things stood, Dean was jealous of my friendship with Oliver; Amy was doing her best to keep me and Dean apart; and I wanted to sabotage everyone's relationships. What a pickle!

*

As I went about my delivery in the hazy sunshine, I mulled over the morning's events. After lengthy deliberation, I decided not to track Oliver down once I'd finished. Neither he nor Dean had apologised following their ganging-up incident and, being typical men, they had left me to stew. Their egos were big enough without me pandering to their every whim, and I had more self-respect than to massage those egos further.

> Lou it's Oliver. Can you give me a hand when you finish. I'm having a mare of a delivery.<

>OK! I'll call you when I'm done
to see where you are. Bye!

Scratch what I said before. Oliver's text was as good an apology as I was likely to get. I was proud of myself for standing my ground, albeit for a few hours. Treating him mean was definitely keeping him keen. For the time being, I was back in the game.

To help give me more time with Oliver, I swiftly finished my round, leaping over a few small fences and flowerbeds in the process. When I called Oliver, he replied with details of his whereabouts. A few moments later, I was pedalling towards him and ringing my bell.

'I can't get the hang of this delivery at all,' Oliver moaned as I came to a halt next him.

'How much have you got left?' I asked, almost out of breath.

'I've still got another full bag in my car. I'm supposed to be at the driving range in an hour.'

'Give me the rest of this bag and you crack on with the one in your car.'

'You're a life saver,' he overstated, sighing with relief. 'Thank you.'

Although I was still puffed out, I set off at pace on Oliver's delivery. Within the bundles of mail, I found two or three letters for other numbers in that road, and a few for different roads entirely. Half an hour later, I met Oliver back at his car.

'I just had a text,' Oliver said. 'My practice session has

been called off.'

'You mean I've come and helped you for nothing?' I said, smiling, though a tad peeved.

'You'll get a lift to the office for your troubles.'

'Thanks,' I said sarcastically. 'But I could've been back at home by now.'

Oliver pressed the button on his key fob that made the side door of his car slide open. I stood behind him as he climbed inside and bent down to make some room for my bike. Skinny bums did nothing for me, but it didn't stop me having a lengthy ogle. Oliver moved his golfing gear to one side, and I passed my bike through to him. Travelling back, he spotted the items I hadn't delivered.

'Did you not feel like posting those?' Oliver enquired.

'These are letters *you* sorted wrongly.' I wasn't going to take the blame for his mistakes.

'Being a postman isn't the best of jobs for a dyslexic,' he said. 'Customers keep coming out and shouting, "Can't you read?" at me while waving a letter I've mis-delivered.'

'People can be so ignorant,' I said. 'Tread on their flowers next time.'

'I read that sixty-one per cent of millionaires are dyslexic.'

'That seems a lot. Maybe you read the statistic wrong and it's only sixteen per cent.'

'You won't be laughing when I'm holding a giant cheque for over one million dollars at the Masters tournament.'

'...just before you hand it over to the winner,' I said. 'It's so touching when they get someone with a disability to present the prize money.'

'At least you can't see my disability, unlike yours,' he said, taking the bait and playfully fighting back. 'You receive lottery funding to help with your disfigurements.'

'All the donations I receive are gratefully accepted and wisely spent,' I said, showing him how best to react to childish put-downs.

The return journey was a short one, as Kath's delivery wasn't too far from the office. When we were back on company property, I clambered into the main part of Oliver's car. I could almost stand fully upright in it. Plenty of room for a cheeky bit of fun or, with a tight squeeze, a romantic candlelit dinner for two, complete with self-playing grand piano in the corner. I wheeled my bike to the side door and passed it to Oliver, who lifted it out carefully so as not to scratch his car's paintwork.

'While you're in there, can you grab my empty bags and take them in with you?'

'You're not playing golf now,' I protested. 'You have to carry your own bags in this job.'

'I *do* carry my own bags when I play golf,' he countered. 'The caddie I was supplied with kept making bad calls, so I told my sponsors I'd rather do it myself. I prefer it that way, as I like to make all my own decisions on a golf course.'

'That can't look very professional. I don't often watch golf, but I've never seen anyone carry their own clubs.'

'If there was a caddie out there that could wheel my bag around and keep quiet, I'd hire them.'

'I can do that,' I said all too readily.

20

Never one to turn my back on a glimmer of opportunity, I helped Oliver as much as possible during the time he was with us. It was my way of showing him I worked hard and was capable of being subservient – qualities I thought a worthy caddie would need. Walking while carrying a bag was something I was good at. I'd done it for the past seven months, so I thought I was well qualified to further my career in it. By aiding Oliver, I was killing two birds with one stone, as I knew my role would ruffle Dean's feathers.

'I've got a six-pack like that,' Oliver said, showing me the front cover to July's edition of *Healthy Men* magazine one Tuesday morning. It wasn't his copy; it was one of the many magazines we delivered. *Dairy Goat News*, *Quality Packaging* and *Bus Shelter Journal* were particular office favourites.

'In your dreams,' I said in return, hoping it would goad Oliver into proving me wrong. It didn't.

I wanted to lift up his shirt and see the rippling abs in all their glory, but flirting was definitely off the agenda. Oliver needed somebody reliable to caddie for him, and if he thought for a second I was only interested in being his sidekick because I fancied him, I'd be swiftly replaced by some other fame-hungry desperado. So that I wouldn't put my new role in jeopardy, I kept a lid on my lascivious thoughts.

Oliver pulled out the stool from under my bench and sat down. I hoped Amy was taking note of what was going on, because I wanted her to tell Dean all about my burgeoning friendship with his pal Olly. Dean was out in the car park, his head under the bonnet of his van.

'I don't know,' I sighed, starting off a mock rant. I wanted to make my point to Oliver without sounding as though I meant it. 'You're quite happy to receive help, but when you get a chance to help in return, you just sit and watch. Typical bloke.'

'That's because I'm more of a receiver than a giver,' Oliver teased.

Would you like to receive a hand job, then?

'So I see,' I said. 'There's no danger of getting any help from you.'

'I know why you help me.'

'You do?' The game was over.

'It's because I give you lifts back.'

If only he knew. The game was still on.

'And will I be getting the chance to help you on the golf course soon?'

Oliver paused. 'It's not that easy... It's tough to find someone to practise with that's up to my standard.'

'There must be plenty of people at your club who you can have a knockabout with.'

'A knockabout? You can't just have a knockabout when you're playing against high-quality opposition,' he said indignantly.

'Then let me know when you're *practising* next and I can follow you round.'

'OK. I'll add it into my phone to remind me.'

And with that, Oliver took out his phone and proceeded to fiddle with it. I didn't need a reminder; it would be one of the most important moments of my life thus far. I was a bit put out that Oliver felt the need to place me on his to-do list. Spending time alone with me obviously wasn't a high priority for him. I also had a to-do list, though mine comprised men's names. At the top of the list, Dean's and

Oliver's names were interchanging daily. If I could merge their best bits together, I'd have my perfect man.

*

Dashing round my delivery had become a daily occurrence, though it gave me little time to chat to any of my customers. My tips at Christmas would suffer, but that was of little consequence. If I played things right, I could be swapping my monotonous life in Crockham for more glamorous locations as a caddie. By the end of the year, I could be touring South Africa with Oliver, carrying his clubs for him while Table Mountain provided a picturesque backdrop.

I was in the process of building up speed so I could jump over a water feature, when a female voice called out from the house I'd just delivered to.

'Lou!'

Expecting a complaint, I stopped and turned to face the music.

'Vicky!'

'I thought I recognised that sexy bum,' Vicky replied as I jogged over for a sweaty hug. 'I didn't know you were a postman.'

'Yeah, it's not really what I want to be doing, but it's OK for now.'

'And how have you been? What have you been up to?'

This is the point in a conversation where the inquirer is dazzled by tales of their friend's achievements and high points since the last time they met.

'Well, my brother got married last year, and he and his wife have a lovely house in Worfield. Both of my parents have retired and—'

'Paige, not while mummy's talking,' Vicky turned away from me and said. She had clearly lost interest. I didn't blame her.

A blonde-haired girl of about three or four – I was useless at guessing kids' ages – came running to the door. I'd not seen Vicky since I quit my supermarket job six years back so, theoretically, the child could even have been five. During those intervening years, Vicky appeared to have aged at double speed. The fresh-faced teenager I'd once worked with now looked as though she had overtaken me in age. But at least she had something to show for her fading looks.

'She's got your eyes,' I offered, not knowing what else to say.

Most people would crouch down to the kid's level and say something less corny. Even touching Paige's hand or cheek didn't seem a natural thing to do.

'Michael and me split up last year,' Vicky said bitterly. 'Bastard ran off with a woman from the gym. He was screwing about with her for over a year before I found out. Can you believe that?'

'Men!' I said, as if demeaning my own sex would somehow make Vicky feel better.

'We used to have a nice house in Worfield, but we had to sell it after *he* upped and left. Him and his trophy girlfriend now live in Guildford, and I've had to move back in here with my parents. It's so unfair.'

Karma had paid Vicky a visit. Back in our shelf-stacking days, all the fit guys who worked with us at the supermarket chased after Vicky. The only one who gave me a second look was Michael. There had initially been a spark between us, a definite chemistry. Yet that faded when Vicky joined the team, and I was soon hung out to dry. Vicky and I had started off as good friends, going out on a Friday night and stumbling into work on the Saturday morning still reeking of cider. It was me who brought her out of her shell and helped her to develop her personality. But by doing so, I was inadvertently displaying Vicky's winsome qualities for all my male colleagues to see. Although she didn't know how I felt about Michael, I still saw it as a betrayal of friendship when she took a shine to him. Soon after their first date, I quit my job. That was all in the past, though. I'd had other men to pursue and further rejections to contend with since then.

'At least you gave it a go,' I said. 'I haven't even attempted to leave home.'

'I take it there's no boyfriend you could move in with?'

'Gay men are a bit thin on the ground around here.'

'You need to get out of the Crockham bubble,' Vicky advised. 'My sister was working as a waitress in town. She got so fed up of her life that she took a break to try and find out what she really wants. Right now, she's backpacking round Australia. It's something I always wanted to do, but I can't now I've got madam here to look after.'

Paige started tugging at Vicky's skirt.

'In a minute,' Vicky looked down and said, before addressing me again. 'And if it's true love you're looking for, remember that the world is a big place. Having him turn up in Crockham would be way too much of a coincidence.'

'Yeah, I guess.'

Paige carried on trying to get her mum's attention.

'Anyway, I've got this one to see to,' Vicky said. 'How about we meet up and go to a gay bar one night? I'll drive, and then you'll be free to have a drink.'

'Sounds like a great idea.'

*

My accusation regarding Oliver's lack of help had evidently sunk in, because he came and found me after he had finished his delivery that morning.

'Either you're getting slower or I'm getting quicker,'

Oliver said as he drew level with me.

'Sorry, one of my customers kept talking at me,' I said, taking a breather. 'I've only got these few houses left.'

'I've been talking too. Because you keep badgering me about it, I've arranged a practice session for next next Tuesday. Are you free?'

My ears pricked up. 'Next next Tuesday sounds good to me.'

Following another lift back to the office, Oliver wheeled my bike to the sheds while I collected his empty mail bags and took them inside. It felt right. I mean, what's not to like about travelling the world, getting paid a stack of cash and meeting famous people? Oliver knew Jamie Redknapp, so that was a start. This was my big break, the one I'd been waiting a lifetime for.

After leaving Oliver's bags under his bench, I came back outside to find him perched on the bonnet of my car.

If the buttons on the back of his trousers scratch the paintwork, there'll be trouble.

'Give me the gossip,' the nosey bugger said. 'What's the story with Dean and Amy?'

'There's no story,' I replied, parking my bum next to his. 'Why, what have you heard?'

'Ignore me. I've probably got it all wrong.'

'No, go on. I want to hear what you've got to say now.'

Oliver hesitated, then aired his thoughts. 'Dean said some stuff about her when we went to watch Spurs. I got the impression he was chasing after her.'

'So, after the match it was down the pub with the lads for a pint and a chat about birds?'

'Something like that, yeah.'

'Dean doesn't need to chase after her,' I argued, trying to convince myself as well as Oliver. 'I've met his fiancée and she's really nice.'

Just as Oliver was about to speak, a work van came

speeding into the car park. After a blast of the horn and a handbrake turn, it came to an abrupt halt in front of Oliver and me.

'I wish I had time to sit down,' Dean said out of the van's open window. Amy was in the passenger seat.

'You *are* sitting down,' I challenged.

Dean wound up his window and jumped out of the van. 'You know what I mean. Stop trying to be clever in front of your boyfriend.'

'Says the man trying to show off in front of his girlfriend,' I said, making the score 2-1 in my favour.

'Yeah, and what of it?'

Silence. I had no comeback for that. Amy afforded me a smug grin, which I hoped Oliver saw. It was us against them. Amy and Dean were back earlier than usual because there was no overtime going. Funnily enough, posties didn't go sick in summer.

'Can you move the van, please?' I asked Dean. 'I'm going home now.'

'Then you'll have to wait until we've unloaded. Won't be a minute.'

Amy and Dean proceeded to clear the van of empty mail bags, undeliverable parcels and shopping.

'Wish I had time to go shopping,' I muttered under my breath.

Oliver snorted.

'Cheers again for offering to drive us up to Blackpool for my stag, Olly,' Dean said.

My eyes opened wide as I turned to look at Oliver.

'That's OK,' Oliver replied sheepishly.

'There must be room for, what, ten people in that beast?' Dean enquired, nodding towards Oliver's car.

'Yeah, roughly,' Oliver said.

'And all this time I thought you were popular,' I mocked. 'Nine friends? Wow.'

Dean went on the defensive. 'It's a bank holiday weekend. People have other things planned.'

'Anyway, it's about quality, not quantity,' Amy chipped in. 'And Olly and I are top quality.'

My throat began to tighten. '*You're* going on the stag night?'

'I sure am,' she said.

21

Dean glared at Amy. She swiftly gathered their parcels and bags, and Oliver gave her a hand to take them inside. He clearly felt uncomfortable at being a pawn in my and Dean's attempts at one-upmanship.

'I wanted my stag night up in London, but what I want doesn't seem to count,' Dean sighed, leaning against the side of his van. 'The things a man has to do just to have sex with his own fiancée.'

'How come I wasn't invited on the stag do?' I asked, ignoring his attempt to lighten the mood.

'I was going to, but Liz said she wanted you on the hen night. She'll be really disappointed if you don't go.'

'Doesn't Liz think it's strange that you've asked Amy to come on your stag night? And what are your other mates going to say when she turns up?'

Dean ignored the first part of my double-headed question. I must remember not to ask two questions at once; my first question had him cornered, but my second made it easier for him to wriggle free.

'They'll be cool with it,' Dean said. 'Amy's met most of them already.'

When was that? During an orgy, I expect.

'And the reason Amy's on your list and not on Liz's?'

'Because she...' Dean started, before his brain clicked into gear and said something less truthful. 'I didn't think Liz's hen do would be her kinda thing.'

'Though it's my kinda thing?' I challenged, mocking his

mockney accent.

'Liz's friends will probably book some hunky fireman to take his clothes off,' Dean carried on, bearing a look that suggested he was trying to claw his way out of a hole. 'I bet you'll be in the front row.'

'I can't wait!' I falsely shrieked.

Dean stressed his point further by saying, 'You'll have much more fun with the hens. I'll probably end up at a strip club on my stag night. Hopefully my boys will pay one of the hot strippers to give me a private showing.'

Stuff the hen party; I wanted to be with the boys. All I needed to do was act more blokey so Dean would feel I fitted in with his crowd of mates. I'd do what my Maths teacher advised and listen more to my 'masculine brain'. The new course of action should hopefully be enough to earn an invite to the stag night. I'd be fine on the stag, provided I went to the toilet and covered my ears during the stripper bit. No, I was more interested in the handcuffing naked to a lamppost tradition. I wanted a ringside seat and a fully charged camera for that event. I mean, why should passing strangers be so lucky to see Dean naked when I'd tried for months and not seen so much as a chest hair? Amy had already copped a good eyeful, no doubt.

I thought about reeling off a diatribe on how stripping belittles women and that Dean should show his fiancée some respect, but I knew he wanted a reaction.

'Amy going on the stag night has nothing to do with the hens hitting the gay bars, then?' I asked.

'Why would that be a problem?' Dean sniffed.

'Come off it, you must've noticed that she's been off with me. She's such a homophobe.'

'Maybe she just doesn't like you. You can't play the gay card all the time.'

'I'm not the one playing games here,' I argued, leaving my car bonnet and standing up straight. 'The fact is she's hardly spoken to me since you yelled out that I wanted to hit the showers with the footballers at your poxy charity match.'

Dean stifled a laugh.

'It's not funny,' I said, getting het up.

'OK, if I'm being honest,' Dean lowered his voice to say, 'Liz told me that she didn't get great vibes from Amy at the football match. I didn't want Amy to feel left out, so I invited her on the stag.'

'Oh, really?' I said, raising a quizzical eyebrow. The balance of power was shifting. 'Liz suggested I bring Amy along to her hen night. Now, why would she say that if she didn't like her?'

Dean and I were eyeball to eyeball, but before he could give me a credible explanation – or snog me, one or the other – Oliver came out of the office and walked over. Talk about bad timing.

'Are you two still going?' he said. 'I thought you'd be in bed by now.'

'What?!' I spluttered.

'You're normally having your nap around now. Because I didn't see you inside, I guessed you'd gone home.'

'We were sorting out stuff for the wedding, weren't we?' Dean glowered at me and said.

I nodded vigorously, which helped shake from my head the image of Dean and me in bed together.

'And now we're finished, aren't we, Lou?'

'Yeah, we're done.'

Dean hopped into his van and reversed a few feet.

'In that case, it must be time to go,' Oliver said, getting in his car. 'See you tomorrow, Lou.'

'Have a—'

Oliver slammed his door shut.

'—good afternoon,' I muttered to myself.

'Tell Liz about Amy coming on the stag and there'll be

trouble,' Dean came over and warned, before going inside to chase up Amy.

I gave Oliver a wave as he drove past, and I was then left standing with only vehicles for company. My dispute with Dean had made me temporarily forget about rebuking Oliver for offering to drive the stags up to Blackpool and not telling me about it. No wonder he made a quick getaway. But there was no way I was going to let Dean off the hook as easily. I wanted some straight answers, but I knew I wouldn't get any if I confronted him when Amy was present. I quickly got in my car before the two of them reappeared, and I mulled over my next move as I drove home.

*

An hour after I left work, I texted Dean. That gave him plenty of time to have lunch with Amy and drop her home. I wasn't expecting an immediate reply – because he might have still been driving himself home – but I wanted to send my text while everything was fresh in my head.

>How long have you and Amy been sleeping together? And don't pretend you haven't, because you've been acting guilty for ages.

It's none of ur business.<

>You're not denying it then?

It only happened once. No big deal. C u 2moro.<

>I knew it! You've been lying to me this whole time. Poor Liz. I wonder what she'll say when she finds out.

146

Bile rose in my throat. When I was having fun with Dean and trying to tempt him, I couldn't have cared less about Liz's feelings – but that was before I knew her. The irony being that I was now fighting her corner and acting as if *I* was his fiancée. If Liz had known about the Amy situation, would she have been as worked up about it as I was? She would have to be told several times over and shown video evidence, as the blinkered moose would never work it out for herself.

I turned off my phone and snapped it shut. I liked to do that; it felt empowering. I put head to pillow, feeling satisfied with my detective work. I couldn't sleep, though – not with all of that governing my thoughts. After an hour's tossing and turning, I dragged myself out of bed and turned my phone back on. Missing out on afternoon naps made me very short-tempered indeed, and while I'd been stewing, I'd thought of some more grievances I wanted to get off my chest. As I texted, Dean's final message from earlier came through.

> Please don't tell Liz. Give me some
> time 2 tell her 1st. If our friendship
> means anything u'll do that 4 me.<

Even after declaring on our date at The Plough that he wouldn't cheat on Liz, Dean had gone and slept with the enemy. I now had to figure out what to do with my findings. Tell Liz and have her call off the wedding? That would be one way for me to get out of going, though it did seem a tad extreme. Besides, Dean would probably thank me for clearing the path for him and Amy to get together. Perhaps that was why he confessed his affair to me, so I'd break the news to Liz gently. No, the wedding definitely had to take place. I wasn't going to do his dirty work for him. Blackmail was another option. But what to blackmail him for? Money?

Sex? Either of those would have done, though I'd have preferred the latter.

I aborted my initial message and started again, pressing each button as if pressing my thumbs into Dean's eyes.

>You can also tell her about the time you
and Amy were at your parents' house.

Are you still going on about this? I already
explained what we were doing there.<

>You're a small man in a large man's
body. Save your smelly breath for
someone worth lying to, like Liz.

Say anything like that again
and see what happens.<

>I might just do that.

(No reply)

22

On a day that I could have done with some support, Oliver texted to say he was running late. It was a bonus in some respects, as I didn't want him to see Dean laying into me, followed by me bursting into tears – that or laughter, which I often did when I was yelled at. Without Oliver next to me, though, I had nobody on my side; everybody in the office loved Dean. Even Oliver was edging closer to the other side. I was even starting to miss Kath and her inane chatter. She would have backed me up had she been around. But Kath's recovery was taking longer than expected, so it meant I had Oliver's company for a little while longer – just not this morning.

Amy and Dean usually turned up at work roughly five minutes after me, though today it was nearer fifteen. I stood at Oliver's bench and started to prep his mail, waiting for what the day had in store. I didn't feel particularly on edge, but the several mis-slotted letters I found when I was delivering my own mail that morning told a different story. Either Oliver's dyslexia was contagious, or I was fretting about what Dean was going to do. After my umpteenth glance up at the office clock, Dean arrived and immediately blustered towards me. The plan was to ignore him and carry on slotting in Oliver's mail, but he grabbed my arm and flung me around to face him. In the process, most of the letters I was holding were jerked out of my hand and onto the floor.

'What was all that about yesterday?' Dean barked. His

149

breath stank of smoke. I'd never known him to have a cigarette before.

'You want me to repeat it? In front of everyone?' I goaded.

I would have gladly revealed Amy and Dean's secret there and then, and for a second I thought Dean was going to keep up the bravado and allow me to. However, his stance soon changed when Amy caught up with him. Just the sight of the mucky tart almost brought up my morning bowl of muesli. She looked so smug. One word from me to Liz could easily change Amy's expression, though. I wondered what she would look like with her eyes scratched out.

Dean leaned in and said quietly, but forcefully, 'Canteen. Now!'

I tossed the few remaining letters I had in my hand onto Oliver's bench and set off for the canteen, with Dean walking close behind me as though making sure I didn't run off and lock myself in the toilets. Steve was getting himself a cup of coffee when I opened the canteen door.

'Hi, Steve. Alright?' I said politely, as if trying to make friends with the good cop.

'Not bad. A bit tired.'

Judging by Steve's terse reply, I gathered that Dean had told him about our argument while they had been outside smoking. I liked that they talked about me and that I stirred such passion, because it showed I was included and involved in life; I mattered. From my schooldays, and on through my work life, I was completely overlooked by boys. I wanted to be the one who the boys talked fervently about, and now, in a round about sort of way, I was.

'Leave us for a sec, mate,' Dean ordered Steve.

'Don't do anything I wouldn't do, lovebirds,' Steve said.

'In his dreams,' I sneered.

Although he was Dean's mate, I wanted Steve around to

pull Dean off me in the event of an attempted throttling. But Steve merely picked up his coffee from the vending machine, gave Dean a wink and left the room. Dean shut the door after him. Fortunately, there wasn't a lock on it. I hoped Steve was listening from outside, just in case things turned nasty. Thinking that I was less likely to receive a punch to the face if I was sitting down, I perched on one of the plastic patio chairs. Dean started to pace up and down in front of me.

'I guess I'll have to find another usher,' he threatened weakly.

'Good luck with that,' I said. 'You must be short of friends to have asked me in the first place.'

'It was Liz's idea to ask you, not mine.'

'That's not what she said.'

I sat back in the chair and looked up at Dean, quite pleased with how the quarrel was panning out. Everything he threw at me I swatted away with ease.

'It was a joint decision,' Dean said, half-admitting his lie.

'You should get your pal Olly to replace me. You seem to like sponging off him and taking advantage of his good nature.'

'That's not a bad idea. And he'll look better than you in the photos. Thanks for the tip.'

My sarcasm was catching.

'You noticed he was good-looking, then? And there was me thinking you were only into schoolgirls. Liz really is clueless.'

Dean smashed his right fist into the side of the hot drinks vending machine. I hoped it was broken – the machine, not his fist – so that Amy wouldn't be able to have her morning brew.

'I've already told you what Amy was doing at my parents' house,' he said vehemently. 'So there's no need to go stirring up any shit between Liz and me.'

'Liz has a right to know what you've been up to,' I said, trying hard not to raise my voice.

Dean marched over and placed his hands either side of me on the arms of the chair. We were now at the same eye level. As he moved his face towards mine, I leaned back.

'Come anywhere near our wedding and there'll be trouble,' he said, his wide eyes penetrating mine.

I couldn't decide which eye to look at, so I flicked between the two. Dean's face was inches away from mine. Normally, that would have turned me on. Not this time. The smell of cigarette smoke on his breath was fading, a hint of morning breath seeping through in its stead.

After his threat, Dean maintained his evil stare as he stood tall – as tall as a short man could – before looking away and walking towards the door.

'I'll have to make a note of that,' I boldly retorted, getting a pen out of my pocket and pretending to write on my hand. 'I've been looking for an excuse not to go.'

'Why don't you get a life and stop interfering in mine, you fucking annoying twat?'

It was a rhetorical question, so I didn't provide an answer. Not that I had time to think of one because, after his final outburst, Dean left the room, and I was left to stew.

Dean once told me that he didn't use the C-word because it showed disrespect towards women, but the hypocrite didn't see anything disrespectful about using the T-word... or sleeping with someone who wasn't his fiancée. All the comebacks I'd conjured up throughout our clash meant nothing now, as the last word had been Dean's. Our wits had been pitted against each other, but it was Dean who had come out as the victor. One good thing came of it, though: my invite to the wedding had been rescinded. I didn't know how Dean was going to explain that one to Liz, and I didn't particularly care. What had I done to deserve getting caught up in all this? I'd led a reasonably normal life up until I met

Dean. Perhaps it was punishment for past misdemeanours. But Dean's misdeeds far out-weighed mine, and his life seemed on track.

*

With Dean's comment about me needing to get a life of my own circling my brains, I marched to Colin's office. The door was already open, so I knocked as I entered. A second or two later, Colin spun his chair round and faced me. There was a splodge of porridge on the corner of his mouth. Tempting though it was to say nothing, I pointed it out to him. Colin wiped off the splodge with his finger, looked at it and put it into his mouth. 'So, what's wrong with you?'

'So, what's wrong with you?' Colin asked. 'The only reason people come to see me this early in the morning is when they're pretending to be ill. It's usually just after they see how much mail there is to prep.'

'I'm fine,' I said. 'Actually, I'm feeling really good.'

'Why's that?'

'I'm off to South Africa in September.'

'Are you indeed? And how long are you planning on being away for?'

'Six months.'

Colin leaned back in his chair, stretched out his arms and rested his hands behind his head. By doing this, he had unknowingly pulled some of his shirt out of his trousers and exposed a bit of pale belly flesh, which my eyes were strangely drawn to. I felt another of my urges: I wanted to bounce up and down on his paunch as if it were a space hopper, pushing his weight to other parts of his body and spreading it out more evenly.

'I can't authorise that, I'm afraid,' Colin said from his more imposing position. 'You know how busy we get over Christmas.'

'But there's plenty of time to put an ad in the paper and get someone trained up.'

'I'm sorry, Lou,' Colin spat. 'But the answer is no.'

There was no way I was going to let someone who couldn't feed himself properly ruin my future. I walked towards Colin's desk and placed my hands on its surface, narrowly missing the bowl of porridge. It was time to bring out the bullshit.

'I know my rights,' I started confidently. 'In the union handbook I was given when I started, it states that staff members are allowed to apply for time off or career breaks as long as they've been with Regal Post longer than six months and give at least two weeks' notice. So, if you don't authorise my career break, I'll go above you and get someone else to authorise it. Now, can you please get me the form I need?'

Colin paused, then nodded over my shoulder. 'They're in the middle drawer over there.'

'Thank you,' I said, my annoyance level dipping.

Getting the form himself would have made Colin feel like a secretary. I was happy to let my boss wield a bit of power over me if it meant I got my form. It was a good job Colin was an inept manager, or he would have known I wasn't part of the union. Three pounds a week membership fee in return for the monthly magazine and talks given by our dozy union rep seemed like a bad deal.

'Has Oliver been in to get his form yet?' I asked, tugging at the middle drawer of the filing cabinet without success.

'No, why would he?'

'Because we're going to South Africa together,' I said smugly. 'I'm going to be his caddie.'

Colin picked up a pen and started passing it through his fingers. It must have been a trick only fat-fingered people could do.

'Of course you are,' he said with derision.

'He probably got his form from one of the other offices he works at.'

I'll show you. You and all the others who thought I'd amount to nothing.

'Try closing the bottom drawer first,' Colin said as I continued to struggle. 'I don't know, you want to fly half way round the world to be Oliver's right-hand man, yet you can't even open a filing cabinet drawer.'

It appeared Colin wasn't the only incompetent person in the room. You would think opening a drawer would be simple, and in the end it was. Having followed Colin's basic instruction, I flicked through the alphabetised folders until I came to the one I wanted. Filing was fun! How was it that a job involving order and labelling could be missing from my CV? Yet it was too late to add that skill now. My caddying career was about to take off.

23

Real men don't need changing rooms – they whip their tops and trousers off wherever they please. Oliver wasn't one of those men, though, preferring to disrobe in a toilet cubicle. It was the day of the golf practice and, having helped him out on delivery, Oliver had driven us back to the office to get changed. Tuesdays were always the quietest day for mail, though I wasn't sure why. Everyone finished early on a Tuesday; even the old duffers managed to complete their deliveries by eleven. It went without saying that I also opted to change into my golfing attire in the toilets, hiding away in the middle cubicle of three. I heard a few knocks coming from Oliver's side of the dark grey partition, but I put that down to him being long-limbed and finding it hard to undress in such a confined space.

The fittest bloke I know is taking his clothes off and he's inches away from me. X-ray vision would be so much better than invisibility.

Thinking about Oliver naked was too much to bear. I was down to my pants, and it seemed like too good an opportunity to pass up. I pulled a couple of sheets of toilet paper from the dispenser and coughed to mask the noise. Being as quiet as I could, I crouched on top of the toilet lid, before straightening my legs and inching towards the top of the partition. When I peered over, Oliver was looking down at what he was doing. Little did he know that I was too. As I watched him standing in his tight blue and white James Tudor briefs, I reached into my tatty Marks and Spencer's pants. Considering he had a tanned face and toned arms, Oliver's pale and skinny legs were a let down. It explained why he didn't wear shorts at work, even on sunny days like today. I was conscious that he might lift his head at any moment and see me peering over at him, but the risk of it happening added to the excitement. Just as I was getting into my stroke, I heard footsteps. I averted my gaze and saw a dark figure through the frosted glass of the main toilet door. In my haste to crouch down, I lost my footing and slammed against the partition as I fell to the floor. My right arm, with loo paper in hand, ended up on Oliver's side.

'What are you doing in there, Lou?'

'Sorry!' I said, swiftly getting to my feet. 'I got my foot caught in my shorts. These cubicles are so cramped.'

'I hope you haven't strained your wrist again.'

'What?! No... No, I landed on my thigh this time.'

'Good, because I need a caddie that's fully fit.'

While this had been going on, whoever had entered the lavs had locked himself in the third cubicle. A few moments later, what can only be described as a lengthy shart reverberated around the gents like an echo in a cave. Talk about pricking the mood. I opened the toilet lid and threw my unused pieces of loo paper inside.

Oliver's cubicle door unlocked. 'Are you nearly done, Lou?' he called over from the basin area.

Done? He thought that stink was me!

'Almost,' I called back as I started to get dressed.

'We've got to be there in half an hour, don't forget. And I don't want to be late. Club personnel are very strict about members teeing off on time.'

'I'll be right with you,' I said, struggling to get my head through the tight collar on my polo neck. I should have tried it on the day before to check it still fitted, as I hadn't worn it since college. 'I've just got to—'

'See you at the car.'

The smell wafting over from the other cubicle must have shooed Oliver out the door. I wasn't so lucky. I had to grimace and bear it while I changed. So that I wouldn't look out of place as a caddie, Oliver had advised me to wear smart dark trousers and a top with a collar. The grey long-sleeved polo neck that was giving birth to my head and the pinstripe trousers I subsequently put on fitted the brief perfectly. Clare dressed in a similar combination when she went to work, and her male colleagues deemed her professional – although, blokes being blokes, I'm sure they were more captivated by her melons than what she had covering them. Therefore, by copying Clare's style, I hoped my outfit would have the same effect on the male colleague I needed to impress.

After donning my smart threads, I stood at the basin area and sorted out my flattened hair in the mirror. I knew we were cutting it fine for time, but a quick spruce up was needed. The lock on the third cubicle switched from 'engaged' to 'vacant', and the door swung open.

'Who ordered the lesbian?' Colin snorted, looking me up and down before joining me at the basins to wash his hands. 'I didn't know you were into cross-dressing.'

'It's called style. Not that you'd know anything about that,' I retorted.

'And you're dressed like that to go and caddie for Oliver?'

'Yup. If all goes to plan, I'll be turning that career break into a permanent break,' I said, putting the final stray wisps of hair into place.

Colin turned off the tap and inadvertently splashed me as he flicked his fingers on his way to grab a paper towel.

'Even though you're one of my brightest workers, you shouldn't get ahead of yourself.'

I stopped preening and looked at Colin in the reflection of the mirror – men should avoid direct eye contact in toilets. It was pleasing to know that Colin could distinguish between me and the office simpletons.

'Why? Are you jealous that somebody in here actually wants to make a go of their life?'

'No, not at all,' Colin said, throwing the screwed up paper towel in the bin before opening the door. 'Just don't forget who's paying your wages.'

'Not you,' I called after him. 'Or else you wouldn't keep letting Amy and Dean get away with things.'

Just as the door was coming to a close, Steve burst through it, unzipping his fly as he hurried to one of the urinals.

'I've been dying for this for the last twenty minutes,' he sighed, leaning back. 'Must've drunk too much water.'

'You could've stopped off and gone behind a tree like all the other blokes do,' I said, talking to the reflection of Steve's half-turned head.

'There's nowhere to hide on my round. I'd normally ask a customer, but then they'd start talking, and I'm in a rush today. Holding it in made me get a wriggle on.'

'That's nice.'

'Were you moaning to the boss about Dean just then?'

Knowing that whatever I said would make its way back to the man himself, I said, 'I wasn't moaning.'

'You'd be wasting your breath if you were. Dean's dad and the boss play bowls together. They're old friends.' Steve bent his knees slightly, zipped up his fly and used an unwashed hand to pull open the door. 'Enjoy the golf.'

*

When Oliver and I arrived at the golf club, most of the caddies I could see were dressed more casually than I was. In fact, the whole clubhouse looked less formal than I'd pictured it. Where I'd expected to see a reception desk, there was a bar – one that wouldn't look out of place in a chav town boozer. Had it not been for the eighteen-hole beer garden, I wouldn't have known any different.

'Why didn't you tell me I could've worn shorts?' I asked Oliver. 'I'm going to be sweltering in this.'

'I've never been to this club before,' he replied, noshing off a banana. 'I didn't know their clothing policy was so relaxed.'

'How come you're playing here?'

'This is where my opponent plays. To give him a bit of a chance, I agreed to play him on his terms,' he said confidently.

'Is he not very good?'

Oliver shrugged. 'I don't know. I've never played Dean before.'

'Dean? Dean from work?' I said with a panicked expression.

'Yeah, he likes his golf. But he seems to think he can beat me. We'll show him.'

A few minutes later, Dean showed up in the clubhouse. He was still wearing his charcoal work shorts, but his top half now sported a lime green polo shirt. We hadn't spoken since he stormed out of the canteen, preferring to look the other way whenever we passed at work.

'Olly, mate!' Dean bellowed in his laddish way as he made his way over.

It was a mystery as to how Dean could afford membership to a golf club. Though, from what I'd so far seen, it wouldn't have cost much to be a member of this particular club.

'Did you manage to get a caddie?' Oliver asked Dean as the pair of them shook hands. 'If not, mine can caddie for both of us.'

'I can't carry around two sets of clubs,' I protested. 'I'm not a donkey.'

'You won't have to carry them,' Oliver maintained. 'Our

160

bags are on wheels. It'll be easy.'

'Look, it doesn't matter,' Dean interjected. 'When you told me who was caddying for you, I thought I'd better get one of my own.'

He knew I was caddying and he still came. He can't hate me that much.

'Where are they?' Oliver asked.

'She's getting changed.'

Please don't say you've brought her along?

At that moment, the door to the women's toilets opened and out stepped Amy. For a tramp, she had dressed rather well, in a salmon-coloured polo shirt and khaki cargo shorts.

'Sorry, everyone. I hope I haven't kept you waiting,' Amy said, showing an uncharacteristic display of altruism.

'Not at all,' Oliver said. 'Shall we crack on with it?'

'After you,' Dean said, opening the door that led to eighteen holes of hell.

24

Everyone being so cordial was already pissing me off, and the afternoon was only just beginning. Even though the sight of the little cow-horse dog-pig made my flesh boil, my resentful feelings towards Amy didn't appear to be reciprocated. She must have left her homophobia at work. I had hoped Oliver and I would be so far ahead on each hole that I'd be able to avoid Amy, but that wasn't the case. For the most part, Oliver walked with Dean; it was only when a shot went astray that Oliver and I separated from the other two. I liked those shots. Yet Amy seemed quite happy to walk alongside me, albeit in silence. It's possible she wanted to keep an eye on me and make sure I kept my distance from Dean. However, this was too good an opportunity to let pass without venting some anger and letting Amy know what I thought about the state of affairs.

'Good delivery today?' I asked Amy when the boys were out of earshot.

'Yeah, it was alright,' she replied. 'But we had to get a shift on so that we could get here on time.'

'No driving lessons or trips to Pizza Den for you two today.'

'Depending on what time we finish, we might squeeze in a random session later on,' Amy said shamelessly.

I stared at her for a few seconds before responding. 'Do you not feel the slightest bit guilty about what you've done?'

'I've not done anything wrong,' she said, picking up her

pace to try to catch up with Dean.

'You slept with a man who's about to get married!'

'Don't take it out on me just because you're jealous.'

Dean must have told Amy that I knew about the affair, as Amy didn't appear the least bit surprised by what I knew. They probably chatted about me and had a good laugh as they carried out their deliveries together.

'Have you been invited to the wedding?' I asked as I fast-walked after her.

Amy failed to answer my question. 'He's only marrying her to keep her happy.'

'I thought not. Keep the grubby little secret hidden away.'

'I'm nobody's secret,' she said resolutely.

'If that's the case, you won't mind me telling Liz.'

On drawing level with Dean, Amy shot me a look that could turn honey sour. So that she could be protected from my insults, Amy stuck to Dean for the rest of the afternoon. She even had the gall to flirt with him, knowing full well it would wind me up. Revulsion pulsed through my veins. Amy was showing absolutely no signs of remorse whatsoever. I clenched my teeth, same as I did when I drove over cattle grids – an obstacle Amy would be unable to walk across.

Though it had been a warm July morning, the sun disappeared behind puffy clouds and a bit of a breeze picked up as the day wore on. I was now reaping the benefits of wearing a polo neck. As Dean took a jumper out of his golf bag, a sleeveless Amy had the cheek to ask him if she could borrow it. Despite the hairs on his arms standing on end, Dean duly obliged. Forced chivalry came at a price. As if sensing what was going on, Oliver asked if I'd like to tee off at the next hole for him. I'd only played crazy golf before, and I hadn't exactly been crash hot at it. I was probably being set up for a fall so that he and the lovers could have a good laugh at me.

Oliver handed me one of his clubs. 'Just give it a go.'

I didn't want to fanny about and appear like a 'fucking annoying twat', so I stepped up to where Oliver had placed a tee.

It can't be too hard to hit a ball. I know I've got good hand-eye coordination, because I can do cat's cradle.

'Take a few practice swings first,' Oliver advised.

I did as he said and took a swing. It can't have been very good, because Oliver told me to open my legs further and keep my head still. He then stood close behind me, put his arms around me and placed his hands on top of mine as I gripped the club.

I bet Amy and Dean are hating this!

After doing a few air swings together, I felt confident enough to take a shot on my own. I did everything Oliver told me to do, yet the ball I struck skimmed across the grass and came to a halt about thirty yards away. I heard Amy snigger.

'Not bad for a first effort,' Oliver said. 'You're almost as good as Dean.'

'Oi! I'm only a couple of strokes behind you,' Dean countered.

I hadn't been taking much notice of what had been going on in the game, as I'd been more interested in taunting Amy. But following my brief golf lesson, I perked up and paid more attention, like a decent caddie should. For someone who had desires to compete in major tournaments, Oliver looked distinctly mediocre. Dean was by no means a quality player and didn't have first-class golf clubs, so Oliver should have been wiping the floor with him. Something wasn't right.

'Are you OK?' I asked Oliver when we were on our own. 'I thought you'd be way ahead by now.'

'So did I,' he confessed. 'But I can feel a pain in my lower back and I don't want to make it worse.'

'Is that why you wanted me to take a shot, to give your back a rest?'

'Yeah,' Oliver said with uncertainty. 'I'm only playing at about fifty per cent.'

'Call it a day. Quit while you're ahead.'

'I can't do that. It's not very sporting.'

'You don't want to jeopardise your career by picking up an injury,' I said, fearing for my place as his caddie.

'There's only a few more holes to go. I'm sure I can make it.'

'I can play some more shots for you, if you want?'

Oliver smiled. 'Don't you want us to win?'

Indeed, I wanted us to win more than Oliver did, so I left the golfing up to him. At least there was an excuse available if Dean did end up winning.

The game was all square going into the final hole. Oliver's tee shot made the perfect 'thwack' sound as his club connected with the ball, sending it down the middle of the fairway and into a bunker. I say bunker, but it was more of a soil pit with beer cans and cigarette butts in.

'You've not had much luck today,' Dean said.

Oliver picked up his tee, looking ruffled. 'I think you've got it all, that's why.'

'It's not luck, it's skill.'

From what I'd seen of the last few holes, the strongest part of Dean's game was his putting. He had no doubt been practising daily in his back garden in advance of this match. Dean's tee shot let him down once more, his ball veering towards some trees on the right.

'Looks like it's going to be a close one,' Oliver said.

'Feeling the pressure?' Dean asked.

'What pressure?' I answered, taking hold of Oliver's bag and wheeling it away.

It wasn't until we reached the green that both pairs met

up again. Dean had already holed out in six, while Oliver was about to take his fifth. His ball was ten yards from the hole, and he needed to down it in one shot to win.

'Go on, Oliver! Stick it in the hole!' I whooped, thinking it would encourage him.

'Shhhh! Keep quiet!' Oliver barked, causing Amy and Dean to smirk.

There was silence as Oliver putted the ball towards the hole. The ball looked to be rolling straight into the centre of the hole, but the uneven green diverted it slightly. Nevertheless, the ball rimmed the edge of the hole before dropping in. A relieved Oliver marched triumphantly over to me with a hand in the air, and I duly high-fived it. Kath's 'Jack Sprat' story echoed in my head. She had been right: Oliver and I did make a good team.

'Well played, mate,' Dean said as he and Oliver shook hands. 'I thought I was going to have you at one point.'

'He would've beaten you by a lot more if he'd not had a bad back,' I said.

'A bad back?' Amy said. 'You looked like you were hitting pretty freely to me.'

'It was only a twinge. Nothing major,' Oliver said, giving me a stern look so I wouldn't say any more.

My perception of Dean's club being a bit of a dive was confirmed when I found out they didn't serve food. Not a sausage. The game had taken nigh on four hours – two hours longer than I'd anticipated – and all I'd eaten since breakfast was a Special K bar.

'That was good fun,' Amy said as we all prepared to leave the clubhouse. 'Can I caddie for you again?'

'I don't see why not,' Dean said. 'Olly, we should make this a weekly event.'

'Yeah, I'd like that,' Oliver agreed wholeheartedly.

'When Oliver's back to full fitness, he's going to need *quality* opposition to get him ready for South Africa,' I chimed in.

'Why, what's happening over there?' Dean asked.

Oliver glared at me. 'Don't!'

'He's taking a break from the EuroGo tour and joining the one in South Africa,' I said with a self-satisfied grin. 'And I'm going to be his caddie.'

Dean stopped walking and looked at Oliver. 'I think it's time you told him the truth, Olly.'

25

Amy and Dean left hastily afterwards – probably so they could fit in a quickie before Dean dropped Amy home – leaving a red-faced Oliver and me in the clubhouse.

'I'm listening,' I said, arms folded.

'Dean's got it wrong,' Oliver said. His usual calm and confident exterior had deserted him. Beads of sweat were gathering on his brow.

'Maybe I should give your sponsors a call,' I harried. 'See when that tour to South Africa starts.'

'You don't have their number.'

'It's on a sticker on the back of the car they bought for you. I'll go and call them now, shall I?'

I took my phone out of my pocket and made to walk outside. Oliver stepped in front of me.

'Lou, if I tell you the truth, you've got to promise not to say a thing to *anyone*,' he said intensely.

'You can trust me.'

Behind my back I had my fingers crossed in case it was a secret too juicy to keep secret.

'Get in the car. I can't tell you here. Somebody might overhear.'

I trailed Oliver as he marched to his car. It made a refreshing change to see him show some genuine emotion. I could feel my libido stirring. Or it could have been my near-empty stomach rumbling.

Maybe he's going to kidnap me, chain me up and force me to do things I've always wanted to do, like the butterfly position or a sixty-nine.

'It's a long story,' Oliver began as he drove out of the car park.

'Make it shorter,' I said. 'The office is only a few miles away.'

In an attempt to mitigate whatever it was he had to announce, Oliver said, 'Don't think badly of me. I just got a bit carried away.'

'We all say things we don't mean,' I said, trying to make it easier for him.

As though ripping off a plaster, Oliver came straight out with it. He clearly wasn't one for foreplay. The sixty-nine was off the agenda, then.

'I'm not on the EuroGo tour,' he disclosed. 'I got kicked off it in February.'

'*February*? But... But what about all these things your sponsors paid for? Don't they want them back?'

Oliver paused. 'There are no sponsors. My dad bought it all. The clubs, the phone, this car... Everything was paid for by my dad.'

I sat there thinking for a few seconds about what Oliver's revelation meant and how it rated on the dishonesty scale. Bearing in mind he was being candid, I didn't want to attack him or shout at him for being a liar.

'But you've got a sticker,' was all I thought to say. As if that was the most cunning thing about this whole deception.

'That's a sticker from the golf club where I sometimes work. Nothing special.'

'And the South African tour? And the psychologist?'

'The story just snowballed. I wanted to sound genuine so I wouldn't get found out.'

My dreams had been shattered. I felt like a kid who had been told at the last minute that he couldn't go to a theme park with his friends, but instead had to stay in and cut his gran's toenails.

'Why start the pretence in the first place? You used to play golf, now you don't. End of story. Who cares?'

Oliver paused as we cruised to a stop at a crossroads. It gave him a few moments of respite from my questioning. Although he was looking left and right, I could see he was thinking about what to say next.

'You know I told you my dad used to be a football manager?' Oliver continued.

'Don't tell me. That was a lie too?'

'No, that's true,' he said. 'But I wish he'd had a normal job.'

Oliver's dad had wanted his son to follow him into the game and become a successful player – something he had failed to do himself. From what I heard, he wasn't crash hot as a manager, either. Oliver's story about his dad capturing David Beckham on loan was complete bull, and the 'complimentary' tickets to the Spurs match Oliver and Dean attended had been bought. It was all coming out now. Playing golf with Jamie Redknapp did happen, though, so it wasn't entirely a pack of lies. I thought I excelled at fabricating stories, but I took my hat off to the new master of deceit.

'The only sport I liked was golf, because I always beat my dad whenever we played mini golf on holiday,' Oliver said. 'He forced me to take up proper golf and paid for me to have lessons. Then he boasted to everyone that I was going to be golf's next big thing. I only went along with it so he'd be proud of me, but now he sees me as a failure.'

'You're still young. I've heard of really old golfers winning tournaments. Maybe you'll get better when you're older,' I said, trying to say something helpful.

'No amount of money or practice is going to make me into a world-class golfer. My heart's not in it. I'm surprised I lasted as long as I did on tour. You saw for yourself how average I am.'

I tutted. 'The things we do to keep our parents happy.'

There were periods in my teens where I'd gone as far as taking girls on dates just to please my parents. Whenever my dad asked why none of the relationships worked out, I used the age-old excuse, 'I haven't met the right girl yet.' My mum never questioned it; she knew. Mum's always know.

Oliver let out a deep sigh. 'Wow, it feels so good to finally talk to you about this,' he said, smiling for the first time since we left the clubhouse.

'I can't believe you told Dean before you told me, though.'

'Dean has been pestering me to play golf with him for ages, and I kept putting him off because I knew he'd see that I wasn't up to standard. I couldn't keep making excuses, so last month I told him I wasn't on the tour anymore.'

A minute or so later, we came to a stop outside the office building. The gates to the premises were shut, but I'd thought ahead and had parked my Peugeot on the side road outside. Oliver, being a gent, got out of his car and walked me the ten yards over to mine.

'Thanks for today. I really enjoyed your company,' Oliver said.

'I guess I won't be needing my passport anytime soon, then?' I said, resting my bum against my driver's door in a casual manner.

'No,' Oliver said sheepishly. 'Sorry.'

'That's a relief, because caddying is the most boring thing I've ever done!'

The exaggeration was supposed to make Oliver feel less guilty about spinning me a line regarding the caddie job, but it didn't have the effect I'd desired. I should have learnt by now not to insult a man's favourite pastime, team or food.

'What did you expect? That we would play a few holes, stop for a light tea and go home when it got cold?!' Oliver said, clearly offended by my slight on his 'sport'.

'Something like that, yeah.'

Oliver threw his arms in the air. 'I *knew* you weren't interested in golf! I should've trusted my instincts.'

'You also should've trusted *me*. If you'd told me your secret before the game, you would've saved us both from humiliation.'

Oliver's lack of response told me all I needed to know.

'You had no intention of telling me, did you?' I challenged. 'If Dean hadn't said anything, you would've kept quiet and let the lie continue. When were you going to tell me? When I'd booked my ticket to South Africa?!'

My empty stomach and the tiredness were to blame for my hysteria. Not that I needed an excuse to act irrationally.

'No, Lou,' Oliver pleaded. 'It's not like that.'

Attack was definitely the best line of defence. We had swapped positions and I was now on top... metaphorically speaking.

'Go on,' I commanded. 'This should be good.'

'I wanted to tell you after I'd spoken to Dean, but he told me not to tell you,' Oliver revealed. 'He said I should make up a reason why I no longer needed you as a caddie.'

My eyes narrowed. 'I bet he did,' I said, transferring my hostility away from Oliver and placing it firmly at Dean's feet.

'Is there something going on with you two?' Oliver asked.

'No! I'd never go near someone like Dean.'

'I didn't mean it like that. It's just that I've noticed you and him aren't as pally as you used to be.'

'Right, well let's just say that Dean has been a very naughty boy. That's all I'm allowed to say because I've been sworn to secrecy,' I said, pulling an imaginary zip across my closed lips.

It wasn't my place to reveal Dean's secret, not even to a bloke whose nipples I wanted to gnaw. I shouldn't even have mentioned that Dean had a secret.

'I'll have to ask him myself, then.'

I unzipped my lips. 'Good. You do that. Maybe he'll explain himself to you. And if he does, you can tell me what he says.'

'Oh, I get it. You want to hear all the gossip but not be responsible for spreading any of it.'

'Think of yourself as my very own *Scandal!* magazine.'

...complete with a picture of you on the week's Bod of a God page.

Oliver smiled. 'So, are we good? You're not angry with me?'

I stepped forward and gave him a light punch on the arm. 'Just stop the golf lies, yeah? If people don't want to know you for who you are, then they're not worth knowing.'

'Thanks, Lou. That means a lot,' he said.

And before anyone could say 'white dimpled balls', Oliver had moved in for a manly embrace. With my nose centimetres away from his neck, it took all the restraint I could muster to not nuzzle into it. Making that urge even more difficult to quell was the aroma of sweet-smelling aftershave still emanating from his skin. The posh stuff obviously lasted longer. Either that or he had been furtively squirting himself throughout the afternoon.

Oliver released me from the hug and asked, 'Do you fancy sharing a room with me up in Blackpool?'

26

Wednesday morning could not come soon enough. Twelve hours had passed since I'd said goodbye to Oliver, and I'd thought about him for at least eleven and a half of them. In that time, I'd performed a total of four hundred sit-ups and two hundred press-ups. My last shave had been on Monday evening, so my designer stubble – which basically looked the same as my regular stubble – was coming on a treat. I put on my work shorts, which my mum had taken up an inch on my request, and made my way into work. I was hot to trot, and I'd never felt fitter.

I'd been in two minds about whether I should carry on helping Oliver on his delivery. On the one hand, he had been guilty of taking advantage of my good nature and playing me for a fool. But, on the other hand, I didn't want him to revert back to thinking that people were only interested in him because they thought he was a future star of golf. He had said that he found it hard to make work friends because he kept getting moved from office to office. But as soon as he mentioned he was a promising golfer, people deemed him important and they talked to him, and that's why he kept up the golf ruse. I settled my inner turmoil by deciding I would only help him if he was struggling, as full subservience isn't an attractive quality.

Before I'd even reached my bench, the familiar smell of Atrixo hand cream alerted me to Kath's return. Oliver had once again become surplus to our office's requirements. The hours of musing and my efforts to look and feel my best had been in vain.

'Louis! My lovely boy,' Kath said, reaching up and placing her chamomile-scented hands either side of my face. 'Oooh, are you growing whiskers?'

I pulled myself away before she could give me a kiss.

'It looks like you are,' she said, as if talking to a boy who had sprouted his first crop of bumfluff.

'I forgot to shave, that's all.'

What's the excuse for your whiskers?

It had been less than a minute and I was already sick of Kath. Her road to recovery had been a long and arduous one, but a couple of potholes to extend her journey by a week or two would have been appreciated. I knew Kath meant no harm, but I wanted to be standing next to Oliver, not her. I'd have welcomed Oliver's comments regarding my appearance, but I had to make do with listening to stories about Kath's surgery and recuperation.

'The doctors said I was lucky,' Kath said as we prepped our rounds. 'People can die from having a ruptured appendix.'

'Do they know what caused it? I hope it's not getting on and off a bike all day that did it.'

'Believe me, I wouldn't be back here if it was. I was in absolute agony.' Kath placed a hand on her stomach as she recollected the pain she had gone through. 'Luckily for me, I was on my way to hospital when the appendix burst and spilt pus into my abdomen. I must have passed out soon after that, because the next thing I remember was waking up in a hospital bed. One of the nurses told me afterwards that it had all been caused by a stomach bug, which had somehow made its way into my appendix.'

I was close to passing out myself after hearing the ins and outs of Kath's illness. My daily trip to the canteen to buy my appetising can of Red Bull suddenly didn't seem essential.

'And how are you now?' I asked, feeling the burn in my right tricep every time I reached up to slot a letter in the top row.

'I'm still a bit sore, so I won't be going out on delivery for a week or two,' Kath revealed. 'I'll be doing light duties within the office, like sorting mail and prepping this round for whoever's doing it on overtime.'

Oliver might still be coming in, then?

Kath could have done with going out on delivery and getting some exercise, as she had become even more comfy over the past eight weeks. During a lull in the conversation, I sent Oliver a text.

>Hey buddy! Are you in today?

> No. I'm back in the Worfield office. The boss here called this morning and said I'm not needed at Crockham. It's well boring here.<

>You're not missing much. Kath is back and she's been telling me all about her burst appendix. Nice! So when will we see you again?

> Not sure. Depends when I'm asked to get you lot out of trouble again! We'll have to meet up before Blackpool though.<

>Defo! Hope your day gets better! Speak soon :o)

Just as I was finishing my last text, Amy and Dean showed up. Judging by Dean's comment, he had assumed the only person I could have been messaging at such an early hour was Oliver. The big grin on my face as I texted also made it less of a mystery.

'Missing your boyfriend already?' he said, taking a seat on Amy's bench.

Dean's sidekick did her customary snort of approval, before going off to get the coffees in. Their relationship had become so routine that there was no longer any flirty arguing over whose turn it was to do the coffee run. The honeymoon period was over.

'Did something happen between you and Oliver while I was away?' Kath asked excitedly.

'No, nothing happened,' I answered. 'Dean's being a moron.'

On hearing my comment, Dean forced his tongue in front of his bottom row of teeth to give himself a fat chin – an action I hadn't performed since I was a child. Clare and I knew it as 'belming'.

'That's a shame,' Kath said. 'For a second I was thinking about what colour dress to wear to your wedding.'

'Sorry to disappoint you, but I won't be getting married for a long time yet.'

'Only because nobody'll have you,' Dean called over.

Two sentences from Dean in as many weeks – I was being spoilt.

'So, what's been going on in here while I've been cooped up at home?' Kath asked, cutting in before a potential argument started. 'You must have lots of gossip for me.'

Revealing Amy and Dean's affair was highly tempting, considering how malicious Dean was being. Before I replied, I glanced over to see if he was sweating over what I might disclose. He was scratching his balls, totally unfazed.

'Actually, there is something you might like to hear,' I started. 'Oliver asked if I wanted to share his room when we go to Blackpool later this month.'

Dean's ears pricked up.

'I *knew* you were lying earlier when you said nothing had happened between you two!' Kath squealed. 'What did you say?'

'I told him I'd think about it.'

Kath put down her mail and edged closer. 'Louis, what is there to think about? You've got the opportunity to share a room with a good-looking young man. And he'll probably be wearing very little in the way of nightwear, what with it being the peak of summer,' she said, giving me a nudge.

Those images had flashed through my mind when Oliver invited me, but all I'd done was gawp at him while I tried to muster a reply. The thought of waking up next to Oliver was enough to make any gay man dribble. Eventually – when the blood had flowed back to my brain – I'd formed the words 'no' and 'sorry', before gabbling uncontrollably about the commitment I'd already made to Jay and how let down he would feel if I didn't share with him. I knew how much Jay was looking forward to our trip away, and I couldn't disappoint him, no matter how keen I was to bed Oliver. The only way I was going to wake up in Oliver's room was if I pulled him on the stag night.

'Don't get too excited,' Dean butted in. 'My mate that Olly was meant to share with had to cancel. Olly's been asking loads of people because he wants to split the cost of the room.'

'He must like you, Lou, or he wouldn't have asked,' Kath said after frowning at Dean. 'Go for it, I say!'

'Thanks, Kath. I'll call him later,' I lied, knowing it would vex Dean.

'If I was twenty years younger, I would've come up to Blackpool and shown you young ones a thing or two,' Kath joked. 'Life gets boring when you're old.'

'You've still got Dean's wedding to look forward to,' I said.

The silence that followed told me I'd gone and put my size nines in it. Before I made the situation even more awkward by asking questions, Dean set the record straight.

'Liz wants a small wedding. Sorry, Kath.'

'It's fine. I understand,' Kath said, though she didn't look fine about it at all.

More lies from the mouth of Dean. He had a way of twisting things to make it look as though he was never at fault, but putting the blame on Liz was a total cop out. Admittedly, Kath wouldn't have been my first choice of guest had I been getting married, but I'd have felt compelled to invite her. She was the mum of the office and should have been treated as such. As Kath had been working there for nigh on thirty years, she would have undoubtedly mothered Dean when he started as a teenager, so she had every right to feel aggrieved at being snubbed.

'You can take my place, Kath, if you want?' I offered.

'Aren't you going?' she replied.

'No, I can't make it. I've got something else on, unfortunately,' I said, catching an animated Dean out of the corner of my eye. 'And I'm sure there'll be plenty of space for both you and your husband at the church. I'll dig out my invite with the times and places on.'

I knew exactly where and when the ceremony and reception were taking place; they had been engraved into my brains the moment I read the invitation. Nevertheless, I wasn't going to recall the information for Kath in front of Dean. He was arrogant enough without thinking I'd memorised the details of his wedding day.

'That's OK, isn't it, Dean?'

Unbeknown to Kath, Dean had been frantically waving in an attempt to make me drop the subject, but that came to an abrupt end when Kath turned around. The expectant look on her face was met with an approving nod from Dean.

'I'll have to run it past Liz first, though,' he said. 'Don't get your hopes up just yet.'

'What is there to check? You're swapping one person for another,' I said.

Dean's hand had been forced. The way I saw it, Dean had two options: tell Liz I wasn't attending the wedding and risk her finding out why he had banned me, or re-invite me and disappoint an old lady. Either way, Dean was going to have some explaining to do.

27

Ordinarily, Roy's birthday would provide the first contact with family since Father's Day, but there had been an untimely get-together in the meantime – if you can call a funeral a get-together. In spite of being a tough old bird, Gran lost her fight against Alzheimer's. I'd visited her on a handful of occasions at the nursing home since I'd become a full-time postie. It hadn't been easy seeing her in that state: pale, weak and without her glasses and teeth. It must have been much more difficult for her. She used to smile and gaze into my eyes, and I would stare right back into hers. Some days she would call me by my dad's name, and I'd play along with it. Other times she would have no idea who I was. It might have been different had I visited her more regularly. But her suffering was now over; Gran was finally at peace.

It was a week on from Gran's funeral, and all of the family were over at Roy and Christina's 'poky' three-bedroom semi in Worfield to celebrate Roy turning twenty-five. All of us except Graham, that is. Clare's excuse for him was that he had made other plans, but not going so far as to divulge what those plans were exactly. Down the pub with his mates, no doubt. Clare, by this point, had all but moved in with Graham at his flat in Northwood. She had managed to cut the apron strings that still bound me. We would occasionally see her on a Sunday evening, depending on whether Mum had cooked a roast dinner. Her room was kept the same, on the off-chance she saw sense and decided to move back home. Whoever I brought into the family fold would be welcomed with open arms when measured against Christina and Graham.

Because she had been the Lawrence children's last surviving grandparent, Gran's death meant that we had been promoted a generation. Middle age didn't seem far off at all. And by the way Christina was talking, it wasn't going to be long until my parents were grandparents and I became Uncle Louis. Coupled with this, Liz and Dean's big day was fast approaching, so having honeymoons, babies and all things wedding shoved in my face wasn't helping my mental state.

'We'll need a bigger house, of course,' Christina crowed. 'This house is lovely, and we really like the area, don't we Roy? But a study or an extra bedroom would be ideal.'

Roy nodded in the right places.

'We've been looking at properties, and we've seen a few suitable ones on the other side of town,' Christina ploughed on. 'It's just a question of waiting until the time is right.'

It was only when the Thai takeaway arrived that the rest of us were treated to a break from Christina's bleating. I'd never had Thai before. It was Christina's choice, as Dad was paying. I wasn't overly impressed with my meal, which was basically a runny Chinese with nuts in.

After dinner, and when Roy had opened all his presents, Mum took an envelope out of her handbag and passed it to Dad.

'Just one more gift,' Dad said, handing the envelope to Roy. It was like a prize-giving ceremony. I felt as though I should have been taking photos. 'It's from Gran.'

Roy opened his final present and revealed a cheque. Christina's eyes lit up.

'Five grand!' Roy exclaimed.

That put my *Star Wars* Cluedo present to shame. It had been the best gift up until that point.

Clare and I exchanged looks.

'Did Gran write that out before she lost her mind?' I asked facetiously.

'I wrote the cheque on Gran's behalf,' Dad said.

'And if she'd held out for another two months, would I be getting five grand for my birthday?'

'The money isn't a birthday present, as such,' Dad continued. 'We just thought it would be a good idea to do all this while you lot were together.'

'Do all what?' Clare asked.

Mum passed over three more envelopes to Dad, who in turn handed one each to Clare, Christina and me.

'Nice one, Gran!' I cheered, waving a cheque for the same amount in the air. I looked heavenward and said, 'Thank you', before giving the piece of paper a lengthy kiss. Bizarrely, it was the most satisfying kiss I'd ever had.

Christina's eyes grew even bigger... until she opened the envelope and saw the digits on her cheque.

'*Two* grand?'

She would have been dead chuffed with that amount had she not seen how much the rest of us had been given. Personally, I didn't think she deserved anything. Gran hadn't been the richest of souls, but she had a kind heart and wouldn't have wanted anybody to miss out. Yet in trying to please everybody, Gran's final wishes left somebody unhappy.

'Gran left all her grandkids five thousand pounds each in her will,' Dad explained, stressing the amount in full so we would respect its value. 'Partners of grandchildren have all been given two thousand pounds. Clare, we put Graham's cheque in with yours for you to pass on.'

'I'll make sure he says thanks when I give it to him,' Clare said, having a thinly veiled dig at Christina's impolite response.

'Her money hasn't come through to us yet,' Dad said.

'You'll have to wait a couple of weeks before you can cash it, hence the September date on it.'

'I'm worth the same as Graham?' Christina said, still coming to terms with Gran's decision. She then turned to face Roy. 'He's a part of your family because of me, and the only time he met your gran was at our wedding. He couldn't even be bothered to come tonight.'

'Just be grateful you got something,' Roy said, risking his wife's ire, before swiftly placating her by adding, 'It goes without saying that we'll be sharing mine.'

Although I would never have said it out loud, I understood where Christina was coming from. For someone who hadn't officially joined our family, Graham had done very well out of us: two grand and a lovely girlfriend. He was also allowed to skip the family occasions he didn't feel like attending. I wished I'd had that option.

'Can I have the two grand that would've gone to my partner?' I asked airily, trying to make a point without causing any unrest.

'But then you'd have seven grand all to yourself,' Christina chimed in before I could be given a sensible answer. 'If Roy and I put ours together, that's only three and a half grand each.'

'It still works out as seven grand if you were to put it towards a new house, though,' I bravely argued.

'But houses cost more than one-bed flats,' Christina retorted, taking a swipe at my relationship status. 'If anyone deserves more, it's us.'

'Nobody will be getting any more money,' Dad confirmed. 'Gran's wishes are final, so can we please leave it.'

Mum and Clare cleared the plates and dishes, then headed to the kitchen. The room fell silent... though not for long.

'Don't get me wrong, I am grateful for the money,'

Christina began. 'I was just astonished that Louis had the nerve to ask for more.'

Christina, having lit the blue touch paper, sat back in her chair and drank from her wine glass. Seeing eye to eye with Christina regarding Graham's payment had been a one-off; she was an adversary once more. I preferred it that way. The money wasn't even central to the argument anymore; this issue was personal.

'Take a joke,' I hit back. 'I wasn't being serious.'

'Good, because it's not like you need the extra money to start a family, like me and Roy will soon be doing.'

That was it. She was done for. By trying to use my sexuality as a means to win the argument, Christina had made a grave mistake. If there was one thing guaranteed to get my dander up, it was discrimination. I stood up – as a sitting rant wouldn't have had quite the same effect – and had my say.

'Reward the normal people and shun the black sheep, you mean? That's not a very Christian attitude,' I said, hoping Dad would pick up on it and be on my side. 'Why should I be penalised for being independent?'

'Independent? You still live at home!' Christina pointed out. 'Try moving out, and then you'll know what independence is.'

'The money you have all been given should help you with your futures *whatever* they may hold,' Dad cut in diplomatically.

'I'm waiting until the right man comes along,' I said, ignoring Dad's attempt to put a stop to the bickering. 'What's wrong with that?'

'There's waiting and there's being delusional,' Christina remarked. 'I've been with Roy nearly four years now, and I've not seen you with anyone. That should tell you something.'

'I bet Roy's wishing he'd waited.'

185

Christina's face must have been a picture, but I didn't dare to look at it. I'd been brave enough to make the comment, but I didn't have the balls to follow it up with a death stare. Before Christina could become apoplectic, Roy piped up.

'OK, that'll do,' he said casually.

'Getting Roy to fight your battles? That's not very independent,' I said cattily.

'Louis, stop being such a drama queen and calm down,' Dad said.

Christina snorted. Even Roy was stifling a laugh.

'Just sit down,' a composed Christina patronised. Her plan to make me look a ninny had worked. 'You're spoiling Roy's birthday.'

'And we mustn't spoil the golden boy's birthday, must we?' I spat.

'Happy birthday to you...' Mum and Clare sang as they re-entered the room with Roy's cake.

Clare walked slowly so the candles wouldn't blow out. My throat constricted as I was forced to obey Christina's orders. I sat down, pulled my chair in and mumbled along while everyone else sang.

'Make a wish,' Mum said when Roy had blown out the four candles.

I bet he really does wish that he'd waited.

Following a slice of cake each and more small talk, Mum started the farewell process. As it was a weeknight, she used my needing to get to bed early as an excuse for us all to leave. It was only eight-thirty, but I wasn't going to contradict her. I gave Roy a hug and, as Mum was watching, Christina and I forced ourselves to share a flimsy embrace.

After dropping Clare off at Graham's flat, I realised how much I missed her being around. Just as Graham had been eager to lure Clare away from the family home, I'd been equally selfish by holding her back and wanting her to wait.

I'd relied on her way too much and taken her constant presence for granted. She had always been on hand to listen, but Clare had moved on and found someone to replace me. It had to happen at some point that we would go our separate ways, and the fork in our road had now been made clear.

Even though I was loath to admit it, Christina had been right. Independent? Who was I kidding? I didn't even know how to turn the water off in the event of a leak. To mask the silence within the car as I drove home, I stuck the radio on. In a gesture of goodwill towards Dad, I tuned it in to Radio 4. It was my way of saying sorry for my infantile outburst. Mum was in the passenger seat, and I managed to get home without catching Dad's eye in the rear-view mirror. All would be forgiven in the morning – that's how it was in our family – but until then it was best to remain quiet... and think about what I was going to spend my five grand on.

28

When Oliver and I had been arranging our pre-Blackpool lunch, we had settled on meeting in Crockham high street at one o'clock on a Tuesday. I'd told Oliver that I didn't mind driving over to Worfield, but he insisted on meeting in Crockham so I wouldn't be inconvenienced. Judging by some of the things Oliver had said after golf, his parents were accountable for his constant need to please people, but they had also instilled in him a kind heart and good manners. I'd have preferred lunching out in Worfield, though, as I liked the anonymity of being outside Crockham.

Following a speedy shower, I styled my hair for the second time that day and walked into town. I passed by the bank and gave one of my ex-colleagues a wave. Fortunately, Amy's dolt of a dad wasn't around to see me. I rarely stayed in contact with people I'd worked with, as I liked to cut my ties with a job when I moved on to the next. Just as I reached the café where I was due to meet Oliver, he texted to say he was running late and would meet me at two.

As I had an hour to kill, I decided to make a dent in Gran's money. Technically, I was spending my own money – as I couldn't cash her cheque for another couple of weeks – but I wanted to pimp myself up in time for Blackpool. I fully intended to go on the hen party, as I wasn't going to let my rift with Dean stop me from having a fun weekend away. My yearly sex was counting on it. I didn't plan to have sex annually; it just happened that way. And the flirting with Oliver was the nearest thing I'd had to intercourse all year.

Most of the men I'd slept with had been summer shags. The combination of looking tanned and feeling confident, men's legs being on show and the fact there was nothing good on TV must have contributed to it.

After having a fifty quid haircut, I tried on a couple of shirts that caught my eye. I hadn't bought clothes in Crockham since I started working as a postie, preferring to order items online instead. The costly process of returning unsuitable goods is what had put me off internet shopping in the past. But that downside caused little hassle to a postal worker who swiped pre-paid envelopes of various sizes from the office stock cupboard. The largest envelopes were A2: the perfect size to hold clothes and shoes. I regarded it as a perk of the job. Having bought neither of the shirts, I made my way back to the café, stopping off at the newsagents to buy my lottery ticket and *Scandal!* mag.

Impatience is one of my worst qualities. That and being ratty when I'm tired. It was a beautiful day, though, so I managed to calm my blood pressure by sitting at one of the café's three outside tables. With the sun on my face, I was close to nodding off when Oliver arrived – a full eighty minutes after the original meeting time. My anger levels should have been through the roof, but the missed nap and all the waiting was worth it to see Oliver again. A couple of subtle digs about Oliver's poor timekeeping did creep into my dialogue, so I obviously hadn't fully conquered my negative qualities. I hoped spending more time with Oliver would eradicate them altogether and that his laid-back approach would rub off on me. I could certainly do with his calming influence after all the arguments I'd been having of late.

As you would expect, Oliver was looking hot. Literally. Although it was the last full week in August, there was still no sign of Oliver in a pair of shorts. I'd just have to look at his face instead, although it wasn't as appealing as usual –

189

what with the sweaty forehead and flushed cheeks.

'Sorry I'm late,' Oliver puffed, pausing for breath when he could. 'I was put on a delivery I didn't know... And then I couldn't find a parking space in town... In the end I parked outside The Plough and ran up here.'

'Aren't the parking bays in town big enough for your caravan?'

Oliver shook his head. 'You'd think I'd be able to park in the huge disabled spaces... what with my dyslexia and everything.'

To let me know he was taking the rise out of himself, Oliver gave me a prolonged wink. He didn't crack jokes often, so he had to trumpet every one he made.

'Sit down and I'll get us a drink,' I said. 'What are you having?'

'Do you mind if we sit inside? I'm absolutely boiling.'

It wasn't the ideal start, but I was impressed with Oliver's efforts to get to me as soon as he could. After downing two glasses of water, Oliver took a trip to the toilets to freshen up. He must have taken his light blue shirt off and run it under the hand dryer, because the South America-shaped sweat patch that had covered his back had vanished when he returned. Lucky hand dryer, getting to blow Oliver in the toilets. When you are starting to feel jealous of an appliance, you know it's time for a kip. Once he had returned, our lunch date went smoothly. In a nutshell: I had a jacket potato with beans, cheese and salad. Oliver had a tuna melt with chips. I spoke about my Gran's money. Oliver spoke about his new gym workout routine, while filling his face with greasy chips. He even noticed I'd had my hair cut... and liked it! Normally, blokes only commented on my hair when it was looking less than perfect; their lack of a comment was a compliment in itself.

After we had finished eating, I walked Oliver back to his car outside The Plough, where we popped in for a couple of ciders. Even though I lived a short walk away, Oliver insisted on driving me home. More time spent with Oliver was fine by me, so I hopped into the passenger seat. Before he started the ignition, Oliver took out a small alcohol tester from the glove compartment. I watched as he put his lips around it, breathing into it until his cheeks puffed out. Not that I needed any encouragement, but Oliver's actions were putting lewd ideas into my head. The tester beeped, and the light on the side of it turned green. In the time it had taken him to do all that, I could have walked home. Anyway, Oliver's positive result meant we were good to go.

'Tell me honestly, would you have helped me so much at work if I hadn't told you I needed a caddie?' Oliver asked during our one-minute journey.

'Yes, I would. You're a lovely guy, and I like spending time with you.'

It was true: I helped him because he was fit, not because of the golf. But now that I wasn't going to be employed as Oliver's caddie, there was nothing stopping me from flirting with him. I lightly bit my lip and turned to look at his profile. In response, he was meant to turn his face towards mine so I could tempt him with my inviting expression. Oliver kept his eyes on the road.

I made Oliver stop a few yards short of my house in case one of my parents was looking out of the living room window. My mum would have been ecstatic if someone as responsible and well-mannered as Oliver was my boyfriend, though it would have taken a bit more – preferably breasts and a womb – to please my dad.

'Thanks for the lift,' I turned to Oliver and said.

'We'll have to do it again sometime,' he proposed. 'Or maybe you can come and caddie for me again? I've got another game coming up, but I'm caddie-less. I know you said it was boring last time, but you did do a good job.'

'You really think so?'

'Definitely. You can hold my clubs anytime you like,' Oliver said, giving me a wink.

Now if that isn't a come-on, I don't know what is.

The cider was kicking in. Mix that with being in a confined space with a fit guy and it becomes difficult to keep one's emotions in check. It was the image of holding Oliver's clubs that made me do what I did next. Damned imagination.

'If I could handle your clubs now, I'd give you a wood,' I pronounced slowly, trying to make it sound breathy and seductive.

'Pardon me?' a flabbergasted Oliver said.

I placed my hand on Oliver's upper thigh. 'I want to down your balls in one.'

'No... Don't do that,' he cut in awkwardly.

From Oliver's expression, anyone would think I'd put a tarantula on his leg. He sat rigid in his seat and didn't even attempt to touch my hand to remove it. My endeavours to impress him with my newly found knowledge of golf had fallen flat.

'Why not?' I said, taking my hand off his leg. 'You've been flirting with me for ages.'

'I think you've misread the signals,' Oliver said. 'I don't like you in that way.'

'You just winked at me!'

'I'm a friendly guy. I must've done it out of habit.'

'You go round winking at lots of people "out of habit", do you? You wink at them and tease them a bit so they'll be your caddie or help you at work?'

'That's not how it is.'

'Now I feel *really* good about myself. I'm such a mug,' I grumbled, hanging my head in the hope I'd be pitied. It worked.

'Hey, it's not your fault,' he said, turning towards me. 'I do like you, but—'

'—not in *that* way. Yeah, you said,' I interrupted, before overdramatically undoing my seatbelt and grabbing my bag of shopping.

Oliver pressed a button on his dashboard and all the doors made a clunking noise. I pulled at the lever on my door, but Oliver had locked me in. I'd been acting like a child, so no wonder the child lock had thwarted my attempt at a stroppy getaway. I relaxed in my seat, folded my arms and stared out of the front window in silence.

A few seconds later, Oliver whispered, 'There's somebody else.'

'You don't have to justify yourself,' I said in a huff. 'It's fine.'

'I want to explain.'

'Who is it? Is it someone I know?'

'I, erm...' Oliver mumbled – a marked admission that I was on the right track.

'Whoever it is, I bet I could hit your sweet spot better than they ever could. If you give me two minutes...' I said desperately, reaching across to unzip his trousers.

Oliver tried to wrestle my hands away from his groin. 'I don't... Stop it! What are you doing? Get off! You're not going to... It's Dean!' Oliver blurted out, batting my now lifeless hands away. He then said with more composure, 'I'm in love with Dean.'

My face dropped. I sat stock still. 'You have got to be kidding me.'

'I wish I was,' Oliver said quietly.

'But you can't. I'm...'

I tailed off before I said something else I'd later regret – though the revelation I made instead was no better.

'Dean's been sleeping with Amy,' I spilled.

'He's what?!'

Oliver leaned forward in his seat so he could look at my eyes and check I wasn't lying. I could tell from his stunned countenance I'd done the wrong thing.

'So there's no point chasing after him,' I added, attempting to downplay what I'd divulged. 'He's totally straight.'

'I know. I'm not stupid.'

'Cool. Same time next week?' I joked. I pressed the deadlock button on the dashboard and pulled the lever on my door. Before I could open it fully, Oliver caught hold of my arm.

'Hey!' he said, raising his voice. 'You can't say something like that and leave.'

'Alright, calm down. Don't go all flouncy on me.'

Trying to subdue my tendency to become ratty when tired hadn't lasted long. In all fairness, though, I had been rejected by someone who I thought was a dead cert to become my boyfriend.

'Lou, this is serious. How did you find out?'

I dug my phone out and showed Oliver the texts Dean had sent me. After he had read them, his tone became sincere again. The news was slowly sinking in. In response, I dropped my confrontational attitude and opened up a bit more.

'If it's any consolation, I don't think Dean even wanted me to know,' I said. 'I challenged him on his relationship with Amy, and it kind of slipped out. A bit like with me a few seconds ago.'

'Slipped out? Text messages don't just slip out,' Oliver reasoned.

'Good point. But it had to come out sooner or later. Juicy gossip doesn't stay secret for long.'

'And now I have to deal with it. Thanks for that.'

'Sorry,' I simpered. 'You've got to promise me that you won't tell *anyone* about this? I could get in serious trouble.'

I bit my bottom lip and looked pleadingly at Oliver, who managed to turn his frown into a slight smile. I needed him to be onside.

'OK,' he said. 'Let's forget everything that happened in the car, yeah?'

'Deal.'

We had both uttered things we would rather not have come out with. I felt like an A-grade cretin for making the demand to lick his balls. Total cringe. I could have easily felt sorry for myself and played the victim, but I'd done that several times in the past and nothing ever came of it – not even a sympathy snog.

After shutting the passenger door, I walked up my driveway, turning to acknowledge Oliver as he drove past. So, Dean had another admirer who wanted a piece of him. That brought his number of admirers (that I knew about) to four. Yes, *four*. And I was struggling to find *one*.

29

Despite my promise to forget what had been spoken of in Oliver's car, I couldn't. There had been no need for me to tell Oliver about the affair; I'd done the difficult bit and told him I wasn't going to divulge Dean's secret. It was pure bitterness that had made me come out with it. I'd lost Dean to Amy, and now I'd lost Oliver to Dean. It would have been easier to take if Oliver had said he was straight. But he was gay, and he *still* didn't fancy me. My gaydar had correctly picked out Oliver – thanks to some re-tuning from Kath – but it hadn't detected where his affections lay. I'd been so sure it was me he fancied.

The reasoning behind some of Oliver's past actions had now become clear. His avid support during Dean's matches at the charity football tournament was the start of it. And the teaching me to play golf episode was clearly geared towards making Dean jealous. Offering to drive Dean and his buddies up to Blackpool was another way of getting closer to his man. I'd been so entranced by Oliver – and too busy fawning over him – that I'd failed to notice these things before. Perhaps it was a good job Oliver was no longer working in our office, as it was nauseating enough having to watch Amy chase after Dean. Being forced to witness Oliver attempting it too would have pushed me over the edge for sure.

Now that there was no need to impress Oliver, and without the caddying job to rescue me, I had nothing other than Blackpool to get excited about. Once the hen weekend was over, that was it. I was one stop from being back in Boredom City. I knew why I was put on the planet: to have a shitty life so people everywhere would feel good about theirs. My introspection spread and made me increasingly aware of how a couple of items of clothing can alter people's perceptions. By simply pulling on a shirt and shorts every morning, I transformed from Louis Lawrence into Lou the postie. I was beginning to get fed up with being looked at like I was a postal worker. The average customer couldn't see the person inside the uniform and frequently looked past me, even when I was wearing a fluorescent waterproof jacket. I believed I was worth more than that.

One thing I did have to look forward to post-Blackpool, though, was Amy starting university. I wasn't sure when she would be leaving Crockham, but it couldn't come soon enough. She'd had Dean wrapped around her little finger from the moment she showed up, and I couldn't wait to kick her dumpy arse out of the office when the time came.

*

With the August Bank Holiday weekend only three days away, Dean and Steve were in a buoyant mood at work, though Amy was less so.

'I hope Olly will let us drink a few cans on the way up,' Steve said as he prepped his mail.

'He'll be fine with it,' Dean replied confidently. 'He knew what he was letting himself in for when he offered to drive us.'

'Oh, I forgot to ask,' Kath said with a start, before turning to look at Amy. 'How did you get on with your driving test yesterday?'

'I, like, failed because of my reversing around a corner,' a despondent Amy said.

'Never mind,' Kath reassured. 'I'm sure you'll pass it next

time.'

'I'm surprised you failed the practical, what with all those *manoeuvres* you and Dean practised in the van together,' I said, revelling in Amy's misfortune.

Nobody said anything; the bait remained untouched.

'Why is it that you don't talk to me much, Amy?' I asked, upping the sarcasm content. 'Surely you're intelligent enough to form your own *random* opinions about someone?'

'Actually, I came to the conclusion that you're a bitch all by myself,' she said, imitating my tone of voice for extra effect.

Steve and Dean made a lengthy 'Oooooooooooh' noise – the sort you would hear from the audience of a trashy talk show when someone on stage was about to kick off.

I jabbed a finger in Amy's direction. 'You're in no position to judge me.'

'We all know what position *you* like to be in,' a protective Dean jibed.

'Yeah, flat on your back with your legs in the air!' Steve needlessly added.

'That's enough of that, thank you!' Kath admonished. 'Now, stop teasing poor Louis and get on with your work.'

The two 'men' plus Amy stopped their laughter. Kath had earned the respect of everybody in the office over the years, and I was pleased I had her on my side. While Kath had been off, the balance of power had shifted towards Dean, Steve and the others. But now Kath was back, she had rightly regained the mantle.

'Can I have a word outside, Lou?' Dean asked a few moments later.

Unless it was an apology, I didn't want to hear what he had to say. And as I knew an apology was unlikely, I brushed him off.

'I'm a bit behind,' I replied. 'Can't it wait until later?'

'It could, but I'd rather do it now,' he said. 'I'll be quick.'

'That's what all your past girlfriends said about you,' Steve quipped, before adding an insincere, 'Sorry, Kath. I couldn't help it.'

'Fine,' I huffed. 'This better be good.'

I plonked down the letters I'd been holding and followed Dean to the car park, eyeing up his beefy calves as we walked. Although the sun hadn't officially risen, it was warm and light outside. There wasn't a cloud in the sky. It would have been a great day for going to the beach.

'That was sweet of you, defending your girlfriend like you did,' I said as soon as we were outside.

'Look, just leave Amy alone, yeah?' Dean said, though it wasn't as fierce as his usual warnings.

'*Me* leave her alone? You're incredible, you are!'

'I know,' Dean boasted. 'I've got two birds on the go and I'm getting away with it. I'm a genius.'

'How can you be so blasé about this? I don't think you realise how awkward you've made things... for you *and* for me. How am I meant to look Liz in the face after what you've done?'

'I've done nothing wrong.'

I stared at Dean for a couple of seconds, wondering where the charming man who had accompanied me to the Christmas party had gone.

'You've changed,' I said with pity, turning to go back inside.

'Olly told me what you said.'

My feet felt as though they had been replaced by bricks; I was rooted to the spot. It appeared that while I'd been licking my wounds after being rejected by Oliver, he had been on the blower to Dean. So much for our secrecy pact. Trying to curry favour with Dean was evidently worth more than our friendship. I heard a plane overhead. I wished I was on it.

If I turn around, he's going to punch my face... hard.

'It's OK,' Dean said. 'I'm not angry. Actually, it's a good job you blabbed.'

'Really?' I said, trusting Dean enough to face him again.

'Me and Amy aren't sleeping together.'

'But I've got texts from you admitting it.'

I took my phone out and passed it to Dean. He grinned as he looked through my inbox at the messages sent from his phone.

'Since when have I used numbers instead of words?' he said, handing me back my phone. 'I can't believe you thought I sent those.'

'Who sent them, then?'

Dean shrugged. 'No idea. Probably someone having a laugh.'

Considering someone had pretended to be him and spread vicious rumours, Dean was pretty composed. Thinking about it, there could only be one culprit: someone who wanted to weasel their way between Dean and me. And their devious tactics had worked.

'It was Amy, wasn't it?' I deduced. 'She got hold of your phone when you weren't looking and replied to my messages.'

Dean looked as though he was about to brush off my accusations. To save him the indignity of trying to fabricate a lie on the spot, I spoke again.

'Don't bother defending her. I know she was behind this, because she didn't deny anything when I asked her about the "affair" during the golf match.'

'Amy didn't tell me any of this,' Dean said. The dumbfounded look on his face seemed authentic.

'But you did know it was her that started these rumours?'

Dean leant against the side of his van and sighed. 'When Olly called me last night and told me what you'd said, I rang Amy and asked her what she knew. She told me that, just as

200

a joke, she'd replied to a couple of texts I got while I was filling up with petrol. I always leave my phone in the car when I do that, because I've read these stories about mobile phone waves setting petrol on fire and blowing up garages and—'

'Hang on,' I said, interrupting Dean before he went off on a tangent. 'Amy thought it would be *funny* to spread rumours about you two? She's sick in the head! Imagine if I'd told Liz.'

'I've already spoken to Amy, so there's no need for you to say anything to her.'

'Tell her to put her claws away, then,' I said. 'Because there isn't room for two bitches in that office.'

Dean smiled, and I found it difficult not to smile in return. He held out a hand. With a mere handshake, everything could be back to normal. Could all our issues be forgotten just like that? As I wanted to draw a line under the whole palaver before Blackpool, I met Dean's hand with mine, and he pulled me in for a manly cuddle. It's true what they say: making up is the best thing about having an argument.

'I'm pleased we've sorted this out. It wouldn't be the same if you weren't at the wedding,' Dean said when our hug was over. 'And I don't know if Liz has told you already, but the ushers are being fitted with their suits next Wednesday.'

30

'We're only going for one night,' I said, putting Jay's mini suitcase in the boot of my car on the final Sunday in August. 'I took less than this when we had that week in Tenerife.'

'You have to prepare for every possible situation,' Jay retorted as he hung up a couple of smart shirts.

'Can you hang those on the back of your headrest, please? I need to see out that window.'

'To eye up the talent as they drive past?'

'And you wonder why you keep failing your test.'

'It's not my fault I always get harsh examiners,' Jay said as he took his place in the passenger seat. 'Nice calves, by the way. All that cycling is doing you good.'

'Cheers, mate.'

'Now crank up the air-con and let's get this baby moving!'

The route I'd planned online stated that the journey from Guildford train station to Blackpool should take a little over four hours – arriving in time for a late lunch. I was fine with that, as long as I focused on the road and not on the conversation. I'd often missed motorway exits due to a lack of concentration. Multi-tasking wasn't one of my strengths. Men lost interest in me pretty sharpish when they discovered I couldn't do two things at once during foreplay.

'How's Marc getting on with those favours?' I asked.

'All finished,' Jay said, stifling a yawn. 'He's been working really hard on them.'

'He's such a trooper. I'll come down next weekend and pick them up, if that's OK?'

'Sure,' was the last word Jay said before nodding off.

Jumping on an early train out of Brighton had caught up with Jay, who slept for the main chunk of the car journey. I wasn't feeling sleepy at all, though; I'd become an expert at early starts. It was during the afternoons that I started to flag. All being well, I'd get a chance to have a nap before the big night out. I'd been to Blackpool once before, when I was about nine or ten. I was flashed by a man who I'd thought was a woman. It shat my brain up good and proper and convinced me that Blackpool was full of weirdos. And with the Crockham crew and friends about to invade, the strange goings-on in Blackpool were set to continue.

*

It wasn't until we were on the M6 that a ratty Jay woke up.

'Is it very much further?' he asked.

'Another forty minutes or so.'

'It would've been quicker to take the train.'

'Why didn't you, then?' I snapped. Being confined to one spot was a source of irritation for me, too.

'Because you offered to drive. I didn't want to appear ungrateful.'

I could have pushed him out of the car there and then but, as we were on a major road, I bit my tongue and turned up the volume on the radio. Jay had queeny moments now and again, and through experience I learnt it was best to ignore them.

'So,' Jay started, swivelling in his seat so he could face me, 'tell me more about this Oliver guy you've been raving about. Gay or straight?'

'Gay.'

'Have you shagged him yet?'

'No.'

'Blow job?'

'No!'

'What? He's hot *and* gay and you haven't even licked his willy? There is something seriously wrong with you, boy.'

'I've been trying,' I said.

'Get him drunk tonight and try again!'

'He's not interested.'

Jay let out a sigh. 'Maybe he thinks you're too fit for him. Guys can feel threatened by beautiful people.'

'That's complete bollocks!'

'You do nothing for me, but I can see why other men might find you *reasonably* appealing.'

'Where am I going wrong, dear fountain of knowledge? How come I'm still sans partner?'

Injecting a dash of levity into my question made it easier to ask; talking about my nonexistent love life always made me feel uncomfortable. Yet I wanted some constructive criticism so I could change whatever it was about me that was putting men off. Perhaps guys could see I wasn't relationship material, hence why they didn't bother coming back for seconds. Or I was crap in bed. One of the two.

'You have to *make* men interested in you,' Jay said.

I screwed up my face. Anyone looking in would think I was driving past a silage farm. 'And how am I supposed to do that?'

'It's simple. Confidence. You need to be more confident around blokes and not act so desperate.'

'Desperate?!'

'You practically throw yourself at men whenever we go out,' Jay explained. 'They can see the desperation in your eyes, and that's not an attractive quality.'

'That's not desperation. That's several double vodka and cokes.'

'I drink the same amount as you, if not more, and you

don't see me clinging on to blokes like a wannabe WAG.'

'I don't cling!'

'Do what I do and act confident. Guys will soon swarm round you. But you've got to hold back. Keep them on their toes. That way, you'll be bought drinks galore. Only pounce when you've picked out the guy you want to shag most. Before you know it, you'll be ripping open a sachet of lube. Give it a go tonight. You've got nothing to lose.'

'...and everything to gain. Blah, blah, blah.'

'You did ask,' he rightly pointed out.

'Why haven't you told me any of this before?'

'You never asked before. And I couldn't share all my knowledge with you, because the whole pub would've been after you and not me. But I've got Marc now, so I can pass on these wise words. They might even help you find a proper boyfriend.'

I had thought of myself as moderately confident, but next to Jay I looked positively timid. Everyone did. Maybe I did need to be more assertive with blokes. And where better to practise than in a gay bar full of potential victims. I blasted some washer at the windscreen and flicked the wipers on full to divert Jay's penetrating stare from the side of my head. It worked.

'Can you speed up a bit?' Jay nagged. 'You're being undertaken by drivers with not very pleasant looks on their faces.'

I glanced at the dashboard. What with my mind being elsewhere, I hadn't realised I'd let my speed drop to 57mph. Jay's catty remark had luckily snapped me out of my daydream just as we were approaching the exit for the M55. The journey had been pretty much plain sailing up until then, but the true test came when we left the motorway and hit the minor roads. I'd printed out the driving instructions the night before, so I felt confident about negotiating my way through Blackpool.

'Bugger. I think I've taken a wrong turn,' I said, knowing exactly what Jay's reply would be.

'If you hadn't been talking so much and concentrated on driving, you wouldn't—'

'Hold on a sec.'

I pulled into a side road and went back up the road I'd driven down, taking the turning I'd missed the first time.

'I've just thought of the perfect gift for your birthday,' Jay said. 'A sat nav.'

'Can you afford one?'

'I wasn't suggesting *I* get it for you. I'm organising a party. That's my present for you, along with a few anti-ageing products.'

'You don't have to do that,' I said, hoping he wouldn't go to the trouble.

'It's your thirtieth! What else are you going to do to celebrate such a milestone birthday? Go into Crockham high street like you do every year?'

Nearing thirty hadn't fazed me much, but judging by Jay's comments, perhaps it should have. Forty was the one that sounded old, and Jay was without doubt nearer to that than he was to thirty. I'd been to many parties organised by Jay, and he always ended up stealing the show, whoever the bash was for. I'd have to ask Liz if I could bring him to her wedding. It might be worth going just to see the chaos he would cause.

'Welcome to Blackpool!' I said, reading the sign on the side of the road.

Jay and I whooped, before executing a mis-timed high five. It was tricky doing it while driving.

'About time too,' Jay said. 'I'm absolutely *starving*.'

'I've got muesli bars in the glove compartment, if you want one?'

'A warm muesli bar? I'm not *that* hungry.'

Twenty minutes later, following a tedious stop-start

drive through the local traffic, we turned into the final road name on my list of instructions. I was relieved to see it, but the nearer we got to the hotel, the more nervous I became. I'd not seen or spoken to Oliver since I'd tried it on with him, so I was a tad uncertain of how he would act around me. And even though him blabbing to Dean had worked out for the best, he had still betrayed my trust.

'Look out for the Tuxbury Hotel,' I told Jay. 'I'm not sure which side of the road it'll be on.'

'It better appear soon, because I'm getting desperate for a wazz.'

'Hold on for another few moments. I think I see a sign up ahead.'

As I drove nearer, it became clear that although the name of the accommodation contained the word 'hotel', the place we would be staying in was most definitely a B&B. It was false advertising of the highest order. Liz and Dean must also have been misled by its name when booking it. Fortunately, the white-walled B&B had a small car park around the back; I hadn't parallel parked in years, and I didn't fancy attempting it while being put under pressure by the already irritable motorists I'd be holding up.

'Looks like we'll be heading somewhere else for lunch,' I said to Jay as I parked alongside the girls' pink minibus.

'As long as this place has got a toilet, I don't really care,' he moaned.

Jay fast-walked towards the entrance of our lodgings, leaving me to carry his baggage. It summed up our friendship rather well. I knew the stags were travelling up after a morning football session, so Oliver should already have them on the road, all being well. I may not have been invited on the stag night, but there was no way I was missing out on it. For me, this trip was all about the boys.

31

The B&B didn't appear big enough to accommodate a family of six, not to mention a party of twenty. With luggage in tow, I walked past the bay window and stumbled up the three steps to the front door. Once inside, I was surprised by the modern décor; a complete contrast to the outside of the building. On further inspection, the laminate-floored entrance hall was the only room that had been given a makeover. Jay briefly stuck his head out of a doorway that led into one of the ground-floor rooms.

'Lou! In here!' Jay called, beckoning me with his head before disappearing.

Feeling light as a feather after putting the luggage down, I breezed across the laminate flooring and through the doorless threshold to join Jay. In a regular house, the room would have been used as a lounge or living room, but that wasn't the case here. Jay was standing at a bar, pouring coke into what looked like a glass of whisky.

'I can't believe this place has got its own bar!' Jay raved. 'And there was you saying they didn't do lunch. Cheers!'

Jay raised his glass to me before drinking from it.

'I thought you needed a wee?' I said.

'I've been. The manager saw how desperate I was and let me use the staff loo.'

'Where is he now? I need to check us in.'

Taking his drink with him, Jay wandered out into the entrance hall. I nestled my bottom into one of the comfy chairs, took off my trainers and ankle socks, then called Liz to let her know we had arrived. The girls were in town getting their hair and nails done for tonight. Liz invited Jay and me to join them, but I told her I needed a power nap so that I wouldn't be knackered later on. In a casual manner, I asked Liz what time the boys were due in. Dean had texted Liz a few minutes before I called, saying they were about to leave and were aiming to arrive around six o'clock.

Following a swift check-in, the manager provided us with two Yale keys each – one for the front door, which the manager locked at midnight on weekends, and one for our room. Jay asked for his own set, in the unlikelihood I pulled a bloke and went off with him without telling anyone.

'Not exactly up to date with their technology, are they?' Jay commented as we hauled the luggage upstairs to our second-floor room. 'Have they not heard of lifts or key cards in Blackpool?'

The task of getting our stuff up two flights of stairs was made all the more difficult by the narrow staircases. It wouldn't have been so bad had I been solely carrying my one and only holdall, but I'd offered to take one of Jay's bags for him.

'I feel safer with a normal key,' I said. 'Otherwise, we might get locked out if there was a power cut.'

'They have electricity here? That's a relief, because I brought my travel iron.'

'Feels like you've brought your own sink, too,' I said, mirroring Jay's sarcasm.

When we reached our room, I unlocked the door and pushed it open. Pink carpet and flowery curtains – it's as if they knew we were coming. The room was pretty basic: two single beds, a wardrobe and a dressing table, complete with chest of drawers and mirror. At the end of the corridor were two communal bathrooms, each harbouring a shower unit, a basin and a toilet.

'Bagsy the wardrobe!' Jay sang as he barged past me.

'And the bed by the window!'

'You can't bagsy the whole wardrobe,' I said, opening the fanlight above the locked window to let some air in. 'I need to hang my shirt and trousers somewhere.'

'Hang them on the door handle.'

It took me all of twenty seconds to unpack my bag. When I was done, I sat on my bed and ate one of my warm muesli bars... followed by another one. Taking the weight off my feet had been a mistake. I couldn't summon the energy to walk to the door, let alone down two flights of stairs and to the nearest eatery, wherever that was. Two muesli bars would have to suffice until dinner.

'I wonder which room Oliver will be in,' Jay mused as he finished off his unpacking. 'Maybe I'll "accidentally" bump into him when he's coming out the shower room later.'

'Don't even think about it,' I said.

'Keep your wig on. I'll be subtle,' Jay said, trying to catch me out. He was full of bluff. 'Anyway, why couldn't we have driven up after lunch like the boys? I could've had an extra few hours in bed this morning.'

'It's OK for you, you had a sleep in the car,' I argued. 'Having to concentrate for five hours solid is tiring.'

'If you're going to get your head down for a bit, I'm going for a wander. I want to see what's so special about this town.'

'Dinner's at half six, don't forget.'

Jay looked at his watch. 'That's five hours away yet.'

'Then you'd better start getting ready now if you want to look your best.'

'It might take me a couple of hours to create perfection, honey, but at least I can do it. You could've started to get ready *weeks* ago and you *still* wouldn't have captured what I've got. Catch you later!'

Jay flounced out of the room. He had out-bitched me once again. I put my head on the pillow – which resembled a deflated raincloud – and made myself as comfortable as possible. My body clock had declared it was time for my routine afternoon nap, and I wasn't going to argue. The cooling breeze from the open fanlight brushed against my face, and before long I was dreaming about the evening ahead.

*

A loud knocking at the door woke me from my slumber. It took me a second or two to figure out where I was.

'Lou? Are you in there?'

I leapt off the bed and dashed across the room.

'Hiya!' Liz chirped when I opened the door. 'I haven't disturbed you both, have I?'

Liz peered over my shoulder and into the bedroom. I knew why she thought I'd been slow in getting to the door. The snoop's face was full of optimism as she looked for signs that confirmed her suspicions. There was no naked Jay hiding behind the wardrobe, but the creased sheets on my bed did make it look as though it had seen some action.

'Hi, babes,' I said, kissing Liz's cheek. 'Sorry, I must have been fast asleep. Have you been knocking long?'

'No, not really. I did try calling you, but the voice on your phone said it was switched off. The manager told me what room you were in, so I thought I'd knock instead. I was beginning to think you'd gone out somewhere.'

'I've not been out yet, but Jay's gone exploring.'

'He'd better get a wriggle on. The taxis are booked for six o'clock.'

'What time is it now?'

'It's just before five.'

'You're kidding! He should've been back ages ago!'

'Where is he?'

'I've no idea!' I said, searching for my phone. 'Liz, there's

211

no way we're going to be ready by six. I'll have to book us another taxi when we're ready.'

'If you need me for anything, I'm in room number one on the first floor,' Liz said as I ushered her out of the room. 'Dean booked it specifically for us because it's the only room with an en suite bathroom. He's such a romantic!'

'Awww, that's dead sweet!' I said, imitating Liz's gushing tone.

After practically shutting the door on Liz, I turned my phone on and called Jay. What was he playing at? He knew what time dinner was and that he needed plenty of time to create his 'perfection' look.

'At last!' Jay yelled down the phone. 'What have you been doing? I've been trying to call you for ages!'

'Where the hell are you?'

'I don't fucking know! I'm lost!'

'How am I meant to help you, then? I don't know the area.'

'Tell me the name of our hotel so I can flag down a cab.'

'It's the Tuxbury Hotel.'

Jay cut me off. The frantic texts he had sent over an hour ago started filtering through, but I didn't have time to read them all. With one hour remaining until dinner, I grabbed my wash bag and walked at pace towards the bathrooms. The sound of hair dryers on full blast emanated from a couple of the bedrooms I passed. One hour before their taxis were due, the girls had finished their bathroom stint and were onto the next stage of getting ready. If these girls were anything like Clare, they still had a few more stages to go. I showered in a personal best time of eleven minutes and then, in my flip flops, squelched across the wet carpet back to my room.

To help me get into the party mood, I plugged my iPod into the speakers I'd brought and mixed myself a vodka and Red Bull. After styling my hair and treating the rest of the

B&B to the greatest hits of Roxette – accompanied by me on backing vocals – I boogied out of my shorts and into my pulling pants. I'd just put them on when Jay burst through the bedroom door.

'There'd better be some hot water left,' he barked, slinging four shopping bags onto his bed. 'Have the boys arrived yet?'

'I haven't heard them,' I said, turning the music down.

'I've spent the last two hours in a state of panic,' Jay said, scrambling to get his bathroom bits together. 'The way I was shouting at the taxi driver to step on it, he must've thought I was about to give birth. And now, thanks to you, we're going to be late for dinner.'

'If you get out the trousers you'll be wearing tonight, I'll iron them while you're in the shower,' I offered. 'Your shirt should be OK, but I can give it a quick press.'

'Don't you dare touch my threads!' Jay scolded. 'No offence, but I'm not leaving someone whose mum does their ironing for them in charge of doing mine. Back in a sec!'

And before I could mount a comeback, Jay darted out of the room.

I bet this wouldn't have happened if I'd been sharing with Oliver. Bloody loyalty.

Taking Oliver up on his offer of sharing his room and telling Jay he had been uninvited now seemed like a much better idea. Jay would have dumped me in a flash if he had been presented with such an opportunity, boyfriend or no boyfriend.

As I went to turn the music back up, I noticed Jay's towel in a heap by the door. I picked it up and dashed along the corridor, hoping that Jay hadn't started his shower yet. It was only when I heard the bedroom door shut behind me that I remembered I hadn't picked up my key.

This can't be happening!

Both of the bathrooms were occupied, but the

unmistakeable mewl of Jay murdering a Madonna song as he showered gave away his location.

'Jay!' I yelled, banging on the door. 'Jay, I've been locked out!'

'Wait your turn!'

'Jay, it's Lou! I need your key!'

'There's somebody in here!' he shouted tunefully. 'That's why the door's locked!'

I hung Jay's towel on the door handle and, on the balls of my feet, hurried across the corridor and down the stairs to Liz's room. If she showed the manager some ID, he should provide her with a spare key. I knocked on Liz's door and prayed that she and the girls hadn't left yet, otherwise I'd have to go down another level and locate the manager myself... in my pants. Like finding an adequate receptacle when caught short in a motorway traffic jam, I felt utter relief when I heard Liz's door unlock.

'Hi, Lou. Nice pants,' Dean said when he answered the door, hair slicked back and a towel wrapped around his waist.

'Oh... Sorry. Hi!' I said, trying not to look at Dean's torso. 'Gosh, this door could do with a lick of paint.'

'What's up?'

I continued to pick at the flaking paint as I described the events that led to me standing at Dean's door.

'...And because I didn't want to look like I was loitering by the showers, I thought I'd call on Liz.'

'The girls left about five minutes ago,' Dean said. 'Fancy coming in for a slurp while you wait for Jay?'

Asking the manager for a spare key no longer seemed important.

32

This was the chance my pulling pants had been waiting for. At long last they were going to appear in the bedroom of a sexy man. Dressed in only this one item of clothing, I passed the threshold of Dean's room. I felt as though I was crossing the border to enemy territory; I was trespassing.

'What can I get you to drink?' Dean asked as I followed him. 'I've got lager, Bacardi Breezers... Or I could open one of Liz's bottles of wine? I'm sure she won't mind.'

'Lager's fine with me, thanks.'

'Good lad.'

On any other day I'd have chosen a Bacardi Breezer, but I wanted Dean to see that we had more than just work in common. It was time to act blokey.

'How was football this morning?'

'Lost three nil. But the team we were playing are top of the league,' Dean said, opening a can of Carling and handing it to me. 'Take a seat.'

There weren't any seats in the room. It wasn't quite as palatial as Liz had made out. If anything, it was smaller than the room Jay and I were in. Yes, it had its own bathroom, but that had eaten into the bedroom space. I parked my bum on the end of the double bed. I knew Dean hadn't slept in it yet, but try telling my perineum that. When it was safe to do so, I had the odd cursory glance at Dean's body, but taking a prolonged ogle whenever he had his back towards me. I was pleasantly surprised by the swath of soft-looking hair that adorned Dean's chest, with a tantalising line of it trailing down to the top of his white towel. Dean wasn't in the best shape, but I liked that. He had a bit of a belly on him, and his bosom resembled two small poached eggs, with yolky nipples that appeared to wink at me. If anyone was lucky enough to see Dean chained naked to a lamppost later, they would assume he had an outside job, owing to the defined tan lines created by his socks, shorts and polo shirt; it was a typical postman's tan. Dean was completely unaware of my lascivious staring, much as he was unaware that he was talking to someone who had a pair of his boxers in a drawer at home.

'That's very proper of you,' I commented as Dean drank from a yellow beaker.

'Liz poured this one out for me before she left. She's always nagging me about drinking straight from the can,' Dean confessed.

'Drinking from the can saves on washing-up,' I said, siding with Dean. At that moment, I'd have sided with him whatever his opinion.

'Exactly what I said to her.'

We could be so good together. I'd never nag or moan at him. I'd let him do anything he wanted. I'm so much better than she is. Pick me!

'If you get bored with the hens, you'll have to come out for a proper drink with me and the stags.'

'What are your plans?'

'We're having a curry, then we're off to the Safari bar near the front. It's got cheap drinks and massive widescreen TVs that show non-stop sport. I'll text you when we get there.'

Liz must have had a word with Dean about his stag night plans, because he had been adamant that a jaunt to a strip club was on the agenda. It appeared I wasn't the only one who didn't trust him.

'Has Liz told you the name of the bar we're going to after

dinner?' I asked.

'Can't say if she has or not... She might've.'

'You'd remember if she had. It's called The Pink Handbag... and it's on Queen Street.'

'You can't get much gayer than that.'

'I know! It's very appropriate.'

From the moment Dean opened the door, my heart hadn't stopped palpitating. I'd tried to calm it down by breathing slowly, but that task became pointless when Dean took a seat next to me on the bed. He sat with his legs apart, like a Scotsman trying to let his balls breathe. In contrast, I crossed the leg nearest Dean over my other thigh to help cover up my embarrassment.

I know what this room could do with: a mirror. A low-hanging one that faces the end of the bed.

'How was the journey up?' I asked. 'Any delays?'

'No, but Olly's air-con packed up. We were sweating like Satan's nut sack. I'd showered after football, but I had to have another one when I got here.'

'I always thought footballers had a team bath?'

'The pros do when they win. We can't afford luxuries like that.'

'It's probably for the best.'

'How come?'

'Because you'd probably cause a tidal wave when you got in and drown the other players.'

Dean held his beaker up as if making a toast. 'You're on form tonight.'

'You know me, I don't like to disappoint.'

'Your joking always seems to be at my expense,' Dean figured out. Had he been slightly more astute, he would have realised I was flirting and not taunting.

'I only make jokes about someone when I feel comfortable around them,' I said in earnest. 'I don't say nasty things to just anybody.'

'That makes me feel a whole lot better!'

'It was supposed to be a compliment,' I said, wishing I hadn't made the final comment.

'If that's a compliment, I dread to think what's in the speech you've written for me.'

I looked at Dean for the first time since he sat next to me. 'I didn't think I was writing the whole thing! You said you needed someone to help you with it.'

'No, I said that I'd give *you* some help with it.'

'But I don't know you well enough to write a whole speech about you!'

Dean put an arm around my bare shoulders. 'We can easily fix that.'

I swallowed. 'How?'

'Come meet us for a drink tonight. That'll give you some material.'

With Dean's warm skin touching mine, I thought it wise to keep my can of Carling at waist level. Another of my urges was coming, and an urge + alcohol = me following through with it.

'Steve's your best man,' I said, giving Dean a manly pat on his towelled thigh. 'He can do all the stories about the stag night. Your speech needs to be about your feelings for Liz and how you met, stuff like that. I can't help you there.'

'Sounds a bit gay to me,' Dean said, removing his arm and finishing off his beaker of lager.

Before Dean could get up off the bed, I said, 'Stay there. I'll get you another.'

'Cheers. And I won't be drinking it out of a sodding beaker.'

He's slowly coming round to my way of thinking.

I stood up and intentionally trod on Dean's toes as I passed him. He shrieked in pain and, as his focus was elsewhere, I tossed my can into his lap. I'd not drunk much of the lager, so the spillage was made to look even more extreme.

'Lou!' Dean shouted, grabbing the can that was pouring lager all over his towel.

'I'm *so* sorry!' I said, putting my hands to my mouth. 'You made me jump!'

I stepped back as Dean got to his feet and hobbled towards his sports bag. 'Don't worry,' he said. 'It's one of the hotel's towels.'

'I think I've had too much to drink. I'm going to be an absolute wreck tonight.'

With his back facing me, Dean removed his towel and threw it in the direction of the bathroom. He had unwrapped the best present ever. I didn't know what to say; I just gawped at his meaty arse cheeks. Dean reached into his bag and brought out a pair of boxers – a pair I'd initially seen in his airing cupboard. As he stepped into them, I could have sworn I saw the emergence of a testicle. Before I had a chance to step out of my pants, Dean's phone started vibrating.

'It's Liz,' Dean said, picking the phone up off the bedside table. 'I bet she's forgotten something.'

Liz must have sensed that her husband-to-be was in peril. As Dean placed his bum – now covered – on the side of the bed, I placed my hands in front of my crotch.

'Hi,' Dean began. He could have been on the phone to anybody; there was no emotion in his voice. Following a brief pause, Dean lowered the phone and said to me, 'What did I tell you?'

I smiled in return.

This conversation better be brief. I don't want this moment ruined.

'Oh, it's only Lou,' Dean said to Liz. 'He locked himself out, so I invited him in for a beer while he waits for Jay to finish showering... Yes, he's using a beaker.' He looked at me and rolled his eyes. 'Lou? Say hi to Liz.'

Dean held out the phone in my direction. Thankfully, it was too far away for me to have a proper chat with her.

'Hi, Liz,' I called across the room. 'Sorry about all this. Feel free to start eating without us.'

'Did you hear that?' he asked Liz. 'Yeah... I know... Whereabouts is it?' Dean walked over to the wardrobe and checked the pockets of a pair of Liz's trousers. 'Found it. I'll give it to Lou and he can give it to you later.'

Dean threw Liz's purse to me. It slapped against my belly and landed open on the floor. I crouched down and picked up the contents, which included a passport booth photo of Liz and Dean looking as if they were joined at the head. Although they were smiling in the photo, Liz appeared to be scowling at me. Reality hit. I had a flashback to Oliver's rejection, and my derring-do dropped.

'I'm going to go,' I whispered, pointing a thumb in the direction of the door. 'Jay's probably—'

'See you later,' Dean said to me.

I nodded, then turned my back on him and walked to the door, like a rent boy who'd had cash thrown at him and was expected to gather his things and leave.

'Love you too,' I heard Dean say down the phone as I left.

Dean hadn't been the least bit unsettled about there being a man in his room, sporting nothing other than tight white undies and a waning semi. My pulling pants had failed. I'd blown the best opportunity I was ever going to have, all because my conscience decided to make a rare appearance. What a time for that to happen. Admittedly, Liz's untimely phone call hadn't helped, but it might have saved me from making a huge tit of myself.

'It's only Lou' Dean said. *'It's ONLY Lou!'* I thought as I made my way back up to my room. *Liz and Dean definitely wouldn't have acted so casual had Amy been in my position. I bet if she'd worn her best undies and walked into Dean's room, he would've pounced on her. I was near-naked... in his bedroom... and he'd*

been drinking. I was there for the taking.

The phrase 'spare prick at a wedding' entered my head. It summed me up perfectly. An evening of drinking and frivolity was about to begin, but I was feeling less and less in the mood to party.

33

Making an entrance was something both Jay and I liked to do, but there were some occasions when showing up late was downright rude. Interrupting a meal when the diners were finishing their first course was one such instance. I crossed my fingers and hoped that our heads weren't going to be served up on a plate as the main course. It had been a ten-minute taxi ride from our hotel to the restaurant – a steakhouse in the heart of town and not too far from the promenade. Considering the amount of money that would be spent on taxis over the course of the weekend, Liz and Dean might as well have booked a more expensive B&B near the front. The steakhouse itself was packed, yet there wasn't much of an atmosphere radiating from the table of hens. Most of them were dressed in black, and there wasn't a pink feather boa or wedding veil adorned with condoms in sight. Maybe they were being saved for later.

Liz spotted us and stood up. 'They're here!'

'I'm sorry we're so late, everyone,' I said as I approached the table.

There was no room for me to get to Liz – she was in the centre of one row of hens, all of whom remained seated on the fixed leather bench that was up against a wall – so I blew her a kiss and handed her purse to one of the girls to pass down. The two empty places were at the far end of the rectangular table. A round table would have been a lot better and made for a more intimate evening. Instead, I had to squeeze behind the chairs that the other row of hens were sat on, trying not to brush my arse against the people at the adjacent table. It gave Liz plenty of time to introduce the hens to the gays and for me to introduce Jay.

'Apologies, girls. Nearly two hours I've been waiting for *her* to get ready,' Jay said, gliding effortlessly through the same gap I'd struggled to get through. 'Can't take her anywhere.'

The ten hens found Jay's comments hilarious. The situation was intimidating enough without being laughed at. Liz knew I wasn't to blame, though, and gave me a smile. But even she had only been privy to half of what had happened to put us so far behind schedule. After twenty minutes styling his hair, Jay decided it wasn't 'working' for him, so he washed it again and started over. All I could do was sit on my bed and watch, as I hadn't brought a magazine or anything to keep me occupied. When I'd been packing, I hadn't envisaged having any time to read. To help me keep calm, I dug my nails into the mattress and imagined it to be Jay's neck. Once the hair had been sorted, a fashion show ensued, with Jay parading up and down the room in a variety of different shirts, trousers and shoes, checking the view from behind in the dressing table mirror. I'm not berating him for that, because I did precisely the same thing. The exception being that I'd done it at home a week earlier to save time. I'd only packed one outfit: a blue and white checked shirt, my favourite pair of dark blue jeans and smart black shoes. My opinion on how Jay looked obviously meant nothing, as he didn't once ask for feedback. Having decided upon a black shirt and skinny black cords, Jay whipped out his iron. His ensemble was then topped off with a brown belt and brown shoes. Personally, I thought it a bit dark for a hen night. Still, based on what the hens were wearing, black was the colour to be in. At the end of it all, Jay told me I should feel privileged to have been given an insight into what went on behind the scenes to create the icon that stood before me. I didn't feel privileged at all. I felt hungry. No wonder Jay seldom found time to eat.

'You're both looking rather smart,' Liz called down to us once we had taken our seats. I was at the head of the table, with Jay to my left on the leather seating.

'Thank you,' Jay said. 'And might I just say that you're looking absolutely stunning.'

Liz blushed. Jay might have gone over the top with his comments, but he was right. Liz's usually lifeless hair had been lightly curled and treated to some blonde highlights. And her thin lips had been coated with gloss, making them appear fuller. The dark purple dress Liz was wearing was a brave choice: a figure-hugging number that finished well short of her knees – though she had the curves to make it work. And as the dress had an asymmetric cut, she clearly felt comfortable showing the freckles on her bare shoulder. OK, so the bingo wings could have done with some toning but, on the whole, cutting out the snacks had worked.

'Sorry we started without you,' Liz said. 'The girls were getting hungry. I'm sure you can add your meals to our order, if you're quick.'

'We're not big eaters,' Jay said. 'A drink or two will do us.'

'Yeah, same,' I said, not wanting to put anybody out. Besides, there were no menus on the table.

A couple of waiting staff came over to the table to take the girls' starter plates away. Jay asked one of them for a double whisky and coke, and I told her to make it two.

'Right, now we're all here, I've got a little something for us,' Liz announced, reaching into her bag and pulling out two packets of pink badges that had black wording on.

The girls sitting nearest to Liz ripped open the packets, and there followed a frenzy of snatching and giggling. Surely it should have been the hens' job to bring the novelty party items? When the discarded badges made their way to our end of the table, I could see why nobody else wanted them.

'I'm having "Miss Flirt",' Jay said, grabbing the better of the two badges.

'And that leaves me with "Miss Horny". Great,' I said.

'Come on, hens! On with the badges!' Liz ordered. 'And you must keep them on for the rest of the night!'

'This better not leave a big hole,' Jay muttered as he pinned the badge to his shirt. 'If it does, you're buying me a new one.'

'I'm sure I can afford the five pounds,' I said.

'This shirt cost sixty quid, I'll have you know!'

'Then you were ripped off,' the hen sitting directly opposite Jay said cheekily.

I had to focus on nasty things to help me refrain from laughing. Her eyelashes were heavily loaded with mascara and her badge said 'Miss Cute', but whoever the woman really was, she had become an instant friend. She was probably bigger than Jay and I combined – which makes her sound mammoth-like, but we were hardly the weightiest of men. But 'Miss Cute' certainly had bigger balls than me for taking on Jay, that's for sure.

An affronted Jay looked at the woman's dress and curled his lip. 'And what have you come as?'

'At least I was on time,' she said, finishing off her glass of wine. It evidently wasn't her first of the evening.

Before Jay could mount a comeback, Liz stood up and clapped her hands together to get everyone's attention. As she did so, the whisky and cokes arrived.

'OK, while we wait for our mains, I've got a game for us to play,' she said.

'Pin the willy on the donkey!' one of the hens called out. Gathering by her skin tone, she was a relation of the bride-to-be.

'Nope. It's one to get you thinking,' Liz said.

To let me know what *he* was thinking, Jay yawned. Luckily, Liz didn't see.

'Right,' she carried on. 'If you could choose any celebrity in the world to have a one-nighter with, who would you choose? Leanne?'

To stem the animosity building at our end of the table, Liz pointed at the woman Jay had been arguing with.

'I'll tell you who I *wouldn't* sleep with,' Jay chipped in, almost polishing off his drink in one go.

'She said *celebrity*,' Leanne corrected.

'Who says I was talking about *you*?' Jay snapped. 'I'm gay, darling. I hadn't even *considered* you.'

Leanne took a sharp intake of breath and put a hand on her cheek. 'You're gay? Who'd've thought it?!'

'Lou!' a now seated Liz swiftly jumped in, her fixed smile starting to drop. 'What about you? Which celebrity would you like to spend a night with?'

'Erm... Only one night? Then it'd have to be someone like, say, Tom Hardy. Him or Bradley Cooper, I don't really mind.'

'Good choice,' Leanne cheered. 'I'd definitely do Bradley Cooper.'

'That's not likely to happen, though, is it?' Jay pointed out.

'I've got more chance than you have.'

In an attempt to break up the quarrel, I quickly cut in. 'Jay, do you want another—'

'You reckon, do you? You're not even on his radar, honey,' Jay carried on.

Leanne sniffed. 'And who are you exactly?'

'I could ask you the same thing.'

'I'm Liz's best friend from college, so I've more right to be here than you.'

'Some best friend you are. Lou's had to do nearly all of

226

the planning for Liz's wedding.'

I kicked Jay hard in the leg, but he ignored that and my attempts to speak over him and carried on with his outburst.

'He even had to ask *my* boyfriend to help make the wedding favours. What exactly have *you* done to help?'

Liz stared at me, eyes wider than her side plate.

'Sorry,' I mouthed. It would have to suffice until we were in private.

'Right, that's enough!' Liz got to her feet once more and shouted. 'Can we *please* all get along, just for tonight. It's not much to ask on my hen night, is it?'

The rest of the meal was a sedate affair – the same sort of evening it looked to have been before Jay and I arrived. He may have been a pain in the butt and a wind-up merchant, but Jay knew how to breathe life into an event. Nevertheless, with Jay on his best behaviour after the ticking off from Liz, the merrymaking nosedived. I bet Liz wasn't feeling the love for gay guys now. Shame, as she had promised her hens a trip to a gay bar. It was time to kick-start the party. The fun and games were about to begin.

34

It was absolutely dead inside The Pink Handbag. The lack of a queue outside should have given us a clue. The flashing lights were working and the eighties music was blaring out, but without those it would have looked closed. It was only *after* we had paid our five pounds entrance fee that we were told about the club not getting going until eleven o'clock. The barman who informed us was the only other person in there, and he was polishing glasses. Another hen party showed up soon afterwards and made the one we were on look second-rate. They were all dressed in pink and were topped off with pink cowboy hats. It was tacky, but at least they looked as though they were having fun. Leanne picked up on this and ordered shots of tangy apple vodka for everyone, including Jay.

'To Liz!' Leanne shouted. 'May your marriage be a happy and long one!'

'And may your sex life be too!' Jay added.

We all raised our shot glasses to Liz before knocking them back. The sourness of the shot made my head shudder.

'Can we go now?' Jay whispered to me when he slammed his empty shot glass on the bar.

'Not yet,' I said when my tongue had regained feeling and I was back in control of my mouth. 'It'll be too obvious. Let's have a few drinks in here to give us a boost for when we go and see the boys.'

'OK. But as soon as this place fills up, we're gone.'

As we all worked our way through the cocktail list, the male clientele started to filter in. Because of that, more shots were downed, the volume within our group increased a few notches and boobs were flashed. I performed my signature 'driving a car' dance move that I'd been doing in clubs for the past ten years, ever since I saw a hot Spanish guy doing it. At one point, all of us were up on the stage and dancing around Liz's handbag. I'd managed to speak to Liz during the walk from the steak house, explaining why I'd delegated the task of making the favours. She was in forgiving mood, luckily, but her face conveyed an expression that suggested any further setbacks were likely to push her over the edge.

While the girls rocked out to 'Livin' on a Prayer', Jay and I had a breather... and another drink. I'd been pacing myself – a drink every half hour – so men would see me as confident rather than drunk and desperate. Jay's advice was worth a try.

'Don't look now,' Jay said as the barman put the finishing touches to our mojitos, 'but there's a guy over there eyeing you up.'

'He's probably staring at me because I'm a bloke on a hen night. And this "Miss Horny" badge isn't exactly subtle.'

'Go and talk to him.'

'You go and talk to him. You saw him first.'

'I've got a boyfriend. You haven't.'

I'd forgotten about Marc. For a moment it had felt like old times, when the two of us used to go out on the pull together, taking the piss out of folk with poor fashion sense and regrettably large body parts. I didn't want Jay to have a partner; I wanted him to be sad and single, like me. Things must have been serious between them for Jay to turn down a guy.

'Quick! While he's not looking!'

I glanced over my shoulder. The guy was about my age,

had dark hair and was wearing a vest to show off his defined biceps. He had a bottle of beer in his hand and was gently nodding his head in time with the music.

'Not bad. Bit of a poseur, though.'

Jay put a hand on his hip. 'You're still thinking about Dean's arse, aren't you?'

'Too right!' I said, giving my drink a stir. 'It was the best thing that's ever happened to me! If Liz hadn't called, who knows what Dean would've done?'

'Did you think he would suddenly turn gay at the sight of you in pants?'

'You told me in the car to act confident, so I did.'

'Lou, you need to get over him. And you can start by chatting up the vest-top guy!'

Following a hearty nudge from Jay – so hearty I almost dropped my mojito – I strode over to the guy who had supposedly been ogling me. Not that Jay would admit it, but he liked having me around because I was unsuccessful with men; I made him look good. However, if I started to pull more frequently and gain confidence from that, Jay would be the first person to slap me down. He didn't like people competing with him for the title of top dog – or top bitch, in his case.

Judging by the vest-top guy's accent, he was a local. So as not to bore him, I left out the bit about me being a postman. Actually, I went one stage further and told him I was a caddie for the future superstar of golf, Oliver Johnson. Funnily enough, the guy appeared more interested after I mentioned this. Rubbing shoulders with someone successful had an effect on people. I could see why Oliver had continued his hoax.

'And where do you live when you're not caddying?' the vest-top guy asked over the music.

'Sorry, did I not say?' I shouted. 'I'm from Crockham. Have you heard of it? It's a little town down South. There's not much to do there. We don't even have a gay bar.'

'Sounds pretty dull.'

I laughed in agreement and carried on blathering into the guy's ear. 'Tell me about it. But I didn't choose to live in Crockham. That's my parents' fault. I mean, if I could afford it, I'd move out and get my own flat in a big city somewhere.'

'A golf caddie that still lives at home?'

I gulped. 'Only when I'm not jetting off around the world, that is. Look... I've even got a caddie's tan,' I said, pulling up a sleeve and flexing a pasty tricep.

'Riiight,' he drawled, his focus drifting towards the bar. Never a positive sign. 'One of my friends has shown up, and I promised I'd have a drink ready for him when he got here. Later, yeah?'

Before I could respond, the guy had sprinted off towards the bar and thrust his arms around an unsuspecting boy in a striped T-shirt. The bewildered look on the boy's face told me all I needed to know. I weaved my way through the crowded dance floor and barged open the door to the unisex toilets. At the first basin was a busty girl layering on some glittery lip gloss and checking her reflection. I headed for the basin farthest from her, slammed my glass down on the counter next to it and stared at myself in the mirror. Jay bustled in shortly afterwards and stood next to me.

'How did it go? Did you get his number?' Jay asked while making adjustments to his hair.

'Nope. I didn't even get his name,' I admitted.

'But I saw you chatting.'

'Yeah, about nothing. I must've bored the poor guy silly. He couldn't wait to get away from me.'

'Oh well. You gave it a go. Next time you'll know what *not* to say.'

It was easy for Jay to be matter-of-fact about what had happened, as he hadn't suffered the humiliation of being dumped after a three-minute conversation.

'Let's get out of here,' I said.

'About time! I've been dying to meet Oliver, and I can't wait to see this bird that's been shagging the groom.'

'I want to say goodbye to Liz before we go, though.'

'She won't notice you've gone. The last I saw of her she was dancing on the stage, surrounded by men. Gays love a fruit fly just as much as a fruit fly loves the gays.'

'You're probably right. And if I go over, she'll never let me leave. It's best if we just sneak off.'

'Do you want me to have a word with that guy on our way out?'

'No!' I said, knocking back the remains of my mojito. 'I don't even fancy him.'

'Then what's with all the fuss? Put it down to experience and move on. Jeez, if I had a pound for every knockback I'd received over the years, I'd be as rich as a real queen.'

The vest-top guy was still at the bar when Jay and I left the toilets, and the only way out of the club involved passing the bar. Jay grasped my wrist and pulled me closer to him.

'Put your arm around me and smile,' Jay instructed.

'He's not even looking,' I said.

'Just do it!'

I did as I was told and put my arm around Jay's tiny waist. In turn, Jay put his hand in my back pocket when we neared the bar.

'You had your chance,' Jay called out to the vest-top guy. 'Your loss is my gain. See you around, loser!'

As we sashayed away, Jay turned and gave him a little wave, before slapping me on the arse. We carried up the pretence until we reached the exit. The air was still warm when we made it outside and, with so many drunken Brits about, it felt as though we were holidaying in Tenerife again. Despite Blackpool's official illuminations being switched on in a few days' time, the amount of lights reflecting off the sea's surface made it look as though the celebrations had already started.

'Was there any need for the butt slap?' I asked as we ambled down the grey brick road towards the Safari bar.

'I got us out, didn't I?' Jay said, though it had hardly been *Mission: Impossible*. 'I bet that moron goes in there every weekend, wearing the same vest and standing in the exact same place. Men like that are so arrogant. They think people will come flocking to them because of their muscles. But when it comes for them to string a sentence together, they run off.'

'And I inflated his ego even more because you forced me to go and talk to him.'

'But he was letching at you, so you must've done something right.'

He had a point, although I didn't actually see the guy looking at me. Throwing me in at the deep end and hoping I didn't drown could have been Jay's way of toughening me up, or perhaps he was bored and wanted some entertainment.

'Hottie at twelve o'clock!' Jay said in a hushed tone. He had said it so quickly that it had sounded like one long word.

'But it's eleven thirty,' I said, a bit slow on the uptake.

'Don't be a numpty. Hot guy! Straight ahead!'

Jay was right: there was a hot guy walking directly towards me.

'Oliver!'

'Miss Horny!'

I promptly removed my name badge. 'What are you doing here?'

'Same reason you are,' Oliver said.

'No... I mean, why are you walking this way? Dean said the stags would be at the Safari bar.'

'We are. But when Dean said you were up the road at The Pink Handbag, I thought I'd come and find you. Anyway, where are you heading?'

'We were on our way to see you and the boys.'

'Aaah, isn't that lovely?' Jay said. 'And you're even wearing similar outfits. That's so sweet!'

I glowered at Jay, before finding my manners. 'Sorry, I should've introduced you. Jay, this is Oliver, and—'

'Enchanté,' Jay said, elbowing me to one side before performing a curtsy. 'I'm Jay, Lou's bezzie mate. He's been telling me *all* about you.'

Jay held out a hand, which Oliver duly shook. Where were these manners four hours ago at dinner? I should have been angry with Oliver for breaking the promise he had made to me regarding Amy and Dean's 'affair'. But I wasn't; I was pleased to see him. Perhaps my name badge was befitting after all.

'I haven't told him everything,' I assured Oliver.

'You mean to say that you two have secrets?' Jay said, clapping excitedly. 'Do tell!'

'It's work stuff,' I said. 'Nothing interesting.'

'How about I decide that for myself? Oliver, you can fill me in on all the juicy details while we walk. And we can give you an update on what you lot have missed so far. Wait until you hear what happened to Lou at The Pink Handbag!'

Jay put his arms around Oliver and me so the three of us could walk towards the seafront in a line, with Jay in the middle.

If he starts doing the can-can, I'm not joining in.

'Onwards to the Safari bar!' Jay hollered. 'For it's time to meet some proper men!'

35

Cheap drinks and free entry brought in chavvy punters, and nobody in the Safari bar looked more chavvy than Dean and his mates. They were all off their faces, spilling drinks everywhere and chanting what sounded like a football anthem. I shouldn't have been surprised. After all, Dean was getting married, so he had every reason to want to celebrate the end of his freedom. Steve was there and joining in, though, so he was proof that there was life after tying the knot... if you can call arguing with your ex-wife, working sixty-hour weeks and spending the rest of the time down the pub a 'life'. If I were marrying a woman, I'd also be drinking bucketloads to help block it out.

'Which one's Dean?' Jay shouted above the din. It was busier than The Pink Handbag, and that had twice the floor space.

'Over there by the pool table,' I shouted back as I dodged a stray elbow.

'The one balancing a pint glass on his head?'

'No, that's Ian,' Oliver replied. 'He plays at centre-half. But he'll tell you he can play in any position.'

'I'm not even going to pretend to know what you're talking about,' Jay said.

Oliver grinned. 'Dean's the one in the half-unbuttoned black shirt.'

'The tubby one? Wow, what a catch,' Jay commented. 'I can see why you wanted to join us up at the Handbag. It's like an episode of *Binge Britain* over there.'

According to Oliver, the stags had been drinking since he picked them up after football, and they had left his car looking and smelling like a bin lorry. Oliver wasn't a massive drinker and thought it pointless trying to catch up with the wasted stags, hence his trip to find me.

'What about Amy?' I asked. 'Where's she?'

'She tried her best to keep up with them, but she was sick about an hour ago,' Oliver explained. 'I last saw her heading outside for some fresh air.'

'I think I'm treading in her vomit right now,' Jay said, looking down at the sticky carpet.

Oliver laughed. 'Don't worry. She made it to the toilets.'

'I suddenly feel extremely overdressed,' Jay said. 'Game of "Spot the Homosexual", anyone?'

Oliver laughed again. I rarely made him laugh, but Jay had managed it twice in quick succession. Jay certainly knew when to raise his game.

'Can I get anyone a drink?' Oliver asked.

Jay turned his nose up. 'How about we head back to one of the other bars we passed?'

I hesitated. 'It seems a shame to come all this way and not meet the stags or buy Dean a pint.'

'Why would you want to? They won't remember it in the morning,' Jay pointed out. 'Try to make your way over there and you'll probably get splashed with beer... or something worse.'

'Look at him. He's enjoying himself,' Oliver said, backing up Jay. 'Getting drunk with mates is what stag nights are all about.'

Jay leaned towards me so only I could hear him. 'Dean's paralytic because he's trying to block out the image of you in your pants!'

'What was that?' Oliver said when he saw me grinning.

'Nothing!' Jay said, grabbing us both by a wrist and dragging us outside. He was stronger than he looked. 'Can we *please* get a move on before final orders?!'

The smell emanating from the kebab shop next door made my stomach rumble. I could almost taste the aroma as the sea breeze wafted it in front of my face. By leaving the Safari bar, Jay had achieved the first part of his goal. But the second part – the part where we found somewhere else to drink – was delayed by the return of a familiar figure.

'Amy!' Jay exclaimed.

'Hi,' a startled Amy said.

Jay was about to give the sick chick a hug, but he thought better of it when he noticed the flecks of vomit in her hair. He took out a tissue and tidied her up.

'Have you two already met?' I asked Jay with confusion.

'Amy's dating my manager. She comes into my bar now and again.'

'But your manager is a woman.'

'Where's the problem?' Jay put to me. Then the penny dropped. 'Oh... This is the Amy you've been telling me about? No, you must've got it wrong. Amy's one of us.'

The sheepish look on Amy's face said it all.

I turned to Oliver. 'Can you believe this?'

'I know,' he said. 'I was the same when I found out.'

'You knew?!'

Oliver cowered. 'Only for a week or two. When I told Dean what you said about Amy and him—'

'The secret you promised me you wouldn't share... Yes, carry on,' I sharply interjected.

'Well, Dean explained everything to me then.'

'Dean knows too? And nobody thought to tell me?!'

'Stop talking about me as if I'm not here!' Amy cried.

Now that he had de-vomited Amy, Jay was free to put his arm around her. 'How about me and Oliver leave you two to talk for a bit? I think you need to sort some stuff out.'

I looked at Amy and, as she didn't appear to be against the idea, I went along with it. Nothing made sense, and I hated it when things didn't make sense. I needed answers, and I certainly wasn't going to get any from Dean the state he was in.

Oliver and Jay made their way back up the road, leaving Amy and me in silence. Because her head was down and her shoulders were dropped, she looked more squat than usual. Although she didn't look it at that moment – what with the smeared make-up and the damp circles on the knees of her jeans from stooping over a toilet bowl – Amy was prettier than a stereotypical lesbian. Perhaps that's why I hadn't twigged sooner. My oft-ignored masculine brain had its say.

I bet she's not a gay lesbian; she's one of those straight lesbians that sleep with a woman once to see what it's like. This whole ruse could be one big cover up to conceal her and Dean's shenanigans. She probably lured Dean in by pretending she was unsure of her sexuality and needed to have a go on a bloke to help her make up her mind. Dean probably jumped at the chance and tried his best to convince her that cock is the way to go. No doubt he asked her to bring one of her lesbian mates over – when Liz was out – so he could watch them at it.

Amy and I crossed the road and over the tram tracks and walked along the promenade. The sea, unlike my mind, was at rest. Although it was close to midnight, there were still people on the front, lying on the sand as if in the midday sun. Most of them were couples. Had I been walking with Oliver or Dean, I'd have been tempted to reach for a hand.

'It's nice here, isn't it?' said Amy. 'I wish there was a beach in Crockham.'

'You'll be living near one soon,' I said. 'It *is* Brighton uni you're going to and not Leeds?'

Amy smirked. 'I didn't want people getting suspicious.'

'What does it matter? Being gay isn't a huge deal any more.'

'Tell that to my parents,' Amy said. 'They don't know about my private life, and I couldn't risk some big mouth at work saying anything to them. My mum chats to our postman most mornings, and all it needs is one throwaway comment from him and, like... I'm not ready for them to find out.'

That's what I hated about living in a small town. It didn't take long for the rumour mills to start. I'd already been the subject of the gossip-mongers Amy feared, but they had soon moved on to the next hot topic.

'I gave Dean such a bollocking when I found out he'd told Steve... and then Olly,' Amy said. 'He knew how important it was to me.'

'Why did you tell him in the first place?'

'My dad overheard me on the phone to Karen, my girlfriend. He questioned me about it, and I told him I was talking to a guy at work. Then when my dad saw me and Dean delivering to the bank and having a laugh, he assumed Dean was my boyfriend and shook him by the hand. I had to explain things to Dean after that, but he was cool with it.'

'Dean probably kept your secret because he didn't want people thinking he'd turned you into a lesbian.'

Amy laughed. 'Probably!'

It was surreal. Amy had been my sworn enemy for months, and now we were sharing a joke beneath the lights of the Blackpool Tower. We were back to how we had behaved during her first week at work. Amy told me about how she met Karen in Brighton the previous summer and that she was looking forward to moving in with her when term started. She also revealed what had happened to my torn postcard. Seeing the picture of the muscular guy atop my bench every morning had made Amy 'want to vom', so she did something about it.

'Why did you feel as though you had to fool me?' I asked. 'You could've trusted me to keep your secret.'

'I was probably being paranoid, but I thought people might think I was gay by association, or something. When I heard you were gay, I kept my distance.'

Amy's last comment resonated with me. When Jay had tried to befriend me on my first day at Pizza Den, I was still in the closet. He was so overtly gay, and I wasn't ready to come out. As it turned out, nobody gave a rat's ring piece about my sexuality. Yet had I not met Jay, my true self might still be hiding away somewhere.

'Telling me you'd slept with Dean was a bit extreme,' I said, unwilling to let Amy fully off the hook.

'I didn't actually *say* we'd slept together.'

'But you didn't deny it when I asked you about it at golf.'

Amy looked out to sea and took in a deep breath. 'When you discovered I was off to Brighton, I thought the game was up. I knew I had to do something. I didn't expect the text to cause so much hassle, but then Dean found out and kicked off at me. I feel so stupid for letting it go as far as it did.'

'Lying always catches up with you in the end,' I spouted, tongue lodged firmly in cheek.

My phone vibrated, and Amy and I stopped walking while I took it out of my pocket and read the message.

'It's Jay,' I said. 'He's found somewhere for us to drink. Do you want to start heading back?'

'Sure. But I don't think I'll be joining you guys,' Amy said as we began our walk towards Queen Street. 'Dean's pretty out of it, and I reckon I owe him one for looking out for me at work.'

'How are you feeling now?'

'A lot better than I did a couple of hours ago. My head feels a lot clearer.'

My head felt clearer too. Things were falling into place. The times I'd lost sleep because I'd been thinking about Amy and Dean had all been for naught.

When we reached the Safari bar, I bent my knees so I could give Amy a hug. It wasn't a close hug; only our arms and shoulders were involved. A ballroom dancing teacher would have ticked us off for the amount of 'gapping' we had created.

'I know I haven't got long left in that office,' Amy said after the hug, 'but could you keep what we've talked about to yourself? I want to tell my parents in my own time, when I feel I'm ready.'

'Yeah, no probs. I know coming out seems scary at your age, but it's the best feeling once you do,' I said, trying to show Amy I understood her plea for privacy, though I probably sounded akin to a patronising elder.

'Thanks, Lou.'

'And I totally understand if you want to carry on ignoring me at work. Or how about a fake argument or two?'

Amy smiled. 'I'll think about it.'

Having spent the last half an hour out in the fresh air, I was ready for my next drink. When I reached the pub next to The Pink Handbag, I saw Oliver and Jay through the window. Even though there was plenty of space in the pub, the two of them were standing unnaturally close to each other. Jay was his usual animated self, while Oliver was finding whatever Jay was talking about side-splittingly funny. Jay adored people like that. And it appeared Oliver adored people like Jay, as the two of them moved even closer and locked lips. Dean and Marc had clearly been forgotten about.

That should be me snogging Oliver! I knew this would happen.

My stomach lurched, which may have had something to do with the lack of food in it. I walked back to the kebab shop near the Safari bar and bought the biggest kebab on the menu. There was a queue of taxis over the road, but none of the drivers would let me in with a stinky kebab.

Since when did taxi drivers become fussy?

As I wasn't willing to forgo my kebab, I set off for the

hotel on foot. The scenic route along the promenade probably wasn't the quickest, but I knew roughly where the hotel was in relation to it. With a beautiful view of the sea, and my belly now satisfied, the three-mile walk didn't feel that far. Along the way, I sent Jay a short text, blaming my no-show on a migraine.

Good job Jay has his own set of keys, although I'm sure Oliver will happily put him up for the night. That space in Oliver's room was meant for me!

Back at the hotel, I climbed up the two flights of stairs and turned the corridor light on. As I reached my bedroom door, it was apparent that someone had been there before me. A note had been stuck to the door.

Lou,
I need to speak to you. Come to my room when you
get this. I can't sleep, so don't worry about
disturbing me.
Liz

36

Just when I thought my long day was over... Was it really so urgent it couldn't wait until morning? Technically, it was already morning, but I would have preferred a sleep and some breakfast first. I put my key in the door. There was a creaking on the stairs behind me.

'Lou!' Liz whispered loudly. 'I heard you come up. Did you get my note?'

I had the note in my hand. 'Yeah,' I whispered back, trying hard not to sound sarcastic. 'What is it? What do you want to see me about?'

'Not here. Come to my room.'

As Liz disappeared back into the darkness, I let my head tip forwards and briefly closed my eyes. After a long exhale, I removed my key from the door and followed in Liz's tracks. When I entered her room, Liz was in her pyjamas and sitting cross-legged on one side of the marital bed. She patted the space next to her so I'd join her. There was an empty wine bottle on the bedside table. Judging by her smeared lip gloss and tramp's breath, I presumed she had downed it recently. I took off my shoes and sat on Dean's half of the bed. It had been difficult to tell from her position on the partially lit stairs, but there was no doubting it in a fully lit room: Liz had been crying.

'Are you OK?' I asked.

'The wedding's off.'

Liz put her head in her hands and started to cry. I moved a bit closer and put my hand on her back. It gave me a few seconds to think of the right question to ask. 'Is the wedding off because your fiancé is in love with me?' probably wasn't the best one to put to her, although it was the only one I wanted to know the answer to. Something must have happened since I left The Pink Handbag, because she had been partying like a diva when I last saw her.

'Shall I get a hanky?' I asked. 'I've got one in my room.'

Great question, douchebag.

'No, I'm OK,' Liz sniffed. 'The bathroom is stocked up with toilet paper. It's lucky, really, because I must have gone through a roll of it already.'

'I'll fetch you some more,' I said, dashing to the en suite. It gave me a chance to look in the mirror and check that my teeth were free of kebab.

'Thanks, Lou,' Liz said when I returned, before she gave her nose a good blow. 'If it wasn't for you, I might've made the biggest mistake of my life.'

My heart started to pick up pace. 'What've I done?'

'I heard you talking.'

'When?'

'You were chatting to Jay in The Pink Handbag toilets... I was in one of the cubicles. I heard everything.'

I racked my brains to try to recall what Jay and I had spoken about. She could have easily misconstrued something we had said in jest.

We didn't slag anyone off, did we? It was only the vest-top guy we were talking about. What's that got to do with the wedding? Is she upset because we left without saying goodbye? Did I say anything about fancying Dean? Come on! Think! Think! Think!

'I'm sorry if we've said something that's upset you,' I said, getting my apology in early.

'You were very quick to leave the club,' Liz said, on the verge of tears again. 'Wasn't my hen night entertaining enough? Am I too boring, is that it?'

'No, not at all. Jay and I both had a really good time with

you and your friends. It's just that I promised Dean I'd go and have a drink with him and a couple of the lads from work. I didn't mean to leave without saying goodbye, but Jay said—'

'I heard what Jay said,' Liz cut in, her tone of voice turning bitter. 'Something about me being a fruit fly? I suppose you both had a good laugh at me.'

'I don't remember us laughing at you. Neither of us said anything bad about you. A fruit fly is just a term we use for a woman who likes to hang around gay men. It's used affectionately on the scene, so don't go thinking we—'

Before I could finish, Liz grabbed hold of my face and planted her lips onto mine.

At last, I'm going to see some titty action!

'What are you doing?!' I said once I'd un-suctioned myself.

Much to my masculine brain's exasperation, I leapt off the bed and used the back of my hand to wipe Liz's Pinot Grigio-tinged saliva from my lips.

'If Dean can cheat on me, why shouldn't I cheat on him?'

'Dean's cheating on you?'

'You know he is! Jay told you he couldn't wait to meet the girl Dean was shagging!'

My face began to glow. There was no chance of me trying to convince Liz she had misconstrued *that* comment. Jay's big mouth had landed us in trouble... yet again. Thankfully, after Amy's revelations, this gaffe wouldn't be too hard to correct.

'Oh, you mean Amy.'

Liz paused to think. 'Amy from the football match?'

'Yes, but she—'

'I shook that slut's hand!' Liz cried out. 'I can't believe Dean invited her on his stag night. And I suppose she's staying here, right under my nose. I'm such a fool!'

Liz left the bed and stared out of the window. If there

had been enough space in the room, she would have no doubt started pacing back and forth.

'No, I'm the fool. I got it totally wrong.'

'Lou, with all due respect, it's too late to make excuses for him.'

I joined Liz over by the window, took hold of her hand and stared directly into her puffy eyes.

'OK, you have to trust me here,' I said. 'Dean is *not* having an affair. I spoke to Amy tonight after we left you, and I *know* she's not been sleeping with Dean. Why would Dean cheat on you? You're beautiful. Maybe not right now, what with the smudged make-up and the runny nose and everything, but on a good day you are.'

A bashful Liz looked down and smiled. Even though Dean would probably tell Liz about Amy's sexuality, I still felt obliged to keep Amy's secret; I'd made her a promise, and I'd no intention of breaking it.

'He still should've told me about her going on the stag night,' Liz said.

'She's only a teenager, and Dean didn't think gay bars would be right for her,' I said, trying hard not to make a verbal slip. 'Yes, he probably should've told you, but that's something for you two to discuss.'

Liz leaned towards me, causing me to recoil.

'You're not going to try to kiss me again, are you?' I joked, knowing full well she was aiming to give me a hug. 'I know you love the gays, but that was taking things too far.'

'I'm never going to live that down,' Liz said, putting her hands up to her cheeks. 'I can't believe I did that.'

'Apologies for my sketchy breath. Had I known that was going to happen, I wouldn't have eaten a kebab first. If it's any consolation, I've had worse. Snogs, I mean, not kebabs.'

Liz smiled and leaned towards me again. This time, however, I accepted the embrace.

'Have you invited Jay as your guest to the wedding?' Liz

asked.

'There *is* going to be a wedding, then?'

I felt Liz's arms slacken. 'I'm sure we'll get there,' she sighed, releasing me from the hug. 'But Dean's got a lot of explaining to do.'

'Don't be too harsh on him. From what I can see, he hasn't done a lot wrong.'

Liz looked at the travel clock on the bedside table. 'He should've been back by now. We made a deal that we'd not get back any later than two o'clock. He'd better not be alone with *her*.'

'His mates have probably tied him to a lamppost or park bench. You know what men are like on stag nights,' I said, deciding not to mention that they were all way too hammered to partake in the handcuffing tradition, as it would only add to Liz's turmoil. 'And if he was planning on cheating, why would he follow you to Blackpool and agree to share a room with you?'

'I suppose,' Liz reasoned. I appeared to have convinced her of Dean's innocence. 'Dean's really lucky to have a friend like you sticking up for him,' she went on to say. 'We both are.'

In the space of a few months, I'd gone from hoping Liz and Dean would split up to playing an active role in getting their wedding back on track; I was practically forcing them down the aisle.

'Right, then,' I said, making my way towards the door. 'I think it's about time we got some sleep. I don't want to be nodding off on the drive home.'

'Do you reckon the boys will get back OK?'

'Oliver's pretty sensible. I'm sure he'll round everyone up and get them into taxis.'

'How come you're not with them?'

'I, erm, had an argument with Jay about something,' I fibbed. 'We do it all the time when we go out. We'll be fine

247

in the morning. Anyway, what about you? Won't the hens be wondering where you are?'

'I ran out of the fire exit and came straight back here. I texted Leanne and told her I felt nauseous and that I wanted them to party on without me. She probably now thinks I'm pregnant.'

There was a fire exit? I wish I'd seen that when I was trying to escape.

Before I went back to my room, I stopped off at one of the communal bathrooms to relieve myself. Sharing bathroom facilities with the opposite sex is one thing, but sharing a loo in an establishment where alcohol is served is just asking for trouble – Liz and I could both attest to that. Bloody unisex toilets: they spoil the only time I'm guaranteed to be alone with men. If women kept their distance for just one moment, it might give me a fighting chance. Still, I'd need considerably more time than a three-minute toilet break for that to happen. After giving the toilet seat a quick wipe, I went to my room and collapsed onto my bed. It had only been ten hours since my last sleep, but I was emotionally exhausted. I may have patched up Liz and Dean's relationship, but my own love life was in tatters. Who was going to come to *my* rescue?

37

There was a poor turnout for breakfast the next morning. The dining room opened for breakfast at eight o'clock and remained open for two hours, and that had sounded quite reasonable when the manager informed us during check-in. However, even I – the person who had probably had the most sleep – found it difficult to rise in time. But I loved my bacon. The only food I loved more than bacon was free bacon. OK, it wasn't strictly free, but as it was part of the whole B&B package I'd paid for, I thought it was worth getting up for. After a quick wash under the armpits and a tweak of last night's hair, I went downstairs for breakfast.

The cook – who also doubled as the manager's wife – must have had little to do for the last hour and a half. None of the stags was up in time to eat, and only two of the hens were in the dining room when I arrived. It must have been one heck of a messy night. I knew Amy wouldn't appear, for fear of bumping into Liz; she would be locked away in her room until the hens left. According to the two hens I had breakfast with, they had all stopped off at a burger van after leaving The Pink Handbag at two o'clock. It explained why they weren't touching any of the greasy food on offer, preferring to stick with cereal and toast. They said Liz had already been down for breakfast and was now having a shower. And when I finished my bacon and egg sandwich, I went upstairs and did the same.

Jay was stirring when I came back from the bathroom. I was dressed, my hair was done, and all I had left to do

249

before checking out was pack my bag.

'What time is it?' Jay croaked.

'It's nearly eleven,' I said, pulling open the curtains.

Bright sunshine shone into the room, causing Jay to groan and bury his head under his pillow. He had stumbled in at around five o'clock – on a standard Monday morning, I would have been at work at that time – and had tried to get under the covers with me. Unimpressed, I'd pushed him out onto the floor. It had then taken him a further five minutes to locate his own bed.

'Good night, was it?' I asked.

There was no response, so I sat on the end of Jay's bed and bounced up and down to prevent him from falling asleep.

'We've an hour until we need to be out of here,' I said loudly. 'You've already missed breakfast. But I don't suppose that bothers you, seeing as you don't eat on Mondays.'

'I need to sleep.'

'You can sleep in the car.'

'What time is it?'

'I already told you. Eleven o'clock.'

A groaning Jay rolled out of bed and onto his knees. From that position, he gradually pushed himself up and onto his feet. He looked like a newborn calf attempting to stand for the first time on its spindly legs. Had I agreed to share Oliver's room, I would have been waking up to a six pack. Instead, I was faced with a matchstick. Jay undressed to his boxers – something he had failed to do six hours previously – grabbed the towel I was holding out for him and staggered to the bathroom.

While Jay was showering, I took my life into my own hands by making a start on his packing. Even a soft tapping at the bedroom door gave me a fright. Liz had come up to see if I wanted to join her and some of the others for a walk to clear groggy heads. The exercise was mainly for drivers Oliver and Leanne who, according to Oliver's alcohol tester, were both over the legal limit. It would also give Liz plenty of time to grill Dean about Amy. Liz was still waiting for answers, because Dean had zonked out when he eventually made it back to his room and had only just regained the ability to form words. Jay and I wouldn't be accompanying them on the walk, though, as Jay was due at work in six hours, so we had to leave ASAP. Whether he would be able to face it was another matter. Following a hug, I shut the door on Liz and carried on with the packing.

With just ten minutes until midday, Jay came back from the bathroom.

'Feeling any better?' I asked.

'A bit,' he said. 'I've still got a killer headache, though.'

I popped out a couple of ibuprofen pills that my mum had packed into a mini first aid kit for me. Whenever Jay and I shared a room, he was the one who ended up dipping into it for plasters, pills or TCP. The only time I'd used it was to squash a spider with the case.

'Cheers,' Jay said, before downing the pills with a swig of bottled water. 'Did you take some of these last night for your migraine?'

'Yeah, they worked a treat.'

I filled Jay in on what happened after I left Amy. He didn't appear to care that his loose tongue had caused last night's dramas.

'Are those my things?' he asked, looking at his open case.

'Look, before you shout at me, I thought I'd make a start on your packing to save you some time.'

'Cool. Just bung it in. It'll all have to be washed. Even the stuff I didn't wear will need a good clean to get the musty wardrobe smell out of them.'

Jay picked out the items he needed and started to get ready, while I folded and packed the rest. I told him Liz stopped by and that Oliver had gone with her and the others for a walk. But mentioning Oliver's name didn't raise so much as an eyebrow; my attempt to glean some information from Jay about his night with Oliver didn't have the desired effect. Even though we were against the clock, there was no urgency about Jay. He even had the nerve to sit on his bed and look at his phone. The noise it made whenever a message came through was beginning to do my head in.

'You haven't got time for that,' I said. 'Can't you do it later?'

'What's with the hurry? As long as one of us is down there on time, it won't matter.'

Jay had a smile on his face as he texted.

'Is it Marc?' I asked. 'Is he checking up on you to make sure you survived the night?'

'No, it's Oliver.'

'Oh... You've swapped numbers already?'

'Yup,' Jay said, texting and talking at the same time. 'He said he wants to come down to Brighton sometime, so he took my number. He's just messaged me to see how I'm feeling.'

'That's nice,' I said, packing Jay's bag with less care. 'And did you both enjoy yourselves last night?'

Jay put his phone down and continued getting dressed. 'It was alright. We met up with the stags. Man, that was a mistake. I don't remember much after that. It's a shame you weren't feeling up to it.'

'Yeah, the sight of you snogging Oliver made me feel a bit queasy.'

Jay looked at me and flared his nostrils. '*He* snogged *me*! Get your facts right.'

'I didn't see you pushing him away, though. And I know how friendly your hands get after a few drinks. Admit it, you love it when guys give you attention.'

'Who doesn't?'

Realising I was having a serious dig at him, Jay stopped what he was doing and sat back down on his bed.

'But you're supposed to be in a relationship with Marc. Remember him? Your *boyfriend*?'

'Oh, I get it. You're jealous. Is that what this is about? You're upset because Oliver laughed at my jokes and not yours? Because he snogged me and not you?' Jay said in a phony caring voice, before belting out, 'Newsflash, sister! Oliver doesn't fancy you! And if you weren't so dull, maybe you'd have your own boyfriend by now!'

I threw down the pair of trousers I had in my hand and faced Jay. He was getting over the effects of his hangover pretty sharpish. I wished I hadn't given him the pills.

'If being well-mannered and considerate makes me dull, then I'm guilty as charged,' I said. 'But I'd rather be dull than be someone I'm not.'

'What's that supposed to mean?!'

'You! You put on this act all the time. Whenever we go out, you turn on the campness and the bitchiness. I felt awful for poor Liz during the meal last night, having to tell you off. I was so embarrassed.'

To make me feel bad, Jay said nothing. He got to his feet and zipped up his deck shorts. After managing to keep his mouth shut for about thirty seconds, he spoke.

'I'm sorry if I've embarrassed you,' he said, looking for pity. 'I'll know not to do it again.'

'You're doing it now! Acting all hurt!'

'I'm not *acting* hurt; I *am* hurt.'

To complete his nautical look, Jay put on a pair of sunglasses, slipped into some canvas shoes and donned a straw trilby to save him having to do his hair.

'Right, have you finished packing?' Jay asked.

'Yes, I have finished *your* packing for you.'

Jay looked me up and down. 'And you're wearing *that*,

253

are you?'

'What's wrong with this? It's what I drove up in.'

'Exactly.'

Amazingly, Jay and I were only ten minutes late checking out. After the commotion in our room, the rest of the hotel was noticeably quiet. It felt as if we were the last ones to leave a party, when in fact we were the first. We stepped over the puddle of sick that had been deposited on one of the front steps, then walked to the car park. Our subdued exit brought the weekend to an anticlimax, and that mood continued in the car.

*

Most of the noise within the car on the return journey came from Jay's gaping mouth while he slept. The radio was on, though I kept the volume low so it wouldn't disturb Jay. A sense of clarity permeated my head as I drove. I'd been an utter fool. It was finally sinking in that nothing sexual was ever going to develop with either Oliver or Dean. I didn't like realism. I was at my happiest when my head was in the clouds; it felt safer up there. Maybe that's why I made a beeline for men with good looks and men who were off limits. They were safe; being knocked back by one of those was nothing to be ashamed of. Yet unless I wanted to sleep alone every night for the rest of my life, something needed to change. *I* needed to change. The 'normal' life I so desperately craved just wasn't meant to happen... not with Oliver or Dean, that is. Anyway, what was so special about normal? Normal was boring, so why did I want that? The grass always looks greener on the other side. Or, as Jay once told me, 'The arse always looks cleaner on the other man.' Speaking of Jay, I gave him a prod when we reached the M25.

'Where are we?' a drowsy Jay asked. 'Are we home yet?'

'We're not far from Guildford,' I said. 'But I don't mind carrying on past and dropping you back in Brighton.'

Jay stretched his arms forward and tried to straighten his legs fully, but it was difficult for a grown man in a little Peugeot. He looked at the clock on the dashboard.

'Nah, it's OK,' he yawned. 'It's already five o'clock. I've got no chance of getting to work on time, even if you stepped on it. Anyway, I bought a return ticket. It'd be a waste if I didn't use it.'

'Sorry. We hit a couple of jams,' I said. 'Can't you rock up to work a bit late?'

'I'm not in the mood. I'll give my manager a call and tell her I'm having boyfriend troubles.'

'And are you?'

'No, but she won't know that,' Jay said, before turning to look at me. 'It's not what you wanted to hear, though, is it? I know you don't think much of Marc.'

'I've only met the guy once!'

'It didn't stop you judging him. I mean, why else would you make up some crap about him not being able to come this weekend because Liz wanted her hens to feel relaxed?'

Blood rushed to my face. 'How do you... Did Liz say something?'

'She did indeed,' Jay said. He then paused so he could watch me squirm for a bit. 'But I didn't ditch you in it, so you can stop cacking yourself.'

Before I could explain, Jay gave his own take on my actions. He attributed my deceit to selfishness, but said he didn't blame me for wanting him all to myself this weekend. I didn't think I had been competing with Marc for Jay's attention, but that's how Jay saw it. To avoid another squabble, I chose not to correct him.

'What did you say to Liz?' I asked.

'Well, when you were trying to chat up the guy in the vest, Liz came over for a natter. She said it was a shame that you only brought one friend with you and asked why I hadn't brought Marc. I just went along with the story. Oh, and I might've added a few embellishments of my own.'

My eyes widened. 'Like what?'

'I told her that Marc had made some of the costumes for the Notting Hill Carnival. Liz was thrilled that someone so creative made the favours.'

'Jay!'

'I then went on to say that most of our friends were drag queens and were camping it up on a float with Will Young and a Lady Gaga tribute act. It's weird what comes out your mouth sometimes. Like you said earlier, I'm good at acting. It's one of the many things us homosexuals are *born* to thrive at,' Jay said, ending his performance with a theatrical flourish.

Jay helped himself to a chewing gum that I kept in the gap under the temperature dials. I wasn't sure what the gap was supposed to be for, but I used it to hold Tic Tacs and gum.

'I still don't get why you thought Amy was shagging Dean,' Jay said.

'Amy didn't want people at work telling her parents she was a lesbian, so she used Dean as some kind of beard to help cover her sexuality.'

'You mean merkin, not beard. A beard would make her look manly!'

Jay and I both howled with laughter. I had no idea what a merkin was, but it sounded like the sort of thing a lesbian would wear.

When we arrived at Guildford station, I took Jay's things out of the boot and gave him a hug. I apologised for my earlier bad mood, blaming it on my inability to pull the previous night.

'Forget it. I love a good argument. And it all added to the drama of the weekend,' Jay said between chews of his gum.

'Ooh, talking of drama, let me know how the wedding goes.'

'I've already told you I'm not going.'

'You'll be there,' he stated. 'I know what you're like. You won't want to offend anyone by pulling out.'

'But I'm—'

'Thanks again for a top weekend, and I'll be in touch about the thirty party I'm planning for you. Speak in the week, Miss Horny!'

Jay turned on his heel and walked away, wheeling his luggage and wiggling his little pert bum as he went.

It's been staring me in the face this whole time.

I knew what I had to do.

38

Of the five posties who went to Blackpool, four showed up at Crockham delivery office on the Tuesday. The sole exception was Oliver, who was no longer needed in our office... or in my life. Part of me hoped Dean's, Steve's and Amy's hangovers would last a bit longer so Oliver would be called upon to cover an absence, but that wasn't to be the case. He didn't need to defend his actions in Blackpool – as most people have made an alcohol-related mistake or two – but I so would have enjoyed watching him scrape an excuse together. Before Amy and Dean arrived, I filled Kath in on the weekend's action as we prepped our rounds.

'...And then the hens went for a meal at a classy steakhouse near the pier,' I said, 'while the stags went for a curry.'

'Ordering the chef's special lamb bhuna was a mistake,' Steve piped up. 'I had an arsehole like the Japanese flag next morning.'

'Must you?' Kath frowned. 'I've not long since eaten.'

The stags' journey home apparently took an hour longer than the journey up, what with the frequent breaks at service stations or grass verges for sick and shit stops.

'Good morning, Dean! Good morning, Amy!' I chirped when the two of them arrived at work. 'Lovely day, isn't it?'

Amy and Dean looked at each other.

'He's been like that since he came out of the office,' Kath said. 'Something's not right.'

'Quite the opposite,' I said, continuing my work.

'Is Oliver in today?' Kath asked. 'Is that why you're so happy?'

'Lou must've pulled someone in Blackpool,' Steve chipped in. 'There were loads of his sort up there.'

On any other morning, I would have challenged that sort of comment. 'You're both wrong.'

'It's because he's excited about being an usher at my wedding, isn't it Lou?' Dean guessed. 'We're being fitted for our suits tomorrow.'

'Actually, it does have something to do with the wedding.'

'Told you,' Dean said to nobody in particular.

I stopped what I was doing and turned to face everyone. 'I went to see the boss this morning and applied for a career break. I've booked a trip to South Africa, so you guys won't see me again until next March.'

'South Africa? Until next March?!' Kath echoed.

'I've been thinking about it for a while... since my gran died, really. And it'll give me something worthwhile to spend her inheritance money on.'

'What's that got to do with my wedding?' Dean asked.

'The thing is,' I said, pausing for effect, 'I can't be your usher. My flight leaves in two weeks.'

I'd purposely waited for an audience before announcing my news. Telling Dean I wasn't going to his wedding somehow felt easier when there were others present. Dean clearly wasn't a fan of this method, because he took me to the canteen to finish the conversation. I virtually skipped after him, passing several dour-looking faces on the way. Those people had nothing to look forward to. I pitied them, because I'd been one of those grumps twelve hours earlier. In the canteen, I took a seat while Dean carried out his daily duty as Amy's personal coffee lady.

'Couldn't you have left your trip until after my wedding?' Dean asked when we were alone, punching in the buttons on the hot drinks vending machine.

'It's my thirtieth soon,' I said, making my early-October birthday sound nearer than it was. 'Jay's organising a big party, and my parents will probably do the same. I just want to get away from it all.'

'Liz won't be pleased that you're missing her big day.'

'I'm sure she'll be fine. It's not like I was going to be best man, or anything. She'll be so caught up in the day's events that she probably won't even notice I'm not there.'

'But it won't be the same without you.'

Dean appeared to be genuinely saddened that I wouldn't be going to his wedding. Either that or his dejection was down to me leaving the country for six months.

'Amy'll be there, though,' I said with a knowing smile. 'I wonder if she'll wear a pretty dress. Has she invited her *girlfriend* along?'

Following a long sigh, Dean said, 'If I'd known how much grief all that was going to cause, I wouldn't have agreed to any of it.'

'It's a good job somebody told me about her lesbianity, or there might not've been a wedding. Liz was in a right state after her hen night.'

'And whose fault's that? You and your mate bitching in the toilet is what could've ruined the wedding.'

'We weren't bitching. Jay just made a silly comment. We weren't to know Liz was listening.'

'Lucky for you no harm was done.'

According to Dean, he explained to Liz all about how and why he helped cover Amy's lesbian trail. The two women even chatted to one another before they left Blackpool. It seemed as though everything had been neatly sorted out in time for the wedding and a veil drawn over the dramas.

'Oh, before you go back...' Dean said as I reached for the door handle.

'Yes?' I turned to say, a hint of expectancy in my voice.

'So that we can send you pictures of the wedding, what's your email address?'

Don't you get it? I don't want anything to do with your wedding. I don't want to know how the day goes, I don't want you to save me some cake and I certainly don't want to see pictures!

Dean took his phone out, and I recited an email address that looked as though it could pass for my real one. After he added it, he started to read it aloud.

'Louis_lawrence_01... I didn't know your surname was Lawrence.'

That said it all. If Dean had harboured any feelings for me whatsoever, he would have taken the time to find out some basic information about me. In contrast, I'd looked up his surname a few moments after he asked me to the Christmas do. It hadn't taken much detective effort on my part to locate the information; I merely scanned the staff register.

'Louis Lawrence. Sounds like a comedian,' Dean commented.

'There's nothing wrong with that,' I said, feeling put out at the slight towards my name. 'Dean Greening is a chav of a name. It wouldn't surprise me if you wear a Burberry suit to your wedding.'

'I've got a pair of Burberry boxers. I'll wear them tomorrow and show you.'

Even after everything that had happened, Dean was still flirting with me. Or maybe I was simply misreading the signs again and mistaking run-of-the-mill conversation for something more. As I walked back to my bench, the downbeat faces I'd passed a few minutes earlier now seemed to have more life in them. Word must have spread that I was leaving. In fact, Dean was the only person who wasn't happy about my decision.

The thought of travelling had excited me when I was researching South Africa and imagining what life would be like as Oliver's caddie. Just heading up to Blackpool had felt like an adventure and, now it was over, it had made me see how dull and empty my life truly was. After I'd dropped Jay and his luggage off at Guildford station, I'd driven home and eaten dinner with my parents. As I sat at the table, prodding marrowfat peas with a fork, I wondered if the scenario would be the same in ten years' time. The moment dinner was over, I dashed upstairs, lay on my bed and flipped open my laptop. Thanks to my friend Visa, South Africa had been booked.

Apart from work, I had no responsibilities. So, after Colin had processed my career break form, there was nothing to stop me from going to South Africa and visiting the places I'd read about, getting a fabulous all-over tan in the process. I definitely needed a time out, and this was the perfect opportunity to recharge my batteries. Running away when things got tough had become common practice for me. This time, however, my fleeing would be disguised as an extended holiday. I couldn't wait to be free, to not have my day dictated by the same routine – a day that didn't involve alarm clocks and uniforms and being somewhere at a certain time. After twenty-five years of that, I felt I was owed a break from it all. I sensed the weight lifting from my shoulders. My escape route was planned and the wheels were set in motion.

*

That weekend, I drove down to Brighton to pick up the wedding favours. Although I'd called Liz on Tuesday and excused myself from all my ceremonial duties, delivering the favours to her door was the least I could do. I'd spouted the same guff to Liz about needing to leave before I turned thirty. She appeared to believe me at the time, and I thought no more of it. Down in Brighton, I was due to meet

Jay at his flat. Once again, it was Marc who opened the door.

'Jay's not here,' Marc said in his standard monotone voice.

'Oh... I'm sure he told me to meet him here,' I said. 'Is he at work?'

'No.'

'Do you know where he is?'

'No.'

My, you're helpful.

Marc scooped up two big cardboard boxes from behind the front door and came at me like a forklift truck. 'These are for you.'

'Thanks,' I said as Marc thrust the boxes into my chest. 'I really appreciate you doing—'

As the boxes I'd been loaded with were stacked high in front of my face, I could only hear the flat's door closing. Marc was laconic at the best of times, but this was pure rudeness. One at a time, I took the boxes down the two flights of stairs and loaded them into my car. I stopped off at the bar Jay worked at but, as Marc had said, he wasn't there. For the hour I was in the bar, calls were made, texts were sent and lemonades were drunk. With no response from Jay in that time, I drove home, stopping at Liz and Dean's to hand over the favours. Taking into account Marc's brusque manner, it wouldn't have surprised me if Jay had been hiding at the flat. Jay wasn't normally one for being upset when it came to goodbyes, although it was usually him doing the leaving. This time it was different.

'Hiya,' I said when Liz opened her front door. The smell of bacon hit me instantly. 'I'm not disturbing anything, am I?'

'No, no. It's fine,' a muted Liz said, stepping to one side so that I'd enter.

'It's OK, I can't stop. My dinner is probably on the table by now.'

'Dean's was on the table five minutes ago,' Liz moaned. 'If he doesn't turn up soon, it's going in the bin.'

It went against my nosey instincts to not ask questions or delve further, but I had a roast waiting for me. Liz was also giving off hostile vibes, and I didn't want to hang around in case I ended up being roasted for missing her wedding. However, her frown swiftly turned upside down when I placed the boxes of favours inside the front door.

'These are totally amazing!' Liz marvelled as she kneeled down and opened one of the boxes. Along with her beaming smile, her face was lit up by the reflection of pink and purple organza. 'You'll have to pass on my thanks to Jay's boyfriend. He's done a brilliant job.'

'Will do.'

'And tell him that he and Jay are welcome to come to the evening do. There has to be at least *one* gay guy coming now that you're not going to be around.'

Before I could apologise for the umpteenth time, Liz said, 'It's OK. I know the real reason why you're not coming.'

'Yeah, it's because I won't be in the country!' I scoffed, trying to make Liz think she was being scatty.

Liz maintained her smile. 'And the reason you won't be in the country is because you fancy my fiancé.'

I looked away from Liz. 'What? Don't be so ridiculous!'

'Lou, I've been there. I've lusted after people that I couldn't have. I totally understand why you don't want to come to the wedding.'

'It's not that I don't *want* to...' I started, before coming clean. I had nothing to lose, other than my front teeth, so I took a small pace backwards. 'Look, I didn't mean to like Dean, it just sort of happened. There's something about him...'

'I know,' Liz said, reaching forward and putting a hand on my forearm. 'Dean tells me some of the things you do and say, and it's glaringly obvious to me. He might not be able to see it, but I can. And don't worry, I won't say anything to him. I think it's sweet.'

'I'd never have acted on it,' I lied.

'And if you'd wanted us to split up, you wouldn't have tried so hard to get us back on track after the Amy fiasco in Blackpool. I always knew gay guys had good taste in men!'

Four quick toots of a car horn interrupted us. It was Dean. He was waiting in his car in the middle of the road because I'd nabbed his parking space. Liz and I shared a brief hug and wished each other well for the major events that lay ahead. As I walked back down the cracked concrete path towards my car, I blew Dean a kiss. I heard Liz laugh. Inwardly, I was laughing too, as my ties with the wedding had officially been severed. Freedom beckoned.

39

My final day at work was the Tuesday before Liz and Dean's Saturday wedding. On my drive in, I blasted out an Ibiza Anthems favourite that I liked to dance to in the privacy of my bedroom. I needed the buzz to get me through the day. In spite of all that had happened during my short stint as a postie, I still regarded it as the best job I'd ever had.

'Hi, Kath,' I said as I walked up to my bench, a few balloons and a shiny 'Good Luck' banner tied to it.

'Morning, Louis,' she responded, putting down her letters. 'I can't believe that'll be the last time I say that to you this year.'

'Thanks for decorating my bench. It's a nice touch.'

'I can't take the credit for that. Looks like someone else is going to miss you too.'

'Can't wait to see the back of me, more like.'

Kath reached into her bag. 'I hope you don't mind, but I got you a little something for when you're over there.'

Even though the gift Kath handed to me was wrapped up, I could tell it was a book. I wasn't a keen reader, and I hadn't planned on taking any books with me. Reading was something I did when I was bored so, what with all the exciting things I was hoping to do while I was away, it wasn't on my to-do list.

'I thought you might like to keep a record of your travels,' Kath said as I unwrapped her gift. 'If you wanted, you could stick a few postcards and other bits and pieces in, like a scrapbook.'

'What a brilliant idea,' I said, feeling guilty that I hadn't initially appeared grateful. 'I'll bring it in when I get back and show you what I got up to.'

'I'd like that.'

I put the journal down so Kath and I could share an embrace. 'Thank you,' I said. 'And thanks for looking after me in here, especially when I started. I don't think I would've lasted—'

'Now!' I heard Dean shout.

'What the...? What's going on?!' I shrieked.

All of a sudden, I was yanked away from Kath and an empty postbag was put over my head. My hands were forced behind my back and chained together at the wrists. How had Dean known about this being a fantasy of mine? I heard laughter as I was spun around three times, before the perpetrators ran off.

'Kath, help me! I'm claustrophobic!'

'Don't do it, Kath!' I heard Steve shout.

'Get off me!' she ordered, though sounding as if she was enjoying what was taking place.

After what felt like minutes, my muffled plea was finally answered. Kath, who had been briefly held back by Steve, steadied me and removed the bag. Most of my colleagues had congregated to see what the furore was about, but Dean wasn't among them. I pushed my way past and jogged round the office looking for the culprit, checking the loos, the canteen and the boss's office. Nothing. I wasn't overly fussed, as it meant I couldn't do any work until I was freed. I leisurely walked back to where the action had taken place, my hands still locked behind me. There, sitting on my bench and looking as though butter wouldn't melt, were Dean and Oliver.

'I bet you were rubbish at hide and seek when you were younger,' said Oliver.

'What are you doing here?' I asked him.

Dean cut in with a reply. 'He changed his shift for you and that's all you can say?'

'Sorry, yeah... It's good to see you. Thanks.'

'That's OK,' Oliver said. 'I was meant to be at the Northwood office this morning, but I wanted to be here on your last day. The boss there is pretty fair, so it wasn't a problem.'

'But everyone's here today,' I pointed out. 'What's our boss got you to do?'

Oliver shrugged. 'I don't know yet. Maybe he'll let me be your helper.'

As my hands were out of action, there was nothing to stop Oliver or Dean from having a free grope. There would have been little resistance from me. I could have easily narrowed my hands – as I did when reaching deep into a tube of Pringles – and slipped the chain off, but where was the fun in that?

'Here, I got something for you,' Oliver said, holding out a present he had been hiding behind his back.

'For me?' I asked, a little taken aback. 'I can't accept that.'

'Why not?'

'Because my hands are locked behind my back.'

Oliver looked at Dean, who unwillingly took the key out of his pocket and unshackled me.

'There's nothing to stop him leaving the country now,' Dean moaned.

'It was a stupid idea anyhow,' Oliver retaliated. 'I bet you can guess who thought of it.'

Dean protested. 'At least I'm clever enough to have ideas.'

'Come on, guys,' I said, giving both a smile. 'Don't spoil my last day.'

The two of them watched as I opened the present. Inside was a black T-shirt with 'WHATEVER' written across the front of it in silver lettering. I put it on over my work shirt.

'If ever you're feeling down or homesick while you're away, wear that T-shirt,' Oliver advised.

'And don't let "whatever" it is trouble you,' Dean added, using four of his stumpy, equal-length fingers to mime air quotes.

'I'll remember that. Thanks,' I said, still a bit gobsmacked by the gesture.

'I found it in Guildford,' Oliver remarked, angry that Dean was trying to claim some of the credit.

'I gave you half the money for it, though,' Dean said. 'And I was the one that sorted out the balloons and stuff.'

'No, Liz did that.'

'Thank you *both*,' I cut in before Dean could hit back. 'And I'll make sure I wear it, whether I'm feeling down or not.'

It wasn't solely the boys and Kath who had gone to the trouble of spending money on me. My parents had bought me a backpack, which contained some travelling essentials; I had a dinner with my few remaining Crockham friends; and Roy and Clare had clubbed together to get me a snazzy passport cover, a straw hat and a huge Union Jack beach towel. I'd have gone away sooner if I'd known presents were heading my way. I was pretty sure I wouldn't be getting married anytime soon, so I had to reap my share somehow. This was my moment in the spotlight.

As there was nothing else for him to do, Oliver was indeed allowed to give me a hand. With two of us on the case, we would be finished well early. Not surprisingly, this arrangement irked Dean, and I heard him grumbling to both Amy and Steve. Yet it was my last day, so to begrudge me having a helper seemed a tad mean.

After queuing up at the secure area to collect my Crucial Delivery items, I walked back to my bench to find Steve and Oliver talking quietly.

'…wearing just his pants outside Dean's hotel room. Didn't you know?' I overheard Steve say to Oliver.

I stood behind the pair of them with my arms folded, a stern expression on my face.

'Lou… Alright?' a jittery Oliver said when he caught sight of me.

At that moment, I could sense all three of us felt rather uncomfortable. So as not to add to the tension, I didn't bother sticking around. I left the boys to it and walked outside to the bike sheds. As expected, Oliver wafted after me.

'All packed and ready for your travels?' he enquired.

'Not quite,' I said as I carried out my daily cycle check. It was the third time I'd done it in nine months.

'Have the nerves started kicking in yet?'

'A little.'

Oliver continued to beat around the bush. I knew the question he really wanted to put to me, but he didn't want to come across as being bothered by Steve's disclosure.

'So, did you enjoy Blackpool?' he asked instead.

'Yes, thanks.'

'Steve told me he saw you going into Dean's room in just your pants,' Oliver said, laughing to conceal his jealousy. 'Surely he's mistaken?'

I continued to inspect my bike, replying nonchalantly, 'No, he's not mistaken.'

Oliver's mask slipped. 'Why were you even there? Did you sleep with him?'

'Course I didn't sleep with him!' I said, standing to face Oliver.

'I know you like him. I'm not stupid.'

'That's ancient history,' I said. It was history, but rather more recent than I made out. 'Nothing happened. Anyway, I fly out tomorrow afternoon. Then you can have Dean all to yourself.'

'If nothing happened, how come neither of you mentioned this before? It's like you're hiding something.'

'It was so uninteresting, it didn't seem worth mentioning.'

I needed some backup. Even though I was telling the truth, convincing Oliver of that was proving difficult. I was more believable when I was lying. As if sensing my need for help, Dean appeared.

'Did you enjoy feeling special in there?' Dean asked, putting an arm around me. 'I thought you were going to cry at one point.'

'They'd have been tears of joy,' I said.

'Yeah, right,' he sniffed. 'You know you'll miss us.'

'It's your fault Lou's going in the first place,' Oliver declared.

'What makes you say that?' Dean asked.

I gave Oliver the hardest stare I'd ever given anyone. He would have felt it bore into his brain if he'd had one. Even so, it wasn't enough to stop him carrying on with his revelation.

'Haven't you worked it out? Lou's running away because you're getting married. It's all too much for him to bear.'

You little shit! I kept your secrets secret!

Dean turned to look at me. I raised my right eyebrow and flicked my eyes towards Oliver to make it known I thought him barmy. For a himbo, Oliver's analysis of people was first rate. Annoyingly so.

'You're way off target,' I said to Oliver. 'I want to do something special for my thirtieth, and I've always wanted to go travelling.'

'And why would Lou go all the way to South Africa just to avoid me?' Dean supported. 'It's a bit extreme.'

Indeed it was.

'Because he wants to get as far away from you and your crappy wedding as possible,' Oliver retorted.

271

'It didn't look like he was trying to escape from me when I was getting ready for my stag,' Dean said, giving my bum a slap. 'His arse looks great in tight white boxers. Ended up naked, I did.'

Oliver glared at Dean. 'Lou has seen you naked?'

'I think my tyres need some air,' I said, trying to change the subject before the argument escalated. 'Oliver, what do you reckon?'

Dean remained silent. He was supposed to be helping me dispel the rumour that something had taken place between us, not adding fuel to the fire.

'But you're getting married on Saturday!' a heated Oliver said.

'Until I sign those papers, I'm still a free man.'

'You hypocrite!' Oliver yelled at Dean. 'After everything you said... I can't believe I fell for it!'

A couple of our colleagues who were smoking on the other side of the car park looked over. They were too far away to hear exactly what was being said, but they could no doubt tell by the raised voices and theatrical gesticulations that trouble was brewing. Oliver was exuding all the emotions that I'd previously felt. He, too, had been trapped in Dean's web.

'Calm yourself,' said an edgy Dean. 'Don't spoil Lou's last day.'

'What's the matter?' Oliver asked without meaning it. 'Worried he might find out what's *really* been going on?'

'Say another word and it'll be your last!' Dean warned.

'Find out what?' I asked. 'What's going on?'

Oliver smirked. 'Let's just say you're not the only man in Dean's life.'

I drew a sharp intake of breath as Dean charged at Oliver and rugby-tackled him to the ground. The pair of them writhed about as they continued to scuffle, but no punches were thrown. Oliver managed to get his hand around Dean's throat at one point, though Dean easily swatted it away. Neither of them looked as though he had been in a fight before. It was almost embarrassing to watch.

There's no need to fight over me! There's plenty to go round!

'OI!' Colin shouted as he tried his best to run over to the action. One of the smokers must have fetched him. He was on the verge of being puffed out when he reached us. 'Break it up, you two! BREAK IT UP!'

Colin pulled the two combatants apart and practically dragged them inside. He was stronger than he looked. Dean had a cut on his cheek, and Oliver's shirt had been ripped and his hair messed up. The unkempt look suited him, but it probably wasn't the best time to tell him. For a gay, Oliver looked pretty menacing, and he had more than held his own against Dean. It was thoughtful of them to have put on such a homoerotic display for my final day, though I feared the repercussions for both.

*

My final delivery took longer than usual. It wasn't entirely the saying goodbye to favourite customers – including old Ron – that slowed me down. Oliver texted to say that he had been sent home by the boss so wouldn't be able to help me on delivery. And, towards the end of my round, I received a text from Dean.

What road are you in?
I want to talk to you.<

The option of not replying was a possibility, but the more I pondered, the more I wanted to hear what Dean had to say. I needed to fathom a reason for his actions before I left, or else it would plague me during my trip.

>Tell me more lies, don't you
mean? Send me an email. I might
get round to reading it sometime.

Pretending not to be interested was a guaranteed way of getting a response from Dean. To make things a little more awkward, Dean drove towards me in his van. What a waste of a free text.

40

Cue embarrassment. If only I could have delayed sending that text for a couple of minutes. As it was, Dean put his hazard lights on and pulled up onto the pavement a few yards ahead of me.

'What's with the Michael Bublé song?' I asked with derision as I drew level with the open passenger window. 'It's not Christmas.'

'Tell that to this radio station,' Dean said, switching the music off. 'They're always playing his stuff.'

The cut on Dean's cheek had started to swell. I wondered what story he would concoct when Liz questioned him on it.

'You didn't get sacked, then? Must come in handy having a dad who's mates with the boss.'

Dean unlocked the passenger door. 'Hop in. I think we need to chat.'

I reluctantly agreed. I propped my bike up against the nearest lamppost and walked back to the van. There were parcels on the passenger seat, so Dean picked up a few and lobbed them – even the ones with 'FRAGILE' printed on them – into the back of his van to make room for my bottom. Dean had dropped off Amy, who was out delivering letters.

'She's working solo? I didn't think she knew how,' I jibed.

'Amy's alright once you get to know her,' Dean said, not going overboard in his defence of her. 'The office will be really quiet next week. Amy's leaving for uni, and you're off doing your thing.'

'It's funny,' I said with a skewed smile. 'These past few months, I've been thinking that something was going on between you and Amy...'

'Because that's what we wanted you to think,' Dean cut in.

'...Except that it wasn't Amy who was getting off with the groom. It was Oliver.'

A couple of chatting mothers with pushchairs walked towards the van. As they passed, they frowned to let known their displeasure at being forced into single file on the narrowed pavement.

'I'm actually quite offended you believe him,' Dean said.

'You mean there's nothing going on between you two?'

Dean let out a long exhale. 'Something did happen, but I wasn't going to say anything because I didn't want to embarrass Olly. But now he's brought it all out into the open, I guess I'll have to.'

'Carry on,' I said, folding my arms.

'There's not a lot to say, really. Olly tried it on with me on the stag night, and I knocked him back. I think he was trying to get me into his room. I was off my face, so I can't say for sure. I didn't even know he was gay.'

'He tried it on while you were drunk?'

'Sick, isn't he?'

'And even though you "can't say for sure", you can definitely say that you turned him down?'

'Erm... Yeah, I think so. I can't really remember,' he squirmed. 'Lou, stop trying to put words in my mouth.'

I glared at him. 'And now tell me the truth.'

'That is the truth!' he laughed. 'I'm not into guys!'

'Then look me in the eye and say nothing happened.'

Dean looked straight at me, before turning his head away. 'OK, so he might've quickly tried to snog me. We were both drunk. I don't know exactly what happened. It's a bit awkward, y'know... talking about it.'

'You had a drunken kiss with a mate. It's no big deal. Loads of blokes do it. It doesn't make you gay.'

'I know it doesn't!'

From what Dean was saying, Oliver had snogged two men – both of whom had partners – on the same night. If I'd known Oliver turned slutty after he'd had a few drinks, I would have stayed up for him back at the B&B and followed him to his room.

'Is that why you started the fight with Oliver? To prove how manly and straight you are?'

'Not at all,' he said, cranking up his mockney accent. 'He was winding me up something chronic. You heard him. And I can tell you this for nothing, he's gonna get more than a slap if this cut ruins the wedding photos.'

'What, that tiny graze?' I said, squinting as if the cut was barely visible. 'With a face like yours, I'm surprised you're worried about a minor detail like that.'

'I know you don't mean that. You love me really,' he joked.

'I always fall for the wankers.'

Even though we were exchanging playful remarks, our banter was bordering on truth. Whereas Oliver was near the top of the class when it came to emotional intelligence, Dean was languishing near the bottom. Still, it didn't take a genius to figure out what had been going on.

'Is it true what Olly said?' Dean asked after a brief silence. 'Are you leaving because of the wedding?'

'Partly,' I said. It would have been daft of me to deny it. 'Everyone my age is moving on with their lives. Everyone but me, that is. I even sleep in the same bed that I've had since I was nine.'

Dean smirked. He had every right to; my life was a joke. Who in their right mind would want to date a grown man whose bedroom wallpaper had kites and clouds on it and who slept with a mouldy old teddy?

'It feels as though life is leaving me behind,' I carried on, 'and I want to catch it up before it disappears completely.'

'Just run a bit quicker.'

It wasn't quite the response I'd have given in his position, but expecting Dean to give a profound analysis of my situation was a mistake on my part. Nevertheless, Dean's pithy advice was effectively spot on.

'How about we go out for a drink tonight?' Dean asked. 'And I promise I won't get rat-arsed this time.'

It was highly tempting, especially now I knew he was partial to a bit of mate-snogging after a long drinking session.

'I can't. We've got the family coming over for a farewell meal.'

'Oh... I guess we'll have to do it when you get back.'

'Yeah,' I nodded. 'That would be good.'

I liked the idea of Dean and me being close friends, but I wasn't sure if it could ever happen. A lot depended on whether I managed to move on from him while I was away. Fit blokes had such a hold over me – it was definitely something I'd have to work on changing. Yet even after all that had occurred, I couldn't foresee a time when I wouldn't want to bed Dean.

Despite there being a perfectly capable timepiece on the dashboard, Dean looked at his watch.

'Right, I best be getting on,' I said, taking the hint. 'One more bag to go and then I'm a free man.'

'Lucky you. In four days' time I'll be waking up a free man and going to bed a trapped man.'

'Hey, you made that bed. I know you'd rather be in it with Oliver, but it's too late now.'

Dean stifled a smile. 'Not hearing your sarcastic comments for six months is going to feel like *I'm* the one in paradise.'

'If I find the man of my dreams over there, I might not

come back at all. That'll please you.'

'Really? But you... What about your family and friends? Won't you miss them?'

'I'd still come and visit, although it would be nice to make a fresh start,' I said, before getting a grip on reality. 'Anyway, it's not very likely. I don't have a great track record when it comes to finding a suitable partner.'

Zero suitable partners by the age of thirty: that must have been some kind of record in itself. Yet, thinking back to something Vicky had said, finding The One in my small home town would have been a mighty coincidence. It would have been incredibly convenient, mind.

'Whatever you decide, make sure you keep in touch, yeah?' Dean said. 'I want at least one postcard a week. I'm sure you'll get a discount on stamps if you say you're a postie in England. Take your work ID card with you, just in case.'

I hadn't intended to send postcards to anyone at work, but one a month addressed to all at the delivery office couldn't hurt. Sending them vistas of blue skies and sandy beaches as they struggled with Christmas pressure and the cold weather would make me enjoy my trip that little bit more.

'Take care out there, mate,' Dean said, leaning across the handbrake and giving me a firm hug. Over his shoulder I saw a Michael Bublé CD cover in the driver's door.

'Thanks, mate,' I said. 'And good luck with the wedding.'

Upon leaving the van, I gave Dean a wave and watched him drive out of view. My mind was settled, and I carried on with my round in a state of contentment. After delivering to my final house, I wanted to rip off my wretched uniform and whirl it around in the air. If I hadn't been wearing such well-worn, saggy-crotched underwear – all my good stuff was waiting to be packed – I'd have done precisely that and flaunted my bits for all to see. Even though I remained clothed, I still felt liberated. No responsibilities until the following March. No more of being confined by a uniform. No more royal blue belly button fluff. I was free to be whoever I wanted to be.

Feeling as though I was missing out on life wasn't only a recent belief. From not being allowed on a week-long school trip to the Isle of Wight due to flu, to seeing Mum making a raspberry milkshake solely for Clare (until I discovered it was Pripsen, because she had worms in her anus): I absolutely hated being left out. But now was my chance to be included. At long last I had a purpose, a focus and a goal. My directionless life had finally located an A to Z. Admittedly, it was more like an A to C at that moment, but I had plenty of time to build upon it.

*

Family and friends had initially been stunned when I announced my travel plans, but all were pleased I was getting out and doing something with my life. For once, this trip would give my mum something interesting to write alongside my name in her Christmas correspondence. From reading the letters my mum received, I could see that my life – on paper – appeared dull and ordinary in comparison. Other people's lives sounded uncomplicated and so much more exciting. People with new homes, additions to the family and jobs that had a title that needed to be explained – like Director of Operations, or Network Integration Specialist. Everyone already had pre-judged ideas of what my one-word job titles entailed, so there was no need for my mum to elaborate. All these people's lives were changing. But now it was my turn to do something noteworthy.

There were seven of us sat around the six-seater dining table at home that Tuesday evening. Graham had kindly parked himself between Christina and Clare at the place that had been set on the corner. As the sole singleton, my days of sitting at the corner would come, but not today. I still looked like the outcast of the group because I was perched on the kitchen stool, so sat half a foot higher than the others. After a brief toast given by Dad in my honour, the seven of us tucked into a roast dinner reminiscent of Christmas – one of ours, not one of Christina's.

'If I didn't have a mortgage and other responsibilities, I'd go travelling,' Christina said out the side of her mouth, what with it being half full. 'But I wouldn't go to South Africa, everyone goes there. No, I'd go somewhere off the beaten track, perhaps in Asia or South America.'

Clare and I gave each other one of our knowing looks.

'What's your plan of action?' Graham asked me.

'I've booked seven nights at a hostel in Cape Town. From there I can decide whether I stay put or trek to another city. There isn't much of a plan, really. I'll just go with the flow,' I said, before casually forking a homegrown sprout into my gob.

'You're staying in a hostel?' Christina said, wrinkling her nose as if she had smelt something rancid. 'You couldn't pay me to stay in one of those places. I read an article about hostels. One man had all his things stolen while he slept. And another guy's face swelled up because he was sleeping in a bed that was infested with bed bugs. Goodness only knows what you might catch. Sharing a bed that some smelly hobo has slept in is so unhygienic.'

Roy's been doing it for the past few years and he's survived.

Mum was already fearing for my safety without Christina's stories adding to her trepidation. On several occasions, Christina had made me feel as though I was hijacking her and Roy's one-year anniversary, so I guess her comments were payback for me stealing the limelight. Thankfully, Graham was on hand to assuage Mum's fears.

'For what it's worth, I think it's great what you're doing,' he said. 'I went to Australia for a year after uni, and it's the best thing I ever did. I met some amazing people who I shared loads of adventures with. Living abroad and being outside of my comfort zone taught me a lot.'

'It didn't teach you about not leaving the loo seat up, though, did it?' Clare said, giving Graham a nudge. 'I had to teach you that.'

'What is it with girls and toilet seats?' Graham remarked. 'I don't moan at you for leaving it down!'

Mum laughed, which was probably down to a release of nerves than actually finding Graham's comment humorous. It was the first time I'd witnessed this jovial side to Graham. I could finally see what Clare saw in him. The two of them were interacting like a proper couple. Clare looked happy. It was then that it hit me: Clare and Graham were in love. Although I was loath to admit it, Graham was a witty and considerate chap. He wasn't a patch on me, of course, but Clare would have to make do. I just wished that Clare hadn't fallen for someone whose sex face I'd seen.

Shortly before the goodbye process began, Clare discreetly gestured for me to join her by the front door.

'You are coming back in March, aren't you?' she asked when we were alone.

'Depends how it all goes. I've only booked a one-way ticket, so I could stay longer.'

'Don't extend your trip by too much,' she said. 'I'm going to need all the help I can get... Uncle Louis.'

It was only when Clare placed her hands on her stomach that the penny dropped.

'No way!' I said a bit too loudly.

Clare put a finger to her lips so I'd keep quiet. I jumped up and down on the spot and lightly clapped my hands together, before hugging Clare.

'Graham doesn't know I'm telling you,' she said. 'I'm only

eight weeks gone, but I wanted to tell you face-to-face instead of writing it in an email.'

Clare hushed her words towards the end of her sentence as the rest of our family had started to make their way towards us from the kitchen. Being an uncle was almost certainly the nearest I'd get to having kids of my own. I hoped South Africa would provide me with some interesting stories to tell my niece or nephew when they were older, otherwise I'd have to make do with recounting tales of jobs I'd done, men I'd fancied and clubs I'd been to. God, there had better be some blimmin' good adventures lined up for me.

Four hugs later – which ranged from a fifteen-second firm hug to a one-second distant hug – and me, my siblings and their partners were saying our goodbyes in the driveway.

'Sorry we can't make it to the airport tomorrow,' Roy said.

'Some of us have to work,' Christina added, getting in a subtle dig before she opened the passenger door to Roy's silver Fiat Bravo.

'And that's what's going to make this trip even sweeter,' I said through a conceited smile. 'Knowing that I won't have to get up early for work will stop me feeling homesick. I'll be thinking of you all shivering through the winter when I'm lying on a beach in the sun.'

'Gran would be pleased that you're putting her money to good use,' Clare said.

The two of us had tears in our eyes as we said our final farewells, but we gritted our teeth to stem the full waterworks. Had we been on our own, we would have let the tears flow freely. Roy and Clare not coming to the airport wasn't a problem. It would have been selfish of me to expect them to take an afternoon off work simply to say goodbye and wish me luck, when we could do all of that mawkish gubbins perfectly well at home. Yet it did feel odd when I waved them off, seeing as I was the one who was leaving. The positive ambience disappeared when the guests did, and the noise level was back to where it was before everyone had arrived. Only three of us remained. Soon there would be just two left. One more sleep to go.

41

Apprehension had set in when I booked my flights, but panic kicked in when I woke on my final morning. What on earth was I doing? I was leaving a loving family and a reasonably cushy life to go backpacking... on my own... in a country far, far away. But events of the past few months had conspired to give me a hefty kick up the arse so that I'd do something with my life. If it hadn't been for my gran dying, my impending thirtieth, Dean's games and Oliver's rejection, my mundane life would have carried on as normal.

Like homework of yore, I always left my packing until the last possible moment. I crammed as many clothes, shoes and toiletries into my backpack as I could, and everything else was left on my bed, ready to be put in my holdall. I hadn't noticed at the time, but the journal Kath bought me had already been written in. Inside the front cover, Kath had copied out a Mark Twain quote:

> Twenty years from now, you will be more disappointed by the things you didn't do than by the ones you did do. So throw off your bow-lines. Sail away from the safe harbour. Catch the trade winds in your sails. Explore. Dream. Discover.

Reading the inscription filled me with positivity, and my feelings of anxiety disappeared. I knew Kath hadn't come up with the quotation, but she must have been quite knowledgeable to have been able to recite it. That's what I wanted: to become more learned and return home a man of the world – one who didn't need to rely on tweezers and hair products.

While I was emptying my underwear drawer, I picked up Dean's boxers. As I buried my nose in them, the smell of the fabric conditioner took me back to being in Dean's bathroom – back to when I had delusions of Dean and me getting together. But what was I meant to do with them now? I didn't want them hanging around, as they would be a constant reminder of what I was trying to forget. Charity shops didn't accept undies, and throwing them in the bin didn't seem final enough. The only reasonable thing I could think to do with them was set them on fire and watch them burn. I didn't have time to perform the 'cleansing' ritual before I left, so I stuffed the boxer shorts into my backpack with the aim of doing it at an appropriate moment in time in South Africa – on a secluded beach when the moon was at its fullest and the west wind doth blow, or something.

After finishing my packing, I had some lunch and replied to texts from Clare and Roy, plus a few others. I hadn't heard from Jay since the day before he stood me up in Brighton, so I turned on my laptop and checked my emails one last time. One thing I hadn't bargained for was bloody MSN. I should have remembered to change my status to 'appear offline'. A message from Oliver popped up. He had called me a couple of times following his fisticuffs with Dean, but I hadn't been in a forgiving frame of mind.

Hi Lou! How are you?<

>Good thanks. You?

I've been better. I tried calling. I wanted to explain about yesterday.<

286

>Sorry. I've had a lot to do.

I can imagine. What time is the flight?<

>4.15pm, so I can't chat for long.

That's fine. I wanted to apologise
for the things I said. I don't know
what I was thinking.<

I did. I'd acted the same when grilling Dean about his
blossoming friendship with Amy. Jealousy made people do
peculiar things. I kept forgetting Oliver was only twenty-
one, so acting stroppy was par for the course. Using age to
excuse my own stroppy moments wouldn't wash. Still,
Oliver's apology was most welcome.

>Dean told me about your drunken kiss after the
stag party. I think he's just a bit embarrassed about
it. I told him it's not a big issue.

That's all he said?<

>Yeah, pretty much.

Just so you know, we didn't kiss after the
stag party. Dean was hammered and I'm
hardly likely to try it on with him then.<

>Why would he say that you did?

To cover up what's been going on.<

>Which is what?

Me and Dean have been seeing each other
on and off for months. We had our first kiss
soon after that Spurs match in April. It
made me really happy at the time.<

There was a brief pause while I registered what Oliver had written. Although his revelation sounded far-fetched, I knew he wasn't lying. At the back of my mind, something hadn't rung true about Dean's 'drunken antics' story. I'd believed him at the time because he had provided some plausible answers. But they had all been lies. I wished I'd given Oliver the bogus email address too; I didn't need to hear all this right now. I had to reply quickly, or else Oliver would know something was amiss.

>OMG!

I know! I was so shocked when it happened. He told
me afterwards he'd never kissed a guy before. I think
he was getting cold feet about getting married.<

>Who made the first move?

He did. I met him for a drink a few days after the Spurs
match. We chatted about personal stuff and I told him I
was gay. Before I drove off he leaned through the car
window and grabbed my face and kissed me!<

>Dean told me he didn't know you were
gay until after the stag night snog.

He's such a liar! We didn't kiss *after* the stag night, but
we did before it. He came up to my room before we got
taxis into town. I told him if he wanted to take things
further he should knock on my door later on. Anyway
he ended up getting pissed, so nothing happened.<

Although Amy had been using Dean to help hide her sexuality, Dean had been using Amy for the same reason – I'd figured as much myself. Yet it turned out to be more sinister than that. Oliver revealed that Amy found out about him and Dean months ago. She had looked through Dean's phone and read an incriminating text Oliver had sent. When Dean had wanted to call an end to his and Amy's charade, Amy threatened to expose his misbehaviour. I knew there had to be more to it for Dean to carry on the pretence and risk his relationship with Liz.

>Has Dean said anything to you since the fight?

Not a word. He's ignoring all my texts and calls. I'm supposed to be going to his wedding but I don't think I'll be welcome. What do you think?<

>I think Dean's a prick. He's the most insecure person I've ever met. He doesn't care about anyone but himself. Forget about him. I have.

It doesn't look like I've got a choice. I've been told I'm not allowed to work in your office again because of the fight. It's probably for the best.<

>Don't take this the wrong way, but I've really got to go. I'm running a bit late.

OK. Keep in touch while you're away. Take care out there.<

>Thanks mate :o)

And after that, I went offline. Considering he told me that he was 'not into guys', Dean had had more luck with the same sex in a few months than I'd had in the past year. He had blatantly lied to my face, even when I gave him the

289

chance to come clean. I knew Dean and Oliver had been getting close, but I hadn't realised exactly how close they were. When I'd been daydreaming about their best bits merging to create my very own uber-fit boyfriend, this wasn't what I'd had in mind. Hearing about their clandestine relationship should have made me feel jealous, but all I felt was pity. Poor Oliver was having his emotions toyed with, same as mine had been. Dean gravitated towards those who deemed him attractive, and that spelt trouble for the people who were drawn to him. But his carefree attitude was now coming back to haunt him.

A lot of things now started to make sense. Right from the outset, Dean had been jealous of Oliver's and my friendship. Except it wasn't me who had stirred those feelings inside him; it was Oliver. As far as I was concerned, Oliver could have him. I'd had enough of them and their games. Both of them had been using me to make the other jealous. It hadn't always been that way, though, as demonstrated by Dean's charming behaviour at the Christmas party. However, he soon went cold on me once he had found someone better looking to take my place. Yet Dean transferring his attention turned out to be a blessing in disguise, as it saved me going through the heartache and guilt Oliver was undoubtedly going through. I, on the other hand, was guilt-free; I could leave with my head held high.

One person had been forgotten in all of this: Liz. She was due to marry a cheating partner in little over three days. Despite the fact I wasn't going to be around to see it happen, I couldn't sit back and do nothing, knowing what I did. By the sound of it, Dean's refusal to speak to Oliver proved he regretted what he had done. But was that punishment enough? I removed Dean's boxers from my backpack, lay them on my bed and stared at them. There was one way of getting rid of them that I'd overlooked: giving them back.

'Louis?' my mum called up the stairs. 'Are you ready to

go?'

'Nearly! I won't be a sec!'

So that my dad could load the Volvo, I lumbered down the stairs with my backpack and holdall, before dashing back up to my room. It wasn't for me to decide whether Dean's greediness was worthy of castigation, so I left the judging up to his fiancée. From my stash of work's pre-paid envelopes, I took an A4-sized one and addressed it to Liz. On the back of the envelope, I wrote, 'Return to sender'. I folded Dean's boxers in half, slid them inside the envelope and sealed it. I gave Mr. September on my calendar a kiss goodbye, closed my bedroom door and hurried out to the car. My mum drove the three of us through Crockham high street on our way to Heathrow, and we stopped by a post box so I could set my parcel on its way. I was on my own way, and it was long overdue. While my Crockham classmates were dealing with the trauma of turning thirty and heading towards a routine way of living, I was bucking the trend – something I wouldn't have dreamed of doing when at school. 'Being different' was the new 'fitting in'.

Even though my emotions were all over the place, informing Liz about Dean's wrongdoing had felt like the right thing to do. But when we hit the motorway, I realised that what I should have done was call Liz from the airport. Once again, I'd chosen the coward's way out. The boxer shorts were rather distinctive, so Liz would know they belonged to Dean when she saw them. Still, Dean would no doubt find some way to snake out of the situation, as he always came up smelling of roses. And if the wedding did go ahead – which I hoped it did – at least I managed to open Liz's eyes, because she would need to be a lot more vigilant in future. Dean wouldn't be able to put a single toe out of line without Liz being on his case. Marriage truly would feel like a prison sentence to Dean.

At Heathrow, after checking in my backpack, Mum, Dad and I sat in a café and watched the planes landing. When it was time for me to leave, we walked to the departures area, where I gave them both an emotional hug goodbye.

'Make sure you keep out of trouble,' Mum said, tears streaming down her face.

The only other occasion I'd seen my mum cry was at Roy's wedding – oh, and the time I accidentally taped a *Sunny Bay* omnibus over Princess Di's funeral. I promptly followed suit, as no amount of teeth gritting would stop this wave of sentiment.

'I love you,' I said – something I'd never said with meaning before.

'I'm proud of you, son,' Dad said during our embrace.

'Yep,' was all I managed to get out.

'And give me a call as soon as you get there,' Mum wailed.

'I will.'

By that point, my voice had trailed off on a note Leona Lewis would have struggled to hit. My parents put an arm around each other, and I gave them a wave as I went through to the X-ray and security check area. After clearing those, I turned around, but my parents were out of sight. I was on my own.

As I waited for the boarding gate to open, I felt strangely calm. I'd done all I could do; my departure was now out of my hands. I scanned the people around me, and I noticed there were four or five others in their twenties who appeared to be travelling alone. A couple of them looked particularly on edge, and I wondered what circumstances had brought them to the same point I was at. Our paths had converged – for whatever reason and for however long – and we were now on the road to discovery. I'd learnt a lot recently, yet there was still so much to find out. All the major decisions I'd thus far made in life had been determined by men, but now was the time for *me* to dictate what happened next; *I* wanted to be in control of my happiness.

Just as I was about to turn off my phone, it vibrated in my palm.

Have an awesome holiday Lou-Lou! You're going to have the time of your life out there. Do exactly what I would do and you can't go wrong xx<

>Thanks Jay-Jay! I'm boarding the plane now. You always did like to leave things to the last minute! I'll text you when I land :o)

Pull as many hot surfers as you can. And remember to ask them their names! Photos would be nice too! Love ya xx<

I took my place aboard the plane and waited to see who I'd have to elbow-wrestle for command of the armrest, but nobody came and sat next to me. I took out the journal Kath gave me, then I wedged my holdall underneath the seat in front.

Wednesday September 11th

I've finally done it. I'm on my way to South Africa! After a brief delay, the plane left the runway at 4.50pm. There are loads of empty seats, which is a bit of a waste. But I'm not complaining, because I have three seats all to myself. I've already made a new friend – I got chatting to another backpacker in the queue at the boarding gate. He's staying in Cape Town for a bit, so we've agreed to meet up. He's not bad looking either!

After putting my journal away, I used the controller in the armrest to flick through the library of films until I reached *Thelma and Louise* – my all-time favourite. I put my headphones in, reclined my seat and grinned wider than the fixed smiles upon the faces of the cabin crew. They must have thought I was odd – I reckoned most people did. But I didn't care any longer. I was leaving everything behind and journeying into the unknown. Life was already looking better.

A few people I'd like to thank:

My family – without your patience and support, I'd never have finished this book.

My friends – for providing me with inspiration during the bleak moments.

Debbie, for your brilliant cover art.
Claire, for your expert critiques.

And, at the risk of sounding mushier than over-boiled broccoli, a final thanks to you for reading my debut novel.

All of you have helped make my dream come true.

Thank You

Andy

The sequel, *Back Down to Earth*, is available in paperback and eBook formats.

To read the blog that accompanies this book, go to www.ASEnovels.com

Follow me on Twitter @AndySextonUK

Any questions? Please feel free to get in contact.

Printed in Great Britain
by Amazon.co.uk, Ltd.,
Marston Gate.